Black Valley

A Novel
By

John Washbourne and
Dewi Griffiths

"Nothing Can Hold Back The Otherworld: Except You"

GARLAND STONE PRODUCTIONS LTD
Wales, UK

First Published in 2020 as an eBook, and in 2022 as a Paperback
By Garland Stone Productions Ltd, Cardiff, Wales, UK

Acknowledgements:
English Language Biblical Quotations taken from
The Holy Bible - King James Version.

Quotation from Arthur Machen's "The Red Hand"
published in 1895 and now in the Public Domain.

Cover Artwork by Christian Pinchbeck.
© Garland Stone Productions Ltd
www.pinchbeckdesign.com

Map Artwork by Sophia Zweiner.
© Garland Stone Productions Ltd.
www.sophiawulf.de

Author Photograph: Ray Kilby
Cover Layout & Design: Gareth Hughes

Identifiers:
ISBN (e-book)   978-1-9999263-6-6
ISBN (Paperback)   978-1-9999263-7-3

Garland Stone Productions Ltd.
www.garlandstonepublications.com
www.garlandstone.com
www.facebook.com/garlandstoneproductions
www.dewigriffiths.com
dewi@garlandstone.com

About the Authors

Dewi Griffiths is a native Welsh speaker from the coast of Pembrokeshire in West Wales, Great Britain.

Pembrokeshire is the setting for many of the stories from the Ancient Celtic Myths written down a thousand years ago in the *Mabinogion*. This scenery, remoteness, mythology and the supernatural were strong early influences on Dewi.

Combined with a love of storytelling, photography and film making, Dewi entered a career in feature film and high-end television drama, working worldwide.

Dewi worked on four continents for such production companies as BBC, S4C, ITV, Sky, Merchant Ivory, and Full Moon.

Dewi was head hunted by senior staff at the AFI and USC Film School to head up Producing at The Red Sea Institute of Cinematic Arts in Jordan, teaching award winning film makers from across the MENA region.

Dewi runs Garland Stone Productions Ltd, which builds on his connections and experience, to produce horror films, TV and literature: contemporary stories grounded in folklore.

Today Dewi is Senior Lecturer in Film Producing at the University of South Wales.

John Washbourne has been involved with film distribution for over twenty five years and is VP Development at Garland Stone Productions Ltd.

John is also an international fencing champion (modern & historical), & martial artist.

John's interest in mythology and history has culminated in co-writing *Black Valley, Blood Eagle, Away Game* and numerous other projects for Garland Stone.

Garland Stone creates Cutting Edge Horror with an Ancient Heritage.

The Setting for Black Valley

Black Valley is set in Gwynedd in North West Wales, setting for many of the mythical stories of the Mabinogion.

Black Valley is a dark fantasy drawing together themes which are reflected in the landscape of these areas of North Wales: Ancient Celtic Myth, and Industrial Decline.

Cwm Du, 'The Black Valley' is a dark land with a dark story.

The North West of Wales saw an industrial revolution based on the mining of slate. The result is a landscape of outstanding natural beauty that remains scarred with quarries and massive slate waste tips.

Black Valley is the story of Cwm Du, a place lost in time, whose industry has been destroyed, now haunted by its history and mythology in the form of *The Gwyllion*.

About Black Valley

Black Valley began as a feature film project.

It was supported by such schemes as Film London Micro Market, Peaceful Fish Berlin, and in Wales by schemes supported by Ffilm Cymru Wales.

We would like to thank particularly Angus Finney, also Paul McFadden & Doug Sinclair of Emmy Award Winners Bang Post Production who were very supportive of the project.

The location for the proposed film was Dorothea Quarry in the Nantlle Valley of Gwynedd, in the area's slate fields.

Our thanks to those in the area who were so supportive of this project including Richard Wyn Hughes of Camera Cymru, Helen Pritchard of the Clic Agency and Jezz Vernon of Metrodome.

Thank you to everyone who helped with what would have been an epic folk horror film with deep Welsh cultural roots.

Thanks to Christian Pinchbeck for his work on the cover of the book.
And thanks to Sophia Wulf for her work on the map of Cwm Du – The Black Valley.

Glossary:

Black Valley is set in the slate quarrying area of Gwynedd, in North West Wales. The mythology is based on our Borderland Mythology, underpinning in a number of our projects at Garland Stone, including *Borderland, Witch Sight* and *Folk Devil.*

The Otherworld – 'Annwn'; the place which lies beneath the world. The subterranean place where all that is no longer welcome in our world goes: the land of the dead, the Old Gods and the previous race who Mankind drove underground – The Gwyllion.

Gwyllion – The Dark Things in the Night. The race Mankind drove away as the world was conquered. Living in the darkness of The Otherworld for millennia they are sightless, stone age people communicating by sound alone. They have a pure hatred of Mankind, wishing to reclaim their lost world of light.

The Borderland - A thin place – a place where the border between our world and The Otherworld is very thin and the creatures of the darkness can break through. Cwm Du is such a thin place.

Cwm Du – Welsh for 'Black Valley.' Black now due to the slate quarries which scar the land.

Gwynedd – the Celtic Kingdom of North West Wales, the setting for many of the British Celtic Myths written down in the *Mabinogion* a thousand years ago.

Eryri – Snowdonia, the mountainous area of Gwynedd. Large areas of Gwynedd are scarred by the remnants of the slate quarrying industry, which was in decline in 1918 when the novel *Black Valley* begins.

Druidess (and Druid) – the priests of the old religion before Christianity was brought to Britain. They were the religious leaders of the Celtic tribes, responsible for driving the Gwyllion underground. They have natural magical powers, understanding the lines of power within the land (now known as ley-lines). In *Black Valley*, the mantle of Druidess passes from Myfanwy to her daughter, Becca, who a hundred years later wishes to pass on the role to her direct female descendant, Laura.

Morwyn / Morwynion – The Maid/s or servants of the Druidess, charged with helping her control the world of Cwm Du. They are Female Warriors in this land lost in time.

Nothing Can Hold Back The Otherworld – Except You

Contents:

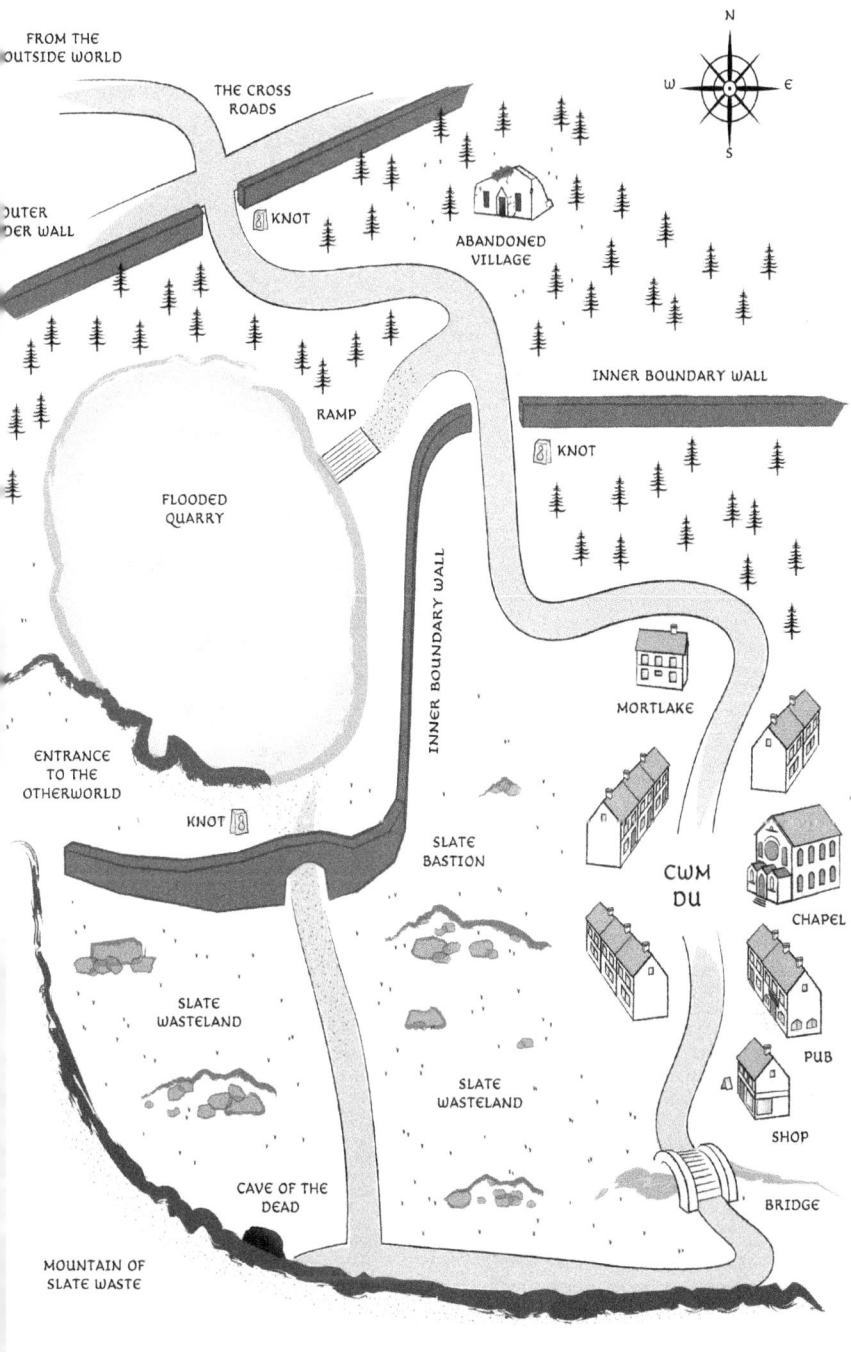

Chapter 1: The Birds of Annwn Take Flight

*"There are sacraments of evil as well as of good about us, and
we live and move to my belief in an unknown world,
a place where there are caves and shadows and dwellers in
twilight.
It is possible that man may sometimes return on the track of
evolution, and it is my belief that an awful lore is not yet
dead."*

– Arthur Machen

North Wales: 1918: During the Great War
The sun rises over the tallest mountain, casting a shadow on a
blackened land. Eryri. Land of the Eagle. A land of myth and
legend, now scarred by industry. Large areas with topsoil
gone, baring the black rock beneath.

Slate. Famous and coveted all over the world. This is the
best slate in the world. Roofing the homes of the British
Empire.

Slate formed of soil millions of years old, holding the
bodies of creatures not known to man when books like the Bible
were written a couple of short millennia ago.

These once living creatures are now buried and preserved
in rock. Rock blown from the earth in these massive pits.
Quarries creating large unnatural valleys and craters in a
country which used to be beautiful, leaving it looking like a
wasteland. Like a black moon.

So much wasted. For every ton of world class slate
exported from the bowels of the country, nine tons are left to
lie in the sun and colour this once green valley black. Black
rock left lying across the land as far as the eye can see.
Creating its own geography.

In this place, everything made by man is made of slate.
Roads, buildings, walls and fences which keep sheep fenced in

at places where the slate has not been discarded on the face of the earth.

Men left this world of slate to fight for Great Britain in the Great War. Those who return know the desolation of mud and ordinance all around them. Now they are back in a world where mud has metamorphosed into slate, which is ripped apart by ordinance daily. The familiar sound of explosions rock the valley as they return to work, treading on the shrapnel of broken slate which lies everywhere. Men broken by war work in this man-made hell to feed their families in this now barren land they call home.

Beyond the rim of the quarry, along the slate track is the Quarry Manager's House. Close enough to allow quick access to the site lest there be more industrial disputes, just far enough away not to be rocked by the regular explosions.

A house built of slate some two dozen years ago, like much of the village just further along the road which grew to house the quarrymen from the countryside all around. Cwm Du. The Black Valley.

The manager's house has been named after his place of birth. Mortlake in London. Within the dark windows is a place between worlds. The manager is named Salhurst. Granted the position of managing one of the largest slate quarries in the country based on an education at the Royal Masonic School for Boys.

Marrying an enchanting local girl, Rebecca, one who could speak good English and seemed to love him. One who preferred the name Becca as it was more Welsh, which reminded him of the Biblical character who the locals used as a figurehead when smashing toll gates in the south west of Wales. The Rebecca Riots. Locals acting against His Majesty's laws. So the name Becca always grated on him.

Rebecca. Or Becca. Living between two worlds, both wife to the Quarry Manager and daughter to the Druidess.

Two brief years ago, like many of the quarrymen, Salhurst
left her and their son to serve His Majesty on the Western
Front. Scarred like so many by the Great War, coming home to
his old job of managing the quarry once more. Trying to hide
his scars, the ones seen on his body and the ones hidden in
his mind.

Finding on his return that the local wise woman, or
Druidess as some would have it, Myfanwy, his wife's mother,
has taken up residence in his home. Myfanwy who never learned
to read nor write, who remembered everything she ever needed
to know, so she claimed. He can hardly say her name, it is so
alien to him. She was the woman all turned to for help, until
Huw the local minister spoke out against her from his pulpit
during the Religious Revival of the chapel a dozen years
before the war. But at times of crisis the people of the area
still turn up at Salhurst's door to see Myfanwy, when they
should be at the Minister's door at the Manse.

This place where the two worlds collide is a strange one
for the little boy. Arthur Salhurst, living in a black world
full of the myths of the once green land taught to him by his
grandmother. A world hidden from view beneath the wasted
slate.

Arthur sitting on his grandmother's knee. His cheek on her
old white home spun dress, looking at the slate amulet around
her neck. Apart from her harsh broken voice the only sound the
ticking of the slate framed clock on the slate mantlepiece.
She finishes the story telling of how thousands of years ago
her foremothers drove back the dark folk into the earth, so
people could raise their animals and crops on this land.
Before the slate. When it was green and open.

In the doorway Becca smiles, recognising the tale she has
heard a hundred times as a child. The front door slams.

Her husband pushes past her. Angry. "What have I told you
Myfanwy? English. I don't want my son brought up like some

wild heathen colonial."

Myfanwy bristles, bending her mouth to speak a language she only learned as an adult. "I'm teaching him history. It is important, yeah."

"History!?! Myth and nonsense! Arthur, to your studies."

The little boy climbs reluctantly from his grandmother's lap. "Yes sir."

Myfanwy looks at her daughter, standing uncomfortably in the doorway. "Tell him Becca."

Becca looks down, not wanting to antagonise her already angry husband.

Myfanwy glares at Becca, storming out of the house 'accidentally' knocking over a photo of Salhurst in British Army uniform. The front door slams. Arthur winces.

Salhurst glares at Arthur. "I said to your studies boy!" Arthur runs out of the room.

Becca rights the photo. "Henry. Please! Don't antagonise my mother."

"She will put this stuff and nonsense into the boy's head! If she taught him something practicable... In English!" Salhurst looks haunted.

"What's wrong Henry? What is this really about? Why are you home?"

"I just spoke to the company accountant. I don't know how long this quarry can last."

"But there are millions of tons of slate there Henry."

"And not an ounce of good slate Rebecca. It's a good thing so many went to the Front. There will be no work for anyone within a couple of weeks unless we find a new seam. We're having to tunnel to find any rock of use."

Absolute darkness. Sounds. Voices in the void. A language long forgotten on the surface of the earth. Clicking. Tongues tapping to let others know where they are. A constant sound in the darkness.

This part of The Otherworld is their darkness. A place not frequented by the Husks of those who live above in light. The living dead of that different race. The race that drove them down here into the darkness hundreds of lifetimes ago.

And there are no other creatures here. There has been safety in this darkness. Until now.

Loud thuds. Hurting their ears. Resounding all around. Drowning out the tapping of tongues. Cries from those now lost in the noise in the darkness.

A dark hand touches the wall of rock, withdrawing as the rock vibrates. What is happening?

Myfanwy walks towards the mountain. Eryri. Land of the Eagle. Given that beautiful name back in the days before the land was torn up for slate. Now there's nothing for eagles to hunt in this ugly world.

Her feet slip on the loose slate, the dust grey on her white dress. She climbs away from the giant hole in the ground, the quarry her son-in-law manages for men who have never been there. If it was in her hands no one would have dug deep towards whatever lies beneath this world. Towards Annwn, The Otherworld, where all that is no longer welcome here are banished. The Dead. The Old Gods. And those half humans defeated millennia ago by her kind so their families could farm this land. So that they could live without fear of those footsteps in the snow, silencing their approach, deadening the screams of those they killed by weapon or pestilence in the darkest of times. Gwyllion. The dark things in the night. Long since banished to The Otherworld but always on her mind these days. Why?

Myfanwy reaches the top of the ridge and looks back at where she has come from. She stands looking out across the once beautiful countryside, now scarred with millions of tons of black slate waste. A black valley she remembers as green.

Beyond the lowlands is the sea. Named The Irish Sea. Even its name taken from her people. Wales seen as an extension to England because it is attached. Her mother told her that the wise learned to swim to Ireland. But there is nothing there. No slate. No good stone. No coal. Nothing but peat and rotten vegetables. There was talk of rebellion there. Good luck to them.

That won't happen in Wales. Here they have forgotten their past. Forgotten their princes, their stories and their language. Her role is not to forget that bigger threat than even those from across the border. The threat which was driven below ground all those centuries before there was a difference between England and Wales.

There are worse things which have walked this land than the English. More evil than the Germans their young men battle some hundreds of miles away.

She turns to climb further up the mountain. A movement catches her eye. A massive flock of dark birds rises from the mountain like a rock face coming to life. It swirls and swarms, flying in her direction. Forming and reforming patterns in the air. Creating a wall of flying bodies which drop like a stone. Flying along the ground in her direction. Rising up as if to swallow her up. Closer, the birds' red eyes, and open beaks screaming out like the cries of a thousand dying men.

Myfanwy looks on in terror. She whispers under her breath in Welsh. "The Birds of Annwn!!!" Birds from The Otherworld. Birds that fly when the veil between our world and the Otherworld grows thin. When bad things are about to happen.

Myfanwy lies on the ground as the birds rush over her, flying barely inches above her head. Thousands of birds spreading out like a black cloud over the valley and the quarry below. Circling now.

Beneath them, the quarry. Another explosion sending dust into the air. In a few seconds the sound arrives. Deadened by the birds in the sky. The birds are an omen of destruction. Myfanwy realises what she is seeing. The quarry!!!

Myfanwy slides her way down the hill towards the quarry, faster than she could run, descending towards the black valley below.

Chapter 2: The Black Wall

The darkness shakes. A rumble reverberating all around. Loose rock falling on them. The sound drowning out their frantic clicking sounds. Confused screams and calls all around. The sound of those lost in the darkness.

And now the sound of something different. Movement. Close by. Just on the other side of the monolith. The perfectly smooth rock. Hands touch it. Feeling the rock vibrate. A large figure pushing the others aside.

The wise one. The one who remembers for them. Placing hands on the smooth rock. Crying out in panic. Talking of those from above who drove them into this dark place.

This is the rock which was spoken of by the old ones. The rock blocking the way into that world of light above. Calls for all to gather at this place. The air filling with the sound of others approaching from the darkness. Clicks and cries drowning out the sound of their own heartbeats. Hundreds of heartbeats converging at this place.

Absolute darkness inside the mountain. Something moving. The light from a miner's Davey Lamp moving in the blackness of the tunnel. Salhurst limps along the narrow passageway.

This new tunnel has been Salhurst's project for the last few months. He discovered the narrow cave. He had the quarrymen cut it high and wide enough to let a man walk through. Weeks of work. Digging deep into the slate and widening the passageway. A tunnel into the mountain following a natural fissure.

Salhurst had the work on this tunnel continue as so little good slate was being exposed by the blasting on the main face of the quarry. It was very difficult for the new geologist to work out the makeup of the rocks here. His old geologist had been killed in war tunnelling in France. This new man, Fergal, had been sent by the London office. No field experience but very reliable. An Irish savage. So he let the man dig to see if there was a change in quality of slate this deep underground as Fergal had predicted there may be.

Now the message from his Foreman to attend at the tunnel. Something must have been found. Salhurst climbs with difficulty over a now shattered boulder which almost blocks the end of the tunnel. Lights moving beyond in the darkness.

Salhurst crawls into a large underground cavern. Slate dust filling the air. There has been blasting. Doubtless the boulder was an otherwise immovable barrier. The minute particles of disturbed slate hang in the dead air, like an unnatural black fog underground.

His eyes become accustomed to the light. This cavern is needless to say a natural formation. Thirty feet tall in parts. Dropping to a couple of feet at the edges. Almost totally clear of debris, apart from dust. Dust deep enough to trip him, his damaged leg catching in the deep loose slate.

Salhurst steadies himself and steps out across the cavern towards the half dozen men who are all congregated at the far end of the cavern. Salhurst wades through the dust, as heavy as trench mud around his feet. His footsteps making a shifting sound.

Lights turn in his direction. A figure steps forward through the gloom to meet him. His Foreman, Idris, who despite being in his mid-forties volunteered alongside Salhurst and was made an NCO in the Friends Battalion at his request. A mountain of a man. Wild black hair and beard now Army regulations no longer applied. But a good man none the less. A local man who understands the desperate need to find a new seam of quality slate which would save this quarry and the jobs of all of the men here.

As he gets closer the features of the quarrymen present become clearer. Some who served with him, some who stayed to work the quarry. Robert, Arwyn and Bryn examining the far wall of the cavern. And Fergal of course. Silhouetted against the far wall of the cavern.

Then Salhurst realises what he is seeing. The light is shining off this wall of slate like a black mirror. Deep black, not grey. Shining. Perfectly smooth. Perfect. Salhurst rushes forward and touches the wall of perfect slate. Almost warm to the touch. Almost alive.

A figure steps beside him. Fergal, his new Irish geologist. An ambitious bastard. The one assigned by London to Salhurst. Salhurst constantly aware of this man's bad reports to the company behind his back. But the bastard has found something here. "So, what have you found here Fergal?"

"It's perfect Mr. Salhurst! By the look of this rock, it is the start of an even harder seam stretching into the mountain."

Idris puts his hand on Salhurst's shoulder. His face white. He shakes his head as tears of fear shine in his eyes.

"My God, Idris. Our prayers are answered."

Idris points to a mark around a foot across on the otherwise perfectly smooth wall off to one side. His hand starts to shake.

"There's a mark. A seal." Idris steps forward towards the marking. Salhurst follows.

Fergal looks at Idris. "What bollocks have you found now you superstitious Welsh bastard?"

A carving in the rock. A Celtic Knot. An ancient endless circular pattern. Lines interweaving and having no beginning and no end. Salhurst thinks of his mother-in-law's pendant. A very similar pattern. But this cavern was sealed within the mountain. She could not have been down here marking this rock in this way. No one has been in this cave for millennia.

Idris steps back. Something crunches beneath his feet in the deep dust. Idris brushes the dust away. Buried in dust at his feet lies a woman's skeletal body. The fibre remains of a white cloth dress. A slate amulet on a leather thong around her neck.

Idris jumps back in fear, crying out. Arwyn and Robert the quarrymen rush forward. They brush away at the slate dust revealing two more white clothed skeletons beside it.

The men exchange glances with Idris. "The Black Wall!"

Fergal laughs in the men's frightened faces. "What in the name of God is the Black Wall?"

Arwyn speaks to Idris in Welsh. "We have to seal this place Idris."

Idris tries to control his fear and nods. "Everyone out!"

The other quarrymen move quickly across the deep slate dust towards the tunnel. Dust whipping up around them, making them appear as phantoms disappearing into darkness.

Fergal roars in frustration. Salhurst beats him to instructions. "Idris! Stop your foolishness! Men! Come back here!" But the men are gone, climbing over the shattered boulder, their lights immediately gone from sight leaving blackness at that side of the cavern.

All bar one. Idris tries to compose himself. Frightened. Pointing. "The Knot... the bodies... it's the Black Wall Mr. Salhurst sir. We must keep away from it or..."

Salhurst cuts him off. The nonsense his mother-in-law has told these men since they were children has now changed from being a joke to becoming a problem. A major problem. This is the best slate Salhurst has ever seen. "The Black Wall is a fairy tale to scare children! Stay where you are! Or this is the last day you will work this quarry."

Idris, the last remaining quarrymen stands torn between his fears for this life and the next.

Myfanwy strides across the black landscape heading downhill to the quarry. Her white dress blowing in the wind.

In the distance three younger women also dressed in white converge on her across the slate waste. Myfanwy waves to her Morwynion, Hannah, Mary and Rachel. Morwynion are Maidens. Servants. The young women of the area chosen to help Myfanwy in her role as Druidess. A role some ridicule apart from at times like this.

The three girls exchanging frightened glances as the thousands of black birds circle over Myfanwy, causing mottled shadows on the ground where Myfanwy walks. Rachel and Hannah are compelled by their roles to follow but filled with fear.

On a nearby ridge Mary stops. Trembling with fear, watching the birds circling over the quarry now, wheeling around like water spinning around a whirlpool. What in the name of God is going on? Does God really have anything to do with what is happening in front of her eyes? Across the black waste slate, the other two Morwynion have joined Myfanwy, all three white figures running now towards the quarry. Mary swallows hard and runs after them.

In the quarry the men down tools. The tapping of hammers on metal spikes splitting the slate for roof tiles stops. The sheds where slates are cut to uniform size empty. Silence below. Above them the swirling birds almost block out the sun. The birds circle and scream. The sound echoing around the walls of the deep quarry.

High above the main work area shouts ring out. People emerging from the cave on the second level which the Manager had them explore, so great is his fear of no good slate being left in the massive hole blown into the land. The quarry is several hundred feet deep. A dark grey hole: good slate is black. This dying quarry has so little time left, each blast feels like it is drawing its last breath. Could there be any good slate left that high above their heads? It makes no sense. So what is all the shouting? Was the Englishman right?

Alarmed shouting from the men who appear from the cave. Others running to them, expecting a fall. Have rocks buried those who have been foolish enough to go within? Including the Manager, Geologist and Foreman!

Robert's eyes adjust to the light, seeing a dozen men rush towards him in panic. He coughs, clearing his lungs. Looking at the questioning faces. "We found the Black Wall!"

The quarrymen stop in their tracks, unclear if they should rush passed him into the cave or run. Run from this place they heard about as children. A thin place. A place where he Otherworld waits to grab you and pull you down deep into the earth to your death. A quarryman runs to the main shed. Moments later the siren rings out. Wailing out across the quarry, fighting with the screaming of the birds overhead.

Becca steps out of the house and looks into the sky. Her face is a picture of terror. The siren is rung if there is an accident. A way to summon help. There are thousands of black birds swirling over the nearby quarry. She remembers her mother's stories of the Birds of Annwn, who arrive at battles and disasters to feast on the bodies of the dead. She takes Arthur by the hand and leads him off towards the Quarry.

Myfanwy and her Morwynion rush through the ornate slate tunnel cut through the massive bastion which separates the village from the quarry. They run out of the darkness stopping at the lip of the quarry. The siren ringing all around. Rachel and Hannah look to Myfanwy for guidance. Behind them Mary is running out of the dark mouth of the slate tunnel. Myfanwy turns to instruct her Morwynion. "Come. We are needed." She leads the way around the lip of the quarry down the steep slate path down into the lower levels of the quarry. Her three Morwynion follow her down to the second level, where the tunnel has been cut into the side of the mountain.

13

Chapter 3: The Black Wall Falls

The dust swirls around Idris and his lamp as he crosses the chamber towards Salhurst and Fergal. Fear in his eyes, wiping his hand on his clothes, trying to get the feeling of the dry bones of the dead Druidess off his hand. The bones of someone who died millennia ago so that he could live. And now he is here with men who do not understand the significance of that sacrifice. Men who would undo that work.

Salhurst looks at the towering quarryman, bent in fear. He never bent in fear on the Western Front. Idris always held his head high. Facing whatever God threw at him in the battle to beat the Bosch. "Idris. What is the meaning of this?"

"Mr. Salhurst. We cannot blow the Black Wall."   Fergal lets out a sarcastic laugh. "Watch me Welshman!"

Idris turns to Fergal baring his teeth. "This is the Black Wall. It holds back all evil driven from this world."

Salhurst sighs. "Idris. Look at the quality of this slate. This seam of slate could keep us all in work for years. Forget your superstitious nonsense man!"

"Me and the men won't work it Mr. Salhurst." Idris turns to leave.

Fergal snarls. "So, you are refusing? I can bring men here from Ireland in a few days Mr. Salhurst."

Idris turns to Salhurst. "We should send for Old Myfanwy. She'll know what to do."

Salhurst looks at him aghast. The old woman! The power she still has over these superstitious people! Time to bring this man into the twentieth century. "And Myfanwy knows about geology, does she? Quarrying? Engineering? Does she put food on your table? My mother-in-law is nothing but an old woman..."

Idris straightens up, towering over the other two men. "Show some respect Mr. Salhurst. Her family have taken care of us for centuries. And if we blow the Black Wall..."

A pause. Fergal jumps in. "What? What will happen?"

Idris growls at him. "The world we know will unravel as the Knot unravels."

Fergal laughs. "Jackeen! You're a fucking peasant!"

Idris pushes passed the smaller man, knocking him aside. He steps carefully around the Druidesses' bodies on the floor and holds his lamp beside the shining wall of slate. "There it is! The Knot!!! Carved in living rock!!!"

Salhurst lifts a finger to silence Fergal. "Listen to yourself Idris. We've all seen true horror. Blowing a new seam of slate is not going to end the world. Is it? I'm in charge here and we push on."

Idris wades across the cavern towards the exit.

Salhurst looks on in disbelief, never thinking he'd see the moment Idris would disobey him in this way. "Idris. Stop! Do you want your men's families to starve?"

But Idris has gone leaving darkness. There should be silence, but there is not. A strange faint thumping sound like a heartbeat coming from somewhere. This is not a sound Salhurst has heard underground before. The acoustics in this cavern are strange. Amplifying every movement of dust at his feet. But the sound is not the movement of rocks. It is movement on rocks. Could it be sound travelling from the workings? Surely not.

Salhurst feels something he feels every night when he falls asleep, whether his dreams take him back to France, or to the company office in London. Fear. The sound seems to grow louder.

Hundreds of heartbeats in the confined space. Hundreds of clicks. Deafening. Hundreds of fists hammering the rock in time with the fists of the Great One. Like a massive heartbeat in the darkness. The hands of a people hammering on the wall.

Wanting to bring it down.

Salhurst stands alone in the dark cavern looking down at the ancient bones lying in the slate dust. A pounding like his heartbeat in his ears, but at a different rate. Slower and irregular. He puts his hands over his ears and the sound stops. That is strange. His mind playing tricks on him down here in the bowels of the mountain. It must surely be the sound of his own heart. What else could it be?

The sound now more like the distant guns of a night bombardment over the battlefield, without the flashes in the darkness. His mind is definitely playing tricks on him. He should not have stayed here alone when Fergal left to bring the equipment needed.

He looks down at the dead bodies found a hundred feet within a mountain of solid rock. No denying they exist. The bones are here. Is there any significance to this? Myfanwy's tales of ancient times are the figment of her imagination surely? There could be no legendary places in this barbaric country. Here the only signs of pre-history are ancient stone rings whose use has been lost in the depths of time. Here in North Wales even these are poor reflections of grander examples like Stonehenge in Wiltshire.

He looks at the skulls staring up at him, white in the black dust. Watching him. He takes a deep breath. Is this really a site of significance? Salhurst scoffs. No, this is merely stuff and nonsense. The less said about this to the men the better. Let Fergal blow the seam to see how deep it is. Payment will put an end to Idris and the men's superstitions. They will be back to work immediately. Grateful for the bread on their tables.

And it will put an end to the stuff and nonsense Myfanwy is teaching his son when he is not present in his own home.

His eyes fall on the carving in the rock. So similar to

the primitive markings on the pendant Myfanwy insists on
wearing. Like some juju thing from the colonies of Africa.
This country, Wales, is in so many ways still as backward as
much of the rest of the Empire.

He runs his finger gingerly along the pattern. No
beginning. No end. A closed pattern. His fingertips feel a
vibration. It must be his racing heart. No. He puts his hand
on the slate edifice. There is a vibration. Like a heartbeat.

Fear growing in his own heart. But why? Where is Fergal?
For the love of God! Let's get on with this! Salhurst realises
he is sweating. Just like in France. Ahead of an action.
Fearing for his very life.

Thank God. The light from a Davey lamp at the entrance to
the cavern. "Fergal? What kept you man!?"

"You need to speak to Idris, Mr. Salhurst. He's agitating
the men. Spewing out folklore and superstition. Frightening
them with stories of the end of the world."

"Stuff and nonsense."

"Yes sir, of course, but these are simple men. They
believe in such fairy tales." Fergal puts down a box
containing charges and detonators. He produces a hand drill
and sets to work on the slate edifice. He looks for a
weakness. A crack. An indentation as a place to commence
drilling. There is none. This slate is perfect. Too perfect.
Fergal turns to Salhurst to see him holding his hand against
the rock. Fergal does the same and feels the vibration. What
in God's name is that?

"Get on with it man!" Salhurst snapping at him. Fergal
pushes the drill hard against the rock and starts to turn it.
Not a mark. No purchase whatsoever. The metal of the drill
starting to burr. But this is a new drill. Possibly faulty. It
is not going to make an impression here. "I need to get
another drill Mr. Salhurst."

"What's the problem Fergal?"

"It won't cut the rock sir. Won't even make a mark."

Salhurst looks at the Celtic pattern again, marked deeply into this rock. So how was that done? Carved by primitives? That must have taken time. The three skulls watch him. He closes his eyes to block them out. "Set charges regardless."

"Sir, you know if..."

Salhurst roars, his voice echoing wildly. "Set charges. Blow this thing. What the devil is wrong with you man!!!"

"Leave it be!"

Salhurst and Fergal jump out of their skins. There is a white shape luminescent in the light reflected from the wall of slate. The shape moves forward towards them, raising dust but not making a sound. Myfanwy, a ghost like figure in white in the pitch blackness.

"How in God's name did you get down here?" Fergal on his feet. Thrown, trying to regain some authority.

Myfanwy ignores him, walking towards Salhurst and the Celtic Knot prominent in his lamp light. "We need to leave here Henry. This is The Black Wall. It is thin place. A very dangerous place." Myfanwy looks at the bodies lying in the dust. Her mind reeling. She has been accepting this to be a true story, as it has been repeated for countless generations. Now face to face with what even she at times has thought may be a myth. But is true. And she is one of the first to see this place since it was created by the women whose remains lie at her feet. She points at the skeletons in the dust. "Those women gave their lives so we could live here in safety."

Her harsh voice echoes around the chamber. The two men look at her in shocked silence. Who let this woman into a working mine?

The echoes of her voice die to silence. But not silence. The irregular beat in the air. Myfanwy's face turns from awe and anger to fear. The same fear felt by these two men who are too foolish to act on it. "You hear it?"

Salhurst and Fergal exchange glances. Unable to answer and give credence to this old woman.

Myfanwy rushes forward passing Salhurst and touches the Celtic Knot. Her face turns ashen. "You can feel it! The sound of The Otherworld. A heartbeat different to our own! Leave with me now! Close this cavern. No one will think the worse of you, Henry."

Salhurst hesitates, confusion on his face. Seeing a way out of this cavern and his unbearable feeling of dread at being here. He closes his eyes, about to nod.

"Shall I carry on sir?" Fergal is looking at the old woman with open distain now that the shock of her presence has dissipated. "We need to report our findings to London sir. We must get on."

Salhurst nods.

Myfanwy grabs Salhurst, pushing him up against the slate wall. Salhurst's head fills with images of soldiers rushing towards him. Thousands of dark figures, running across a black earth. Not the Bosch. Not in France. Here in his quarry. They are unclothed savages. They have no guns. Rather rocks made into weapons like clubs, swords, knives. Quarrymen falling like men walking into machine gun fire. Salhurst screams, throwing Myfanwy off him. She falls into the dust on the floor of the cavern.

Another voice. "Henry? What are you doing!?!"

Salhurst looks on in disbelief. Two other figures in the cavern. He tries to focus through the tears of fear filling his eyes. He steps away from the wall of slate. It's affecting him.

Fergal trying to keep polite control in the circumstances. "Mrs Salhurst. You should leave immediately. It's not safe. I'm setting charges ma'am."

A figure runs at Salhurst. Small, low, fast, raising dust. Salhurst makes to defend himself. Arthur runs past his father, looking in awe at the skeletons on the ground. He picks up a slate amulet from beside the bodies.

Salhurst watches his wife helping her mother to her feet after he has thrown her to the ground. Anger on both women's faces. The boy too excited to notice the family drama coming to a head around him. "Rebecca, for God's sake! Take Arthur and your mother and go home! Immediately!"

"Henry! Have you lost your mind? What are you doing here?"

"We are merely doing our jobs Mrs. Salhurst. Please. Leave the area. We shall be blasting shortly." Fergal doggedly forcing sticks of dynamite into cracks in the slate surrounding the black wall. He connects the detonator and strides away from the wall. Wires trailing. Arthur getting to his feet and watching the man work.

Myfanwy back on her feet, glowering at the Irishman. "Stop fool. You have no idea what you're doing!"

"You want to stay? It'll be the death of you old woman." Fergal runs the wires back beyond the broken boulder at the entrance of the cavern.

Salhurst stands alone with his family in the strange light reflected by the Black Wall.

Fergal places the detonators. "You should leave sir. The charges are now live."

Salhurst stands like a man with shell shock. Deeply affected by what he saw whilst pushed up against the wall of slate. Those images. So alien yet so familiar. Similar to his experiences in France, but different. That wasn't a memory. That was something much deeper. Images of things not of this world. Human perhaps, of a kind. Rather, inhuman sentient beings meaning him and his people harm. Just like the stories Myfanwy told his boy. But he heard little of those tales and remembers nothing like this. So what has he seen?

What he sees right now is Fergal carrying the plunger detonator across the cavern. Salhurst grabs his boy, still

holding on to that slate amulet and heads for the cavern
entrance, leaving his lamp at the rock face. A figure racing
towards him. Rebecca. She claws at him, he catches her by the
hair and pulls her across the cavern, screaming. The boy
starting to cry. Salhurst carries and drags his family back to
the cavern entrance where Fergal is busily readying to blow
the slate edifice.

Myfanwy walking ghost like in the other direction. Towards
Salhurst's lamp. She reaches the Black Wall. Studying the
Celtic Knot. Identical to the one on her amulet. She touches
the carving. A shock going up her arm into her mind. Images of
dark hordes rushing towards her out of the darkness. Figures
like her mother and her Morwynion, all long dead, milling
amongst them. All moving towards her so fast now. The dark
figures catching her. Overwhelming her.

Myfanwy falls to the ground beside the long dead bodies.
Face to face with the figures of legend she first learned of
on her mother's knee before she could even speak. Her name
being called. Myfanwy! Myfanwy! She turns her head. Her
daughter calling her from across the darkness of the cavern.

Myfanwy gets to her feet and runs. Across the cavern. Away
from the monsters in her mind. Running to stop these foreign
fools from letting these creatures out after millennia of
festering their hatred of Mankind. A hatred that could bring
the end of all of the people of the earth. The sheer numbers
of these diseased creatures wishing to reclaim their world.
Followed by the dead. Their own fathers, mothers, brothers and
sisters who have left this world and also want to return to
the world of light. To turn the entire world black, in the
same way these workings had turned this once beautiful valley
black. Turning the whole world into a black desert to reflect
The Otherworld below. Cities would become Necropolises. A
world of the dead. A world of the dispossessed arisen. A world
of dark gods long forgotten, ruling over an inhuman world. A

world of gods and monsters.

Fergal connects the cables to the plunger, as Salhurst pushes his wife and son into the hollow behind the boulder. Myfanwy jumps on Fergal, her unexpected strength overpowering him for a moment. She scratches and bites at him and is pulled away. Salhurst rolls on top of her behind the boulder. "For the love of God, Fergal! Do it!"

Myfanwy struggles with him. "Becca!!! Stop him!!!" But she is trapped and holding on to Arthur who is screaming.

Fergal raises the plunger.

The light seems to go out of Myfanwy's eyes. "Nooooo!!!!"

The plunger drops. Nothing. Silence. Then the blast hits. Dust blinding everything. Blowing out Salhurst's lamp. Blowing out Fergal's lamp. Dust ripping at them and covering them even in the shelter behind the boulder.

From the second level of the quarry the plume of dust blows out of the narrow tunnel into the air, scattering the birds swirling overhead. Driving them away from the quarry for a moment. Idris and the Quarrymen watch the huge plume of dust erupt from the tunnel.

A figure runs across the quarry. A middle-aged man. Huw, the local Minister. "Idris, what in God's name is happening?"

Idris bows his head in respect. "Sir, we found The Black Wall. Myfanwy has tried to save it. I think she has failed."

"That is superstition Idris. That woman follows the Devil's ways. She cannot help you. And be honest. Do you expect God to ever allow the Devil's creatures to walk the earth?"

"I've seen the Black Wall sir. It exists. Now it's been blown up. Mr. Salhurst and the others are all within."

Huw puts his hand on Idris' shoulder. "God help them!"

Idris looks him in the eye with fear. "God help us!"

Chapter 4: Emerging Into Light

An unimaginable silence. The loss of the sense of hearing is
terrifying. It is all they have. Impossible to know where they
are or to communicate. Mouths full of dust meaning it is
impossible to breathe. Trying to clear the dust from their
lungs. And a weight on top of them. Stopping them moving. This
weight being pushed away in the instinctive fight to survive.
Sometimes it is the weight of warm bodies. Sometimes the
weight of cold rock. Faces pushing upwards through the dust,
rock and bodies. Gasping for air.

But this air tastes different. Full of dust but also
strange. The air turning to wind. Wind rushing over them.
Blowing the dust everywhere. The sense of hearing slowly
returning. That strange sound. Wailing. Above it the hiss of
the fast-moving air turning into a howl. The wailing of those
who survived all around. Those with rocks still upon them.
Those with limbs shattered. Those without limbs. Clicking
starting all around but not the same sound as before. Not
echoing. The sound travelling outwards into a new space. Dark.
But then something new. Something told of in stories handed
down across countless lifetimes. Light. Hands reaching out
from beneath the rock. Reaching for the light.

Fergal holds up his lamp. Its pale light illuminates the
cavern. The air is like a sandstorm of black dust. Swirling
and moving, being sucked away into the void that is now at the
far end of the cavern. A roaring of wind as the dust and air
is sucked into the hole in the mountain he has just created.
So there is no vein of perfect slate. There is no future for
him in this God forsaken place. He needs to find a new
position at another quarry.

Myfanwy pushes passed him. Her hair being dragged before
her by the rush of air from the outside world into what must

be The Otherworld beyond. Where there is just darkness. Momentarily the rush of air stops. Silence. Apart from the ringing in her ears. Drowning out everything. Except the strange clicking noise.

She can just see her daughter and grandson walking out across the cavern, as if through a black fog. Stepping over the debris of pure black slate.

Myfanwy studies the rock at her feet. The slate is not very thick. A few inches maybe. The whole edifice seems to be shattered into thousands of pieces. Was this really The Black Wall? Was this all that was holding back The Otherworld for millennia? Myfanwy stares into the darkness and begins to doubt. Is she really the foolish old woman that her son in law tells her she is?

Myfanwy bends and picks up a piece of the shattered monolith. It shines in the dim light. It has The Celtic Knot engraved on it. Becca joins her, taking the piece of rock from her mother. She turns it so that she can see the design in the dim light. A design she instantly recognises from her mother's amulet. She runs her finger over it, clearing the dust out of the grooves.

Becca turns around to find her son and husband. But another face appears in the gloom. Dark skinned. Big eyes straining to see anything in the dim light. As frightened of her as she is of it. Naked. Scarred. Thin. Wiry. Not human. Different. Reminding her of that book she read in her husband's library about the origin of species. The creature bares its teeth worn away by a lifetime of use. Becca raises the rock to defend herself. The creature reaches out and burns momentarily, screaming as it runs into the swirling darkness.

Becca breathes hard, choking. Coughing, retching in fear. An arm around her. Her mother. Dragging her away towards the cavern entrance.

Myfanwy watching the moving darkness within the swirling

black dust. People, of a kind. They exist! Just like in the old tales. Gwyllion! The dark things in the night. The things long banished from this world into that world beneath, The Otherworld. Bound beyond the Black Wall. The Black Wall she has just seen destroyed.

Myfanwy's hearing returning. Rocks moving. Footfalls in dust. That strange clicking sound everywhere. Echoing all around. And now the howling of a wind, coming back from within the earth. A hot fetid rush of air coming from where the Black Wall once stood. "Becca. Arthur! Run!!!!"

They run back towards the light. The light held by Fergal. He staring beyond them at the movement in the swirling dust. And then the movement along the side of the cavern nearby. It's as if the slate is coming alive. Grey shapes hardly visible moving across the slate towards him. His hearing clearing enough to hear clicking sounds getting louder. As the shapes become people. A kind of people. Much like those pygmies and dwarves in the circus freak shows he saw in years gone by. Coming towards him. Naked. Grey skinned. Nightmarish. Some carrying weapons made of slate. Blunt clubs. Sharp knives. The light he holds drawing them like moths to a flame. Their clicking sounds getting louder. Cutting through the whine in his ears after the explosion.

Salhurst stares wide eyed in horror at the creatures approaching. Myfanwy, Becca and Arthur rush by him. Myfanwy says one word, "Gwyllion", before disappearing down the tunnel with her daughter and grandson.

Salhurst stands at the entrance to the tunnel as the creatures approach. Gwyllion. The unpronounceable name the old woman called the monsters in her fairy tales. So much for fairy tales. Salhurst thinks about running after his family. With his damaged leg he will not be able to get far. All he can do is hold the line with Fergal until his family are safe. The thin red line he read about as a boy. That red having a different meaning when his turn came to go to war in France. "Fergal. Come to me. We hold them here!"

Fergal runs towards him before falling under a mass of these grey creatures. They pound him with rocks as Fergal's dead eyes are buried in the slate dust. The Davey lamp goes out.

All Salhurst can hear is the clicking in the darkness. And the rush of fetid air. The rush is getting louder. The clicking becoming deafening. Then a deeper darkness than Salhurst has ever imagined.

Myfanwy and Becca's hands scrape on the slate as they find their way back up the newly cut tunnel. Light starting out the size of a postage stamp becomes the size of a book, and in moments they stumble out into daylight, carrying Arthur.

Mottled daylight as thousands of the Birds of Annwn circle low overhead. A handful of quarrymen led by Idris rush to help them. Myfanwy's Morwynion, Hannah, Mary and Rachel gather around them protectively.

Myfanwy's harsh voice carries out over the quarry. "Salhurst opened the door to The Otherworld!!!" She takes the slate with the Knot engraved on it from her daughter's hands.

Idris pushes passed them. "Let's get Salhurst and Fergal! Before they die in there!" Idris sees he is alone. He looks down the tunnel. Suddenly his eyes fill with slate dust. He steps back, clawing at his eyes. A cloud of dust roars from the depths of the mountain. Something moves in the dust.

A grey skinned creature. Naked. Blinded by the sunlight. It screams. The miners pull back in alarm. The Morwynion step forward ready to face the threat.

Thump! The creature is gone. A jet of black water washes it clean off the side of the mountain and cascades down onto the quarry floor over a hundred feet below. Water with such force, like a huge mighty waterfall falling over the side of the mountain. Idris sees dark bodies spin in the water as it falls in torrents into the quarry below.

In moments Idris sees quarrymen drowning in the waters far below. He drags Myfanwy, Becca and the others away. "Climb up there. It'll be safer". No one can hear him over the roar of the water. He points to the first level a hundred feet above their heads. The quarrymen rush up the steep narrow track cut into the mountain, heading for higher ground. Myfanwy and Becca follow carrying Arthur in their arms. The Morwynion exchange glances, taking in what they are seeing, before running to join Myfanwy.

Beneath them the quarry is filling with pitch black water. Already filling the quarry to the third level. In moments the depth of water is nearing the second level. Quarrymen below trying to escape but being caught by the cascading black water. Men rushing up the steep tracks like ants, their screams drowned out by the thundering water which submerges them.

Their bodies floating on the surface of the foaming water. And other bodies. The grey men, also killed by the flood. Bodies floating like twigs on the boiling swirling maelstrom. This once huge quarry being turned into a lake of the dead in moments. While above the birds swirl around darkening the sky.

The earth shakes as the black water thunders out of the cave entrance on the second level, spraying out over the edge of the quarry. Idris and his men help the quarrymen who have avoided the falling water to the top of the quarry, the first level. Men young and old wide eyed in panic. Some talking of the water. Some talking of what is in the water.

Myfanwy's Morwynion help tend to the injured men. Joined by the village women who have run all the way from the village of Cwm Du arriving through the ornate slate tunnel through the huge slate bastion. Hugging their loved ones or standing frantically on the higher ground staring down into the whirling water which used to be one of the largest slate quarries in the world. Straining their eyes for any sign of husbands and sons as the water rises below, filling the massive quarry.

Becca's widowhood is dawning upon her. She holds Arthur in her arms, cradling the crying child as tears run down her face at her own loss. And the loss of her world. She looks for her mother. For the advice of the wise one. There is no sign of Myfanwy.

Rachel is lying on the ground at the edge above the spout of raging water. Below her the quarry is now almost full of the swirling black water to the second level a hundred feet below. Myfanwy is held by a rope, slung under her arms, held tight by Rachel. Myfanwy climbing down over a hundred feet beside the roaring water spurting from The Other World. The smell. The taste. Almost overpowering. The spray turning her dress black.

Myfanwy looks at the piece of slate in her hand, engraved with the Celtic Knot. The seal which held the Black Wall for Millennia. It must hold again. Myfanwy works on the loose rock inches from the powerful stream of water. Loosening rocks until there is enough space for the Celtic Knot. She pushes it into place, using other loose rocks to seal it in. Pushing it so hard her hands bleed. Her blood covering the Celtic Knot. The red blood turns black. The light goes from Myfanwy's eyes.

Myfanwy slumps and falls towards the water. Suddenly she is pulled upwards by Rachel and by Becca. Others join them pulling Myfanwy upwards to safety. Myfanwy hanging like a blackened rag doll over the churning lake beneath.

Myfanwy is dragged onto the first level as the water level reaches the cave below. Myfanwy looks at her bloodied hands and staggers to her feet. "I have replaced the seal on the cave. I have given my blood to seal the cave as my forebears did thousands of years ago. The Other World is sealed. But there are creatures of the Other World in these waters. They cannot return to whence they came. They must not become a part of this world, or this world will be lost to us. Stand and fight!"

Idris shouts out across the lake. "Take up your tools. Turn your tools into weapons. It's time to defend our land!"

The Quarrymen pick up whatever tools they have carried or are lying around. Hammers, saws, chisels, rocks. Idris has them move out around the rim of the new lake and stand watching. Others follow Idris to the one place where the water is not constrained by tall cliffs, the ramp.

In moments the water rises over the cave entrance, and over the Celtic Knot Myfanwy has put in place. The water stops rising. Still churning for a moment. Then out across the massive new lake the water settles. Almost calm.

For the first time since the explosion there is near silence except for the thousands of birds weaving overhead.

Chapter 5: Creating New Boundaries

Myfawny looks at her bloodied hands. The hands which pushed the slate knot into the rock beside the cave. Sealing the cave and The Otherworld from Cwm Du. Putting the world back in order. She looks at the slick black lake stretching out beneath her. Then she realises. The world will never be back in order. Everything has changed.

This water has come from The Otherworld. Who knows what properties this water has. The thick black water does not reflect the Birds of Annwn circling overhead. The sheeny surface lying unnaturally smooth now. Then the surface breaks. A Gwyllion head, then another appearing on the surface of the water below. All is not in order. All is lost.

She has sealed the cave. No more Gwyllion can leave the Otherworld. Any Gwyllion in the lake now cannot return to their home. So how many Gwyllion are out there? How many could survive the water? More heads appearing on the surface of the water tell her it is too many. Dozens now. There are only a couple of dozen quarrymen who have found their way to this top level. The others are dead beneath the water.

She remembers the old tales of how vicious the Gwyllion are, and how they carry a pestilence strong enough to kill anyone they touch. Now they are here in Cwm Du.

From her vantage point Myfanwy realises as did the old soldier Idris, that the sides of the quarry are now sheer cliffs around the lake that cannot be climbed. The only shore is where the slate is pulled up a steep ramp to the track above.

The Gwyllion will soon find that landing stage. If they get to shore they will reclaim this land. And then Eryri. And then Wales. And then the World.

Myfanwy feels the weakness in her arm since she pushed home that seal. The cloudiness of her vision. At first she thought it was tears. Now she knows it's something else. Then she remembers a line from the old tales. How the Druidess sealed the Black Wall and then had to die. She is now the Druidess who has sealed the cave; she will now die.

Out on the lake there are even more Gwyllion to be seen. Everywhere she looks there are more. Clicking in the air, audible even above the screams of the Birds of Annwn overhead.

This very water is of The Otherworld. Alien to this world. What it contains and what it could do to people is not known. Could it kill all who drink it? Has it already poisoned this valley forever, seeping through the cracks in the slate, making Eryri a place where no one can live? Is Cwm Du now dead?

On the cliff side nearby, Becca is with the Morwynion standing ready with rocks to fight the fierce creatures in the water below. Are they ready for this kind of fight with the monsters of myth and the power of The Otherworld? Myfanwy lets out a sob. She has no energy to scream.

Even if she is not the Druidess anymore, it is now her role to do something. She cannot fight these creatures. She cannot cure this poison. She cannot kill these creatures. There is only one solution. Only one way to save the world even if it means this valley is lost to it. If she must hide this black valley from the outside world; that is how things must be, but she must also save her family, so they continue to exist in the world beyond Cwm Du.

Through her tears and clouding vision she sees Arthur, watching her, upset. He runs forward and hugs his grandmother's legs. She picks up the boy. "Ssshhh. We are going for a walk Arthur." She cradles the boy in her arms.

Myfanwy walks passing Becca on the cliffside. Becca is distracted watching the Gwyllion in the waters below. In a moment Myfanwy and Arthur are gone.

Myfanwy walks briskly through the trees to join the track.

There is no familiar birdsong now. The birds have already fled
this doomed place. Above her it is the Birds of Annwn which
circle like vultures over the dying valley.

She walks down the track near the empty abandoned village.
Old houses, built on the side of the mountain when the quarry
was new, before the village of Cwm Du was built a mile away to
house those who came here to work in the quarry as it grew.
She walks passing the ramp down to the quarry, the new lake
shore, unnoticed by Idris and his men who stand watch down
there.

Myfanwy continues along the lane which is the only road in
and out of Cwm Du. Her grandchild crying gently in her arms.
Walking as quickly as she can along the long narrow track to
the old gateway at the western end of the road. The gateway at
the boundary of three parishes at the crossroads, where years
ago the villains of the area were hung. Heol y Plwcca - The
Gallows Lane. The setting sun now almost blinding her, though
she has not been able to see clearly since placing the slate
knot. She blinks as her vision gets ever more cloudy. It is
happening. She is dying. Myfanwy sobs.

Becca stands on the cliff edge. Tears flowing. Watching
quarrymen used to trench warfare stand ready on the new lake's
shore to repel the inevitable attack.

Strangely shaped heads bobbing on the water, slick with
the sheen of the black water running off their grey skin.
Getting accustomed to this new place. This light and the land
that lies before them. Clicking changing into a more guttural
language in the open air. Talking to each other. Planning.

One warrior moving under the water towards the entrance to
the cave. Looking for a way back to the place she knew.
Looking for her sisters and brothers to lead them into the
light. Swimming in the dark water, seeing the opening from
whence water is still moving. And then the Knot in the cliff

face beside the opening. She cannot pass. Losing her breath
she surfaces.

At the ramp a Gwyllion warrior crawls from the water.
Rising to her knees at the lakeshore. Slam!!! A heavy iron
hammer shatters her head. Smoke seems to rise from the body.
For a moment the water around her turns a different shade of
black. The grey body sinks back out of sight beneath the black
water.

Idris watches the body disappear from sight. He weighs the
heavy iron hammer in his hands. "Remember what Myfanwy taught
us! Iron will kill them!"

A roar as the quarrymen take comfort from what they have
just seen. These monsters die like any enemy. Like the Bosch.
Like anyone.

More movement in the slimy black water as the Gwyllion
begin to move towards the shore. The shore, the land held by
these creatures since the lifetimes ago when they drove the
Gwyllion underground. These beings are unfamiliar to the
Gwyllion in this form. Beneath the earth where the Gwyllion
were banished these creatures' dead Husks wander mindlessly.
These creatures on the shore will soon become more of those
dead Husks.

Becca suddenly aware of her surroundings once more. There
is something missing. There is so much missing. No more
husband. Where is her child? Where is her mother? Something
falls inside her body. Her heart falling, crushing her
stomach. "Arthur? Mam?" Becca looks around desperately. There
is no sign of them. She runs along the cliff edge towards the
ramp where the villagers are congregating.

Becca runs down the ramp. She sees Idris watching her,

holding his bloody hammer. "Where is she?"

Idris whispers to her. "She's gone. She was finished when she sealed that cave. You are our Druidess now. Lead us!"

Becca looks out across the surface of the lake at the creatures poised to attack. Dozens of warriors ready to overrun the quarrymen standing at the shore of the slimy black water. Quarrymen heavily outnumbered but standing ready to fight.

Becca has seen what the Gwyllion can do in the cavern. She is a widow as a result. If normality ever returns, she is finished. As a widow she will have nothing. Soon to be homeless with no family to look after her. Left to live wild in these mountains, just like her mother. She feels desperation rise from the very ground beneath her feet. Flowing up through her body. Filling her mind as her eyes fill with tears.

Becca screams!!! The wave of sound knocks over Idris and the others nearby. The Morwynion stand covering their ears in terror. The sound moves out across the surface of the water like a wave front, pushing the Gwyllion under the black water. The wave carries out across the surface of the huge lake, leaving the surface behind it still. Deathly still.

Then the sound returns, as powerful as before. The echo reverberates and swirls around the valley distorting wildly. The Birds of Annwn scatter overhead before falling from the sky into the black water.

Myfanwy hears the scream and smiles. Knowing her daughter has taken up the fight. Buying her time as she prepares her final task. Hiding Cwm Du.

Myfanwy is leaning on the slate gatepost at the crossroad. She is carving the Celtic Knot, using her amulet made of hard slate. The pattern matching the one on the amulet, matching the one in The Black Wall and matching the one she has made in the opposite post. Arthur is sitting on the floor watching her. "Mamgu. What are you doing?"

"Making things safe, Arthur bach. Making things safe."

"Don't be long, please."

Myfanwy smiles. "Don't worry. Everything will be well." Her amulet cuts deep into the softer slate. The Celtic Knot is almost complete.

The Morwynion surround Becca protectively. She is lying onto the ground. All energy drained by the scream. Crying like a child. Tears of blood running from her eyes.

The quarrymen and the villagers surround her, turning their back on the calm water. Knowing that there will not be a battle now. Knowing that the Gwyllion are now dead. Knowing that their new Druidess has saved them.

The scream is something only the true Druidess can possess. Something they learned in the tales Myfanwy used to tell them when they were children. But if Becca has the power of the scream, something must have happened to Myfanwy.

The Morwynion help Becca as she staggers to her feet. Idris and the others look on with a mixture of awe and fear. The bloody faced woman hardly able to stand because of what she has just done. Destroyed their enemies. Her dress now turning red with her own blood.

Becca whispers, hoarse and barely audible. "The Black Wall is no more. These Gwyllion will come again. We need to make new defences. A boundary to keep Cwm Du safe. It must be done. We must hold back The Otherworld. We must make new Knots. Make it the only battleground the Gwyllion will ever see. My mother will know what to do. Where is my mother? Where's Arthur?"

Myfanwy's hands are bleeding badly. Her blood is visible on both of the Celtic Knots she has carved into the gateposts at the end of Heol y Plwcca. Arthur is watching her. Watching

her quietly. Looking askance. Knowing something is deeply
wrong.

Myfanwy smiles at the little boy as she staggers to her
feet. "Come Arthur bach, we need to go down to the big town."
She holds out her bloody hand. She can no longer hold the
amulet she has used to carve the new Knots. It drops to the
ground.

Arthur does not move.

A tear runs down her cheek. "Hurry."

Arwyn runs along the track. Behind him Bryn is out of
breath and stops. Arwyn runs on alone, crying out Myfanwy's
name.

Out on Heol y Plwcca. Not a place Arwyn likes to be around
sunset. They say the ghosts of the hanged men are abroad
around this time, heading to meet their deaths again at the
crossroads and torment anyone passing this time of night.

The sunlight in Arwyn's eyes is blinding but he runs on.
He trips and falls headlong over a stone in the road. He lies
there, catching his breath, and picking the fragments of slate
from his hands. Blood. He hates the sight of blood.

Bryn catches up with him and helps him to his feet. The
two men walk onwards towards the setting sun. As they round a
bend they see two figures at the gateway at the end of Heol y
Plwcca. Ghostlike in the half light. Bryn makes to call out.
Arwyn stops him. "No! They could be ghosts."

Myfanwy is gently pushing Arthur along the track through
the gateway.

The little boy is blinded by the setting sun. "Where's
Mam?"

"Don't you fret Arthur bach. You'll be fine. It's a great
world out there. You will find your way in it. Forget about
Cwm Du. It has gone from the world."

Myfanwy watches the sun dip over the horizon. She drops to her knees between the gateposts. She places her hand on the Celtic Knot roughly carved into each gatepost. Her blood starts to flow down the gateposts. The little boy looks on in horror.

Behind Myfanwy two figures are running towards them, but Arthur cannot hear them. They seem to be shouting but they are making no sound.

Myfanwy wilts and drops to the ground. The two men try to reach her.

Arthur looks away in terror. Through teary eyes Arthur sees the sun setting on the horizon. Dropping out of sight. An open mountain. Featureless. Low sun hiding any detail in the world beyond Cwm Du. Arthur sobs in terror.

Arthur turns around to run back to Myfanwy, but he is on open mountainside, where two footpaths cross. He is standing on the crossroads at sunset. A place his grandmother told him he was never to go at this time. He steps off the roadway as shadowy figures approach in the falling light. The phantom figures are gone.

Everything has gone. The little boy is alone on a mountainside. He starts to cry in terror at his abandonment. "Mamgu!!!!! Mam!!!!!!!" Arthur is tiny in the majestic empty landscape, screaming for his mothers.

As the sun sets, Becca knows. She knows that her child has gone. And something else has come to fill that void of responsibility in her life. Responsibility for the people around her. Responsibility for Cwm Du. Responsibility for this borderland between this world and The Otherworld. Responsibility for the safety of world beyond. Responsibility for everything.

Becca knows that she has become the new Druidess as she watches Arwyn and Bryn carry her mother's amulet towards her.

Becca knows as they place the amulet in her hand.

Becca turns to Idris and the rest of the villagers. Her long jet-black hair even darker. Her once white dress dark with slate dust and red with her blood. "It is done. We are the lost in time. We are the people of legend now. It is we who must hold back The Otherworld. We must build defences. Come."

Chapter 6: A Hundred Years Hence

2020: The same distinctive long black hair flowing down the back of a young woman's supermarket uniform. She is moving through the unwelcoming twenty first century street on a dull late spring evening.

The street showing all the signs of a dozen years of austerity since the economic crash which changed Britain. Shook the world. Shaped her childhood. Put everything on hold for everyone. Including her; Laura Salhurst.

And just when her prospects seemed brighter, being the first girl in her family to get into university, in comes 2020. A new decade and her twentieth year should bring hope, but instead it brings more hardship. A pandemic. A lock down. Her part time job at a supermarket till transforming her into an essential worker. Her university work cut back to a series of essay submissions which are long since done. Laura is stuck here. Her entire life put on hold.

A second-year student living with her boyfriend in a dingy student flat with nothing to do. Not able to rent one of the new high spec student residences. Saving her money. Her only real possession is her car. The car that can get her out of this shit-hole town when this lock down eases. She is lucky. She has a letter from the government giving her permission to travel. But she is unable to return home because of her mother's poor health, so Laura is still stuck here with nowhere to go.

Laura moves quickly down this street. Once a busy high street, now the shops are mostly boarded up and empty. The others closed due to virus restrictions. It will be time to move on from this place in a year's time, when she graduates. Anywhere but here. Off to London maybe when the virus goes. London is always booming. An island in the wasteland of what the politicians left of the rest of Britain.

Something moves beside her. Laura jumps out of her skin. Something moving in the darkness of a doorway. Something small. It yelps. Laura stops and crouches down. A small mongrel dog limps out to greet her. Tail wagging. Laura strokes the dog.

A face appears in the darkness. Laura jumps back in shock. A homeless man stares at Laura from the gloom. Laura takes a second to compose herself, ready to run if she needs to. "What's her name?"

The homeless man smiles. "Whatever you want miss. I don't give things names. Things don't last, do they?"

"OK. How about Laura. That's my name." Laura plays with the dog for a moment and gets to her feet. She rummages in her pocket and passes a £5 note to the Homeless Man. "Here. Buy her some food." Laura continues on her way.

"Thank you. Miss. Er, thank you Laura." The homeless man watches Laura walk away down the once proud High Street.

Laura turns into a side street in the university quarter of the town. A student street, where those students who can't afford to live in the shiny new tower blocks by the university have digs. Nothing has been done to these student houses in years.

Laura passes her rickety old Japanese car and produces her keys to open the door to a rough looking student house. She enters the house and heads into the kitchen, putting on the kettle. She opens her cupboard and takes out a sliced loaf, popping two slices of bread into the toaster.

The kettle gets louder as it heats up. Rattling and bubbling. Laura closes her eyes, waiting for the toast to pop and for the kettle to boil. Thinking of the homeless man. How close she was to him. She should be more careful, the virus is still out there. Hundreds of people dying every day now. Even people her age. Someone grabs her. She screams.

Her boyfriend Jimmy hugs her playfully. "Got something for you." He has something behind his back.

'What's that? Show me."

"It came in the post this morning." Jimmy hands Laura a handwritten envelope. Laura studies the letter post-marked 'North Wales.' The letter readdressed from home. Laura feels the weight of the envelope. Heavy for its size. Something wrapped in the middle. Laura opens the envelope and produces a gold sovereign.

Jimmy looks at the shiny coin with surprise. "What's that? Welsh money or something?"

Laura shakes her head in surprise. She starts to read the letter. Incredulity on her face. Handwritten in ink. In the style of writing she recognises from old letters she studied for school projects on the First World War. When writing had style. Before everyone typed on computers or phones. There is also a roughly drawn map. Laura puts it on the worktop and studies it intently.

Jimmy looking over her shoulder. "What's the letter say?"

"'If you come to Cwm Du and stay for no less than three days, a substantial inheritance is yours'"

"It's a scam Laura. It's probably in Nigeria."

"No, it's in North Wales. My dad's side of the family came from North Wales. The Salhurst family. I never met any of them... Oh here we are. 'You are known to be the only direct descendant of Mr. Arthur Salhurst, who was born in 1912.' So, what could I have inherited?"

"This looks dodgy Laura. They got your name right. But how many other Salhursts are there? Not like Jones or Smith is it? It's a scam babe."

Laura feels the weight of the coin in her hand. It's so heavy. "But they know so much about me. And this is solid gold Jimmy!"

"Let me see that". Jimmy takes the coin from Laura.

"That's a gold sovereign. Right?"

Jimmy looks at her askance. It seems to be a gold sovereign. Queen Victoria on the back. Dated 1890. It seems real. Very heavy. Shining in his hand in the otherwise dark kitchen. "I didn't think you had two pennies to rub together."

"I don't..."

"Didn't." Suddenly the penny drops for Jimmy. "Laura, this could be goodbye student loan!"

Laura is still studying the letter. Looking for any catches. No, none apparent. She has to travel there and stay for three days to claim her inheritance. But where is this place? "There's a map. Of a kind... Of North Wales. To er... Coom Doo. There's a cross there for... I can't make it out. Mort Lak?"

Jimmy takes out his phone and Googles the name. Nothing. He takes the map from Laura's hand and types in the correct spelling. "Cwm Du. How the hell do you say that? I've found it on Google Earth."

Laura looks at Jimmy's phone. The phone screen shows a black featureless area on the map. "It's just a blank."

"Nowhere on earth is just a blank. What the??? There's nothing there. Could it be a secret army base or something?"

"Let's find out. Nothing to lose is there?" Laura smiles excitedly. She continues to read the second page of the letter. "'You must arrive before 1st May 2020, or the offer of inheritance is withdrawn.'"

"That's tomorrow! The bloody post has taken weeks to deliver this."

"So our luck is in. Let's get down there tomorrow. I've got the government letter if the police are stopping people travelling. We have to get down there, Jimmy. Are you coming?" Laura feels Jimmy's arms around her and smiles. She takes the gold sovereign and feels the weight in her hands.

Laura lies on her bed, talking on the telephone. "Yes Mum. It arrived today. Do you know who sent it?" Laura rolls her eyes as her mother rants on about how the hell is she supposed to know who sent the letter. Or how long it had been before Mum posted it on to her? Or why the address is in a different handwriting to her name? The name beautifully ink calligraphed first line in an almost nineteenth century hand, whilst the address is in shaky block capitals, in biro. Her Mum telling her it's just a letter. But Laura doesn't get letters.

"Did Dad ever talk about his family in North Wales?"

Her Mother's voice growls from the other side of the phone. "No. Never had anything to do with them. No one came to our wedding, nor your Dad's funeral. Not even a card in the post. Your Dad did one of them 'Find Your Ancestors' websites. Nothing. It's like that family don't exist. Couldn't find them even with a ridiculous name like Salhurst. And that's not a Welsh name is it. So if they sent you something, be happy. It's more than your Dad and I ever got from them."

Laura nods. She remembers nothing of the Salhurst family. The couple of photographs of her grandfather. A man she never met. "I'm going to North Wales tomorrow. See if I can find them."

"Can you do that? Oh Laura, do what you like! They're a strange lot. Don't be building up any expectations. And don't go by yourself. Take a friend. And wear your mask!"

Jimmy breezes into the room. Laura gives him a look. He stays silent.

"Yes Mum, OK, I'll be careful."

"Phone me. Let me know what they want."

Laura ends the call. None the wiser, but more intrigued.

Laura and Jimmy asleep. The window open to the still spring night. What has become a new normality; silence at night. No cars, no passers by. Laura stirs in her sleep.

Laura is wearing a long white dress, walking in the night through the empty streets. She rounds a corner. A figure in the shadows. The homeless man Laura met that morning. He steps out into the middle of the street before her. Laura stops in alarm.

"Don't go down there miss. Don't go there." The man is mutating in front of her eyes. Skin greying. Teeth rotting. Voice breaking until he is barely snarling. His voice becoming a series of clicks of his tongue. His posture drops, his arms swinging. A beer bottle in his hand, now held as a weapon. Laura darts around the man and runs. The familiar street opens up.

Sodium light turns to moonlight. The buildings disappear. Space all around her. The sky is full of swarming black birds. She is by an ancient standing stone. Stunning mountain scenery stretches out below her, falling away hundreds of feet. The ground turns black across the valley before her.

Laura looks up at the birds in wonder. Then she looks down: she is standing on the massive area of black slate waste. The black valley now stretches out before her. Black ground as far as she can see. The moon is obscured by the birds. Darkness.

Laura is completely alone. The mountain seems recede. The landscape around flattening out into a plain. The sky is replaced by rock. She is in a massive cavern.

Laura looks around the vast cavern. Different sounds now. That clicking again. Hordes of figures moving in the distance. And then the sound of water.

The plain begins to flood. Water rising around her feet, to her ankles. To her knees. To her chest.

Arms reaching out of the water all around. Laura panics and tries to avoid them.

A dark grey figure rises silently out of the black water behind her. What was once the homeless man grabs her.

Chapter 7: Going Home

Laura struggles wildly as she snaps awake. Jimmy is holding her tight.

"What's wrong babe?"

Laura tries to make sense of her reality. Back in her student bedroom, squashed in a single bed with her boyfriend. Bedclothes tangled around her. It is already light outside, but only shards of that daylight to be seen here in her cave. "Hold me."

"Nightmare?"

Laura nods. "I was in a cave. It was flooding. There were... things there. I don't know, I can't remember. What time is it?"

"Stupid early. Ten thirty."

"What!!! We have to get going. It's a long way!"

Jimmy watches Laura pick at her bowl of breakfast cereal. Pale and sweaty. Engrossed in her thoughts. Looking at the letter which arrived the previous day and seems to be changing her life. "Are you OK Laura?"

Laura snaps out of it. "I'm feeling a bit sick, that's all."

"Are you fit to drive? We don't have to do this you know."

"Yes I do. I have to go. This is a family thing. My Dad's side of the family are never in touch, so this must be important."

Jimmy gives Laura a hug. "OK. Are you sure your heap of junk will get us there?"

"It may be old, but it's mine. You're navigating."

"But I've never been to Wales, and I don't have a map."

Laura hands Jimmy the handwritten map which was in the letter.

Jimmy looks at the scrawl, with drawings of a mountain,

and a standing stone, ending at a crossroads and then dots. "How the hell am I supposed to find this place. There's no post code or nothing."

"Use your phone. Like you did yesterday. We just need to get to this crossroads..." She points at a crossroads at the end of the route marked out on the map. "How hard can that be?"

"It's almost two hundred miles babe. Even if we know where we're going."

"How big can North Wales be? Come on. We'll be there by lunchtime."

Laura puts her overnight bag into the back of her car. Jimmy fills the rest of the space with his sports bag, tossing his bright coloured logo covered coat in on top. Jimmy gets into the passenger seat, fastens his safety belt and reclines the seat. He turns up the car radio, closing his eyes. Laura gets into the driver's seat and gives him a dirty look. She switches off the radio. "I need you to navigate. Would it kill you to make some conversation on the way? "

Jimmy shrugs and opens up the maps app on his phone.

"And keep hold of these." She hands him the map in the letter and her government essential worker letter.

The car pulls away. In a couple of streets the little car is driving along a main road which usually would be clogged by rush hour traffic. There is absolutely no other traffic. In five minutes the car has left the town, crossing a narrow green belt to join the empty motorway.

The sun scorching overhead, the heater on the car jammed at 'On'. Windows open. Jimmy falling asleep. Nothing on the motorway except the occasional heavy goods vehicle.

Laura watching the country slide by. Featureless towns in the distance. A giant petrochemical works. Industry stretching out between the motorway and the sea. Bright flames from tall chimneys.

Then modern industry ends. The Welsh mountains loom ahead. Black greenery on the hills, bright greenery in the fields below. Some bright yellow fields. Laura nagging Jimmy to pay attention through some motorway junctions before he falls asleep again.

He snaps awake. "Are we there yet mum?"

Laura gives him a dirty look, before seeing a road sign. 'Welcome to Wales.'

"Bloody hell! We're there." Jimmy looks at the phone app, showing an ongoing road for miles. "OK. Maybe not." He closes his eyes.

The car drives along the deserted dual carriageway, built to get traffic to and from Ireland. Drab empty lifeless seaside towns lie like flotsam at the edge of the water.

Then the sea opens up on their right. Overlooked by the hills and mountains on the left. The car going through tunnels which could be in continental Europe. That broke up the monotony of the trip. Laura smiles, beginning to enjoy the journey now.

Jimmy sits up. "It's the next turning Laura."

A different landscape. A different land. The car struggles up the steep hill into the open countryside. The road narrowing. Sheep watching from over low walls and hedges.

Jimmy looking at the road signs. "That place has no vowels in it!"

"Welsh has a different alphabet Jimmy."

"Oh great." He closes his eyes again, fighting to keep awake as the sun burns through the windscreen and the heater churns.

Laura yawns and looks in wonder as the car goes over the crest of the hill. Green spreads out ahead of her. Rolling hills. Little villages here and there. She keeps driving.

So this is where her great grandfather came from. It's beautiful. Miles upon miles of open country. Rolling hills. To the right mountains rising up. A *Lord of the Rings* style magical land.

Questions rolling over in Laura's mind. So why did her great-grandfather leave here to go to London a century ago? There is obviously some family still here who want to get in touch with her. Did he fall out with them? Some sort of family rift or feud? If so, why is she being invited back? And why did they not contact her father when he was alive? Laura is just a girl after all. A student. Not having made her own way in the world yet. Just starting out. Scoping out the possibilities, even when most of her friends have not even thought about what the future could be.

But what future out here? Obviously the only thing to do is to work on farms. And what would she know about farms, apart from what she sees in the news about farmers struggling, going out of business? Even before this lockdown.

She slows down behind a tractor. The driver hasn't seen her, obviously not used to traffic these days. Laura follows for a couple of miles, mesmerised by the pattern on the large rear tyres as they turn in front of her. The tractor turns into a farmyard and the countryside opens up once more before her.

Laura drives on into a little village. The houses are small and squat. Centuries old most of them. Lights in the small windows against the gloom within, even on an early summer's day. A scowling old man watches the car pass. Laura looks away, uncomfortable. This is the first person she has seen. Hostile.

"Fuck me. That's welcoming." Jimmy has woken up. "Turn right up here."

The little car turns westward towards the expansive mountain scenery.

The mountains seem to get no closer. Four hours into the trip and Jimmy is asleep again. Not even reacting when Laura turns on the radio to a wall of static. The radio is not picking up any signals. Laura switches it off feeling very isolated. On her one holiday to Greece there was even sound in the mountains outside of the resort town. There is always sound. No sound here apart from the whoosh of wind through the open car windows.

The space around her slowly closes. It's as if the world has risen up around her in her tiny car. There must still be miles before the car reaches the foothills of the mountains which now dominate the landscape ahead. The mountains are black against the sun. Unyielding. Towering. Majestic if it wasn't that Laura is getting nervous. No road signs. And the ones she sees mean nothing. Jimmy out cold beside her.

Then something else. A red light on the dashboard. A red thermometer. The car is overheating. She notices it stutter slightly on the next incline. It'll be OK. Surely it's not far to go now? The car struggles as it sets off up a steep mountain pass. Laura watching the dashboard on the car as much as where she is going.

"Shall I get out and push?" Jimmy. Awake now.

"We may have to, the car is overheating, I've got to stop."

"You can't stop here Laura. We're in the middle of nowhere. No one will find us here."

Laura nods, pushing the accelerator harder. For a moment a battery icon on the dashboard glows red. Then back to normal. Laura swallows hard. She hasn't seen the car do this before. The car begins to squeal. Laura's face goes white.

The car makes it over the brow of the hill. Laura takes her foot off the throttle and lets the car coast down the other side. It seems to be running fine now. The odd squeal and then a thump.

Jimmy looks at Laura. "Great! We're going to break down."

Laura pats the steering wheel. "No, we'll be fine." Did she really see some steam come up from the front of the car? A mile later, there is no doubt about it. Steam pouring from the front of the car, and a load of red icons on the dashboard. Laura is in tears.

She brings the car to a halt in a lay-by overlooking a spectacular valley below. The sunshine lights up the incredibly beautiful open mountain scenery. But neither Laura nor Jimmy are paying any attention to that.

"Great. Bloody great. Eight hours it's taken us so far." Jimmy gets out of the car and has a pee beside the road.

Laura gets out of the car and watches the steam rise from the front of her car. "How far now?"

"I don't know."

"What do you mean you don't know?"

"My phone hasn't got a signal. The map has frozen."

"So when did this happen?" Laura frowns as Jimmy shrugs. "How are we going to find the crossroads?"

Jimmy getting irate. She has never seen him irate. She likes him because he is unflappable, sometimes to the point of being comatose. "I don't know Laura. We better ask someone."

Laura looks around the miles of empty mountainside. "Duh! Who?"

"Maybe we'll find a shepherd."

Laura bursts out laughing sarcastically.

"There are loads of sheep. There's got to be a shepherd, right?"

Laura stands in the middle of the road, head in hands. "OK, I'm going to see if I can spot something. A landmark." Laura's stomach tightening. She is in trouble. The £30 in her purse is all she has. It must cost more than that to fix the car. It may be more than that to get petrol to get back home.

She just didn't realise it was so far. It's late afternoon, she thought she would be at the crossroads a couple of hours ago. She's hungry, hot and pissed off. Very, very pissed off.

Jimmy walks forward, trying to make peace. "Don't worry, it'll be OK. How lost could we be? This is England in the twenty first century, right?"

"No. This is Wales Jimmy!" Laura walks off in anger. She spots a pathway leading up the mountain. More of a sheep track really.

"Jimmy, try to fix the car!" Laura climbs the hill.

"I'm not a mechanic Laura!" Jimmy opens the car bonnet. Steam rises. He jumps back in shock.

Laura climbs the incredibly steep path, often using her hands to help her up the next section. She has gone over a ridge, so Jimmy and the road are no longer in sight. The higher she climbs the less she feels she sees. Then she climbs over the next ridge.

A standing stone. Standing overlooking another as yet unseen valley in this landscape. Far below a narrow track snaking between massive areas of black slate lying out on dead grass as far as the eye can see.

Laura has a sense of Deja vu. She knows this place. Recognising the incredibly beautiful mountain terrain that stretches out below. Laura stands catching her breath, taking in the landscape. It's dream like.

Then she sees it. A reclined leg at the side of the standing stone. There's someone there. The someone jumps to his feet in alarm. Using the standing stone as support. Coughing wildly. Shaking. Wild eyed. Frightened even. The old man must be seventy. "Hello. You're here!"

Laura stands for a moment, considering running. But running back down that path would be the death of her. She's climbed maybe a hundred feet. That's a long way to fall. And

it's an old man. Who is obviously not well. And not
threatening. "Hi."

The old man watches Laura with a mixture of fear and awe.
Her black hair. Those eyes. It has to be her. She is
unmistakable. And who else would come to this spot? Three
weeks from when he posted the invitation. At dusk on the last
day before her invitation expires. He was afraid she would
come. More afraid she wouldn't come. What would they do to him
if she did not arrive? But she's here. One more task, and they
will leave him alone. At least for now. "Are you lost Miss?"
    "I'm trying to get to a place called Coomb Doo".
    "Cwm Du? It's right down there." The old man points down
to the valley beyond the standing stone.
    "How do I get there?"
    "You can walk. If you hurry you can get there by
nightfall. You have to get there by nightfall Laura."
    "But I'm driving. My car has broken down".
    "Where is it?"

Laura's car sits forlornly with its bonnet open in the
high mountains. Jimmy fishes out his brightly coloured coat
from the boot. "This is the middle of fucking nowhere."
    "Overheated?" A man's voice in his ear.
    Jimmy jumps in shock.

Chapter 8: Meeting the Locals

Jimmy spins around. In the road stands a dark, brooding man, dressed in work clothes. He looks at Jimmy intensely.

"Oh my God! You scared the shit out of me mate!" Jimmy weighing up the man. He looks and is behaving like a character from one of those horror films in which city kids leave the city to be killed by psychos in the woods. No woods around here luckily, but this guy may not be playing with a full deck of cards. Something slightly wild in his eyes. Unfriendly. And he talks funny.

"Overheated yeah?"

"Yes mate". Jimmy backs away, trying to keep further than the regulation coronavirus distance away from this stranger.

"I'll fix it for you. Don't get your nice shiny coat dirty." The farmer brushes passed Jimmy and starts looking under the bonnet.

"I'm Jimmy. I'm going to a place called Comb Doo."

The farmer stops in his tracks. "Cwm Du. It's called Cwm Du! Why do you want to go there? Cwm Du is gone."

"Eh? What do you mean?"

"Cwm Du's quarry flooded about a hundred years ago. Everyone died."

"So it's a ghost town?"

"It's not there."

"But I have a map."

"No such place anymore." The farmer keeps working under the bonnet. He looks up. Jimmy is holding the map. "Let me see." He snatches the map from Jimmy's hand. Reading it. His eyes opening wide. Tracing his finger over the standing stone, down the thin line into the next valley. Onwards to a crossroads. He takes a mobile phone from his pocket and takes a picture of the map.

"Hey, what are you doing mate? Can I have my map back

please?" Jimmy snatches back the map.

The farmer squares up to Jimmy. "Why are you going to Cwm Du? How do you know about it?" He advances on Jimmy who backs off.

"I'm just going there because my girlfriend has family there."

"It's dead. They're all dead in Cwm Du!"

"Look mate..." Jimmy is backing away to the edge of the drop. Unaware that he is stepping closer and closer to the precipice as the farmer moves angrily towards him.

"GARETH!!!!" A thin voice straining. The farmer turns at the sound of his name. Laura is helping the old man down the track towards the road.

Jimmy steps away from the edge, walking back towards the car. A couple of minutes ago he was alone on a mountain. Suddenly it's a zoo. "Laura! Who the hell is that? Keep away from him!"

"This is Wyn. He has sheep on this mountain. He's shown me the road to Cwm Du."

Gareth freezes. Rage boiling. His father has told this girl how to get to Cwm Du! A place that is not meant to exist. But a place to where this London bastard has a map! Gareth has lived here all his life being told by his father that Cwm Du is just an old wives' tale. He looks at Wyn with murder in his eyes. The old man mutters angrily to his son in Welsh. "Gareth! These are our guests!"

Gareth walks back towards the car, crest fallen. "I was fixing the car."

"Is it fixed?" Wyn eyeing his son angrily.

"No."

Wyn is furious. "Well fix it! Help them! They need to get on their way. They need to get to where they are going by sunset!"

"It needs water. The radiator is buggered. It won't go

far."

Laura walks to the back of the car and pulls out a bottle of water. Gareth takes is and slowly pours the contents into the radiator cap. It hisses and there is a dripping sound. Water drips onto the road.

"See that? It's buggered. Always let it cool and keep filling it with water until you can get it to a garage."

"Thank you, Gareth." Laura smiles. "What does Cwm Du mean?"

"Black Valley. Because of the slate, yeah. There used to be thousands of people working there. Now it's just... stories."

Laura gives Gareth a questioning look. "My family live there. What are the stories Gareth?"

"Fairy tales. Nonsense like that."

"Fairies? It's a very beautiful here. I can believe that."

Gareth frowns. "These are dark stories. The Black Valley is a gate to Annwn. The Otherworld. They're not make believe, Laura. Those stories are true."

Laura is transfixed.

Wyn is getting agitated. "You best be on your way, if you're going to get where you're going by sunset. Gareth, get back to work." Wyn starts to fiddle with the radiator to see if there is any way of plugging the hole. Jimmy looks on with confusion.

Gareth steps away and walks off passing Laura.

"Thanks for your help. I owe you one."

Gareth stops and produces a piece of paper from his pocket, holding it out for her. Laura takes it at arm's length. She looks at the piece of paper. A Missing Person flyer obviously homemade. On it is a photograph of a pretty blonde-haired woman. 'Missing Person - Sian Wyn Hughes'

"Who's that?"

Gareth whispers furtively, pushing it into Laura's hand.

"She disappeared a year or two ago. If you ever see her around anywhere, ask her to give me a call, will you? She's not well. My number is on the poster."

"OK Gareth, if I see her, I'll call you."

Gareth turns around and jogs off down the road. Laura watches him go. Behind her the car starts.

Wyn steps out of the driver's seat. "Hurry. You need to get going if you are going to get there by sunset."

Wyn sets off up the hill shakily, watching as Laura's car heads up the road. It turns off as directed onto the mountain track around a quarter of a mile up the road. Wyn lets out a sigh of relief. His job is done. Maybe he'll get some peace now.

Laura's car struggles up the steep slate track. Already the scenery is changing around her. So different from the open mountains of the valley they just left. Any landscape hidden by a wall of waste slate. It is like driving through a black gorge. The car reaches the top of the rise. The scenery opens up. A world of black. The mountainside is black with slate waste as far as the eye can see. What grass there is seems to get whiter as they travel. Dark clouds move in overhead.

From high on the mountain above, Wyn watches the car's progress as he leans for support on the standing stone. He watches emotionlessly and closes his eyes. He turns away but his eye has caught something. Way back on the slate track a quad bike is following Laura's car. Keeping back as not to be seen. Wyn puts his head in his hands. The old man is crying. "Gareth. Leave this alone. You're not ready yet!!!"

Laura's car drives along the track as if crossing the surface of a black moon. Laura concentrating on the road, trying in vain to avoid potholes and the occasional large piece of slate which has fallen on the track.

Jimmy looks around in worry. "A bit forbidding isn't it?"

"Spectacular mind..."

"In a desolate and miserable suicidal Emo sort of way..."

"Up there, look!"

Up ahead of the car a crossroads comes into sight, and beyond it a wall made of slate. Straight across the crossroads is a gateway through the slate wall where the track continues. "I could swear that wasn't there a moment ago."

"No... Must have been a trick of the light." Jimmy notices the gloom descending across the plain - the sun disappearing replaced by the shadow of the mountain.

Laura brings the car to a halt at the same gateway that her great grandfather stood a century before. Visible in the gloaming. "This must be it. What does it say on the map?"

"Nothing there's just a dotted line."

"There are no signposts?"

"What can I tell you Laura? That's what the map says."

Laura's car heads off up the rough single-track road which leads into woodland which opens up ahead of them as they drive through the gateway. "This is weird Jimmy. I couldn't see these trees from back there."

The sun dips below the horizon as Gareth brings his quad bike to a halt. A look of wonder and fear on his face. He takes out his phone from his pocket to take a photo but when he looks up the wall and the track have disappeared. Gareth is alone on the crossroads to nowhere on the open mountainside. The same empty mountainside where Arthur lost his home.

Gareth turns around. The sun has disappeared behind the mountain. He looks at his watch. He smiles. He laughs. "Cwm Du!!! I found Cwm Du!!! You old bastard! I know where it is now! I'll see you tomorrow, Sian!!!" Gareth whoops, spins his quad around in circles and rides off back down the track away from the now empty mountainside and the hidden road to Cwm Du.

Chapter 9: Entering the Forgotten Land

Laura's car drives slowly over the slate, heading downwards along the rough track. The trees are getting thicker on their left. The slate wall getting higher on their right. The near darkness of twilight descending overhead. The car continues into the gloaming.

Laura and Jimmy are rocked violently from side to side. The occasional scrape on the bottom of the car makes them both wince.

"Slow down Laura, you don't want to damage the car."

Laura tries slowing the car down - it is close to stalling. The car drops on a rock with a crunch. Laura winces, tears in her eyes. Then the red light comes up again on the car's dashboard. The temperature warning light glows brightly. "Oh no, no, no! It's overheating again. I'll have to stop the car if we can't find any water." Steam starts to rise from the car bonnet. Laura swallows hard.

"You think there's enough water down there babe?" Jimmy points to a large lake a hundred feet below.

"Oh thank God. Does the road go down there?"

Jimmy shrugs, then sees is a fork in the road up ahead. "Try there."

Laura steers the car onto the narrow steep track which leads downwards. In moments she is struggling to keep the car from skidding on the wet slate. The track is now a ramp leading down to the lake, dead straight, the loose slate crunching beneath the tyres. Laura remembering how her father used to take her out on those mad mountain tracks in his old Landrover, which is what he considered a holiday. Swallowing hard, gripping the wheel too tightly, trying to remember what he used to do. Keeping the wheels from locking as the car makes its way straight down the ramp. The lake opens up ahead of them. The road ends at what looks like a beach, with a VW

Camper Van parked up. "There are people here, thank God."

The car moves slowly down to the beach, stopping on the water's edge. Steam billows out of the front of the car and the engine clatters to a stop.

Laura steps out and kicks the car tyre in frustration. She puts her head in her hands. She looks up across the perfectly smooth lake surface ahead of her. The water is deep and black, like a black mirror ahead of her. Above it reds and mauves colour the sky.

Beyond the lake is the cliff edge. A hundred-foot-tall wall of grey slate, and beyond it the open mountains of Snowdonia turning black in the twilight. In the falling light Laura can see huge shapes near the edge of the quarry cliffs. Large black structures. There are more around much of the lake. Huge slate walls and large towers, not dissimilar to in the half-light to ziggurats she remembered from her school history classes. They must be a part of the quarry. Some seem quite ornate. "This must be the place. The flooded quarry. This is Cwm Du."

Behind her Jimmy is trying to see inside the camper van. He probably hasn't heard her over the hissing of the car radiator and the ticking of cooling metal.

Then Laura notices it. Apart from the noises from her car there is silence. No birdsong. Nothing. Laura listens intently for any other sign of life. Car engines. Anything. It was never silent even up on the mountain by that standing stone. The silence is almost deafening. Frightening. No sign of life. Nothing.

Jimmy tries to open the bonnet of the car, not understanding that you need to pull the bonnet release by the accelerator pedal. He sits on the bonnet, jumping up as it is so hot.

Laura looks for the water bottle she used to fill the car. No sign of it. Laura shrugs. What's the point? She wanders

over to the camper van. She knocks on the door. "Hello?" She
looks into the dark interior.

Near darkness. Muffled silence. Sound and light finding it
hard to get through the heavy medium. The black water.
Bubbles. The sound of his breathing through a regulator. For a
moment he is alone. Another diver beside him. Tracey. The
missus. Where did she go just then? She scared him. You can't
be on your own quarry diving. It's too dangerous. He told her
that. But when does Tracey ever listen?

Something coming up ahead in the gloom. Dave switches on
his torch. The quarry wall. They've swum further than he
thought. How deep is he? He checks. Twenty feet. It's so dark
in this water. Totally disorientating. Beneath him the water
here must be a couple of hundred feet deep at least. It's cold
even this close to the surface. The deeper you go the colder
it gets. Guaranteed there are layers of bitterly cold water
down there, enough to give the unwary diver a heart attack.

But this is worth it. The drive from Liverpool. The hours
driving on mountain tracks trying to find this place. He and
Tracey are probably the first to be down here since the day
the quarry flooded over a hundred years ago. Everybody said
this place was a myth.

He reaches out and touches the far wall of the quarry. OK,
time to turn around. There'll be more time to explore
tomorrow. Then he sees it. Just above him. He swims closer and
feels the force. The water moving through it and pushing him
back out into the lake. A tunnel. Going deep into the mountain
into total blackness. He uses his hands to climb up the quarry
wall beside the tunnel. Oh my God! The force of the water
coming out is huge.

He wants to go inside. No, not enough air, they have to
turn back. He puts his hand on another rock. It's loose in his
hand. It feels different. Warm. Smooth. Shining in the torch

light. Out of place. Rammed into the rock face by the look of it. Markings on it. It's darker, blacker than the slate all around. Dave runs his fingers over it. Grooves. There is a pattern on it. Cut into it. Dave pulls out his diver's knife and tries to prise the stone free.

Tracey looking at him. He shows her the piece of rock. Rubbing the surface. The pattern showing clearly. Tracey motioning to her watch.

Dave digs his knife deeper around the slate.

Laura sees the sticker on the van window. NWEDC - North West England Diving Club. The campers must be diving. Hence no people here.

Jimmy playfully grabs Laura and drags her towards the water. "Time to cool off babe."

Laura laughs but then her smile disappears. As she gets closer to the water's edge fear grips her. The black water is not welcoming. Almost oily. Dirty. Dangerous. And Jimmy doesn't seem to notice.

Laura starts to panic. What is in the water to make it so black? How deep is the water? It's a quarry for Christ's sake! They could step off the edge into the depths. It's black. So black. Anything could be in there.

She sees movement across the lake, over above the ziggurat structures a black cloud of birds rises into the sky. She thought birds only flocked like that in the autumn, before migrating. There must be thousands of them.

The dark things. The dark things in her dreams. The darkness that lies beyond the water. Them! "Jimmy, let me go!"

Jimmy drags Laura into the water. Laura starts struggling wildly. "Nope. You're coming in with me."

Laura is very frightened now. "Jimmy, no, that's enough!" She starts thrashing in Jimmy's arms. She bites at him.

"Jesus, calm down babe!" Jimmy lets her go.

Laura wrestles free of Jimmy and runs back on shore. She screams at him. Her entire body shuddering. All her energy being thrown at Jimmy. Jimmy is thrown back into the water with a huge splash. He disappears under the deceptively deep water. He surfaces coughing and spluttering. Laura drops to her knees.

Whoosh! Thousands of black birds swoop across the lake, above the water. Laura jumps back in alarm. The birds circle over the lake before her. Her voice hoarse after the shout. "What the hell? What the hell?"

Jimmy gets to his feet. "Laura?"

Laura looks at Jimmy. Shocked at what just happened. "Are you OK?"

The piece of slate is now in Dave's hand. Shining slightly in the near darkness, glowing when Tracey points her torch at it. The pattern clear now. Intertwined circles. It looks Celtic. Dave and Tracey swap glances. Tracey points at her watch. Dave nods. He puts the piece of slate in his bag. They swim away from the underwater tunnel back towards the centre of the lake.

Laura is sitting on the ramp beside the car. The bonnet open. Less steam now, the rapid clicking of cooling metal like tribal sticks beating out messages. The sound drowned out by the birds crying out as they circle over the lake. Jimmy watches them as he wrings his soaking clothes. "You know you can trust me, right?"

"I just got scared."

"Of me? Come on..."

"Of the water."

"You're a good swimmer."

"But that water. It's so black. Ever so black. It's so deep Jimmy. This is a quarry. People die swimming in quarries."

"But I'm here and we're just at the edge of the water. What can go wrong?"

"It's wrong to go in there. Hundreds of people died when the quarry flooded. It's a graveyard Jimmy."

Jimmy walks over to Laura and kneels in front of her. He hugs Laura tight. "It's OK. We'll get the car going and we'll get to this village. You'll feel better when you have something to eat. It's been a long day."

Laura looks out across the lake. The silhouettes of the slate constructions high above the lake. The birds circling. Something new. A disturbance on the water fifty yards out from the jetty. Something moving towards the shore. Now another one beside it.

Laura tries to get to her feet, but Jimmy is holding her too tight. "Let me go Jimmy." The two forms moving closer still. Laura starts to panic. "Let me go!!!!" She punches Jimmy who backs off.

"What's wrong now?" Jimmy follows Laura's stare. Two divers emerge from the black water. Moving gingerly towards the shore, walking along the submerged part of the ramp. One waves, removes her regulator and face mask. The other diver does the same.

The athletic looking young couple walk towards the shore. The man's strong Liverpool accent makes Laura smile. "How you doin'? Good here, eh?"

Laura gets to her feet. "Hi. We were just leaving. My car needs water."

"Well I'd say you were in a dead good place for water. Give me a hand with this will you lad?" Dave is struggling to undo his jacket. "Hold me tanks mate please." Jimmy steps forward into the water and holds onto Dave's air tanks as he struggles out of the harness. "Thanks kid." Dave puts down the tanks and helps Tracey with her equipment.

"Have you got a water bottle or something we could use? I need to put water in my car."

"Yeah, no problem. I'll fetch one for you." Tracey smiles at Laura. "How long have you been here?"

"Five minutes. We just arrived."

"Which way did you get here? We're a bit lost. We've been driving around in circles since we got here first thing this morning. We can't find the road out of here."

Dave gives her a look. "Well you were navigating!"

"I got us here, didn't I?"

"Only after she had us driving across the bloody mountains all night. If it hadn't been dawn, we would never have seen the gateway into here."

"It doesn't matter babe. It's getting late. We need to set up a pitch for the night. This will be boss, Dave. It's so beautiful. You staying here? Er..."

"Laura. This is Jimmy. We're on our way to Cwm Du. Do you know the way?"

Dave points back up the ramp and to the right. "I'm Dave. It's just up the track there. Right Trace?".

"Tell them Dave!" Dave shrugs his shoulders. Tracey sighs. "I'm not trying to be funny like, but... avoid. We were told this place was flooded and no one lived there. That's not true."

Dave nods. "Funny people. We were glad to get out of there to be honest."

Laura looks puzzled. "I'm going there to meet my family."

Tracey is mortified. "Oh no offence like. Honest. Me and Dave, we're creepers."

Laura looks nonplussed.

Tracey continues. "Creepers! Creepers, you know? We explore places off the beaten track. Forbidden. The bizzies call us trespassers. But we prefer Urban Explorers. But we can't find our way back out. How did you get here again?"

Laura points back the way they came.

Dave shakes his head. "Nah, can't be. We tried up there half a dozen times... There's no road out that way."

"We came through there ten minutes ago! Through a gateway on the mountainside."

"See I told you. You're bloody useless Dave!"

"You were navigating. Anyway, we'll pitch up here tonight. It's dead romantic."

Tracey passes Laura an empty plastic water bottle from the back of the camper van. "Is this OK hun?"

"Brilliant. Thanks very much." Laura takes the water bottle and walks towards the lake. She stops short of the water's edge. Her nervousness returning. Jimmy takes the bottle and fills it from the lake.

Laura watches the birds circling overhead. "Let's get going Jimmy."

Tracey calls out from the back of the camper van. "You sure you brought enough corned beef love? There's buckets of it here."

Dave is examining the piece of carved slate which he is removing from his bag. "My brother got a van full last week. You know we need to keep up supplies with the lockdown and all that."

"Dave! Why not get something useful like toilet roll?"

Dave washes the piece of slate in the lake water. He is engrossed in the pattern carved into it.

Laura watches entranced. "What's that?"

Dave keeps cleaning the knot. "Don't know. It was in the quarry wall. Must have been some sort of sign. Or decoration maybe."

Laura takes the water bottle from Jimmy and pours it into the car's radiator. A little steam rises, and there is a hissing and cracking sound. "The sooner we get to Cwm Du the better. Thank you both. I hope you find your way home soon."

She slams the bonnet and gets into the car.

Jimmy climbs in as Laura turns the ignition. The engine struggles into life, and Laura turns the car around on the narrow ramp. The car struggles up the gradient, slipping and sliding on its way, the engine roaring. In a few moments it disappears into the trees.

Out on the far side of the lake, beneath the far wall, in the shadows, on the dark water, a Gwyllion head surfaces momentarily. The sound of the birds flying overhead intensifies, as if all of the birds are screaming in unison. In a moment the head is gone.

Chapter 10: Return to the House on the Borderland

The sun setting over the lake. Thousands of jet black birds circling above it. Not exactly circling though. The birds are making patterns in the air. The two men watch them from their vantage point overlooking the flooded quarry. A blissful scene if it wasn't for the sound of a roaring engine. The two men exchange glances. "What's going on Robert?" The younger man speaking in the thick harsh local accent, in his native Welsh.

Laura's car pulls itself slipping and sliding up the muddy ramp before heading gingerly up the rough track towards the village. The occasional scrape as the car grounds itself on the slate waste which makes up the track. It rounds the bend out of sight.

The two men emerge from the trees. The older man, Robert, in his mid twenties, dressed in mismatched worn old clothes. This makes him look much older than his years. His hair close cropped at the back and sides, longer on top. A style which died out eighty years ago. He shoulders his shotgun as if on parade. Deep in thought. The other is no more than a teenager, same haircut, same worn out old clothes. Tom. He looks at Robert, worried. Awaiting instruction. "How did they get here? That's two of these charabancs today. Do you think that is her?"

Robert fires brief shortened words, already mutated in his thick dialect, like old style Cockney. A language out of time. "How do I know? Am I a fortune teller in a Fair? Go find Becca. Ask her. Ask if she has seen these birds. I'll keep watch on these by the water."

Tom stands nervously watching as smoke rises through the trees from a fire the man with the charabanc is lighting at the water's edge below.

Robert looks at him. "Tom."

"Yes Robert?"

"Run!"

Tom sprints off along the track into the woods, while Robert heads down for the lake. Robert keeping tight to the side of the ramp, gun in hand. In the shade of the cut. Watching the campers to make sure he is not seen as he approaches them from above.

Behind Laura's car the sky is brightly coloured. Twilight is falling fast. The birds are circling like black shadows in the darkening sky.

Laura's car drives along the track. On one side the hundred foot drop into the lake below, with the view to the south of the lake and the circling birds. On the other side of the road are thick trees.

Jimmy looks at the large slate constructions at the end of the quarry ahead and to his right, realising their size as the car gets nearer to them. Walls rising several storeys above the ground at the lip of the cliff edge. Black and monolithic in the failing light. He swallows. They make him nervous.

Laura is engrossed watching the track, and increasingly looking into the trees to her left. Looking back at the track when she hits a particularly bad pot-hole. Then looking back into the trees. On edge. Feeling like she is being watched by someone. Someone in the trees.

The track narrows. Each side of the track narrowing to a gateway. Just wide enough to drive through. The wooden gate long gone. This gateway was probably only just wide enough for the large carts to move the slate out of the quarry in the days when this was done by road.

Laura brings the car to a crawl, not wishing to damage it passing through the narrow gateway. She notices an ornate carving on the right hand gatepost just outside her window, as she drives through. A lot like the carving that diver found on the piece of stone in the lake. No time to think about such

things. The light is dropping fast. She has to find the house
before it gets dark.

Laura's car passes through an even darker stretch of road.
Trees on both sides of the road now. Near darkness. Laura puts
the car headlights on. Up ahead something moves in the trees.
A shape. Then it's gone. Laura looks at Jimmy. He hasn't seen
it. A trick of the light probably.

As Laura's car rounds a bend out of sight a figure,
dressed in a white dress, walks onto the twilit roadway from
the thick trees. She pushes back her long black hair and
follows the car. In seconds she is lost in the gloaming.

Dave looks up and notices a mist rising across the lake.
It's already obscuring those birds who have been circling
since they came back on land. He turns his attention back to
the piece of slate he took from the tunnel entrance, which he
guesses to be several hundred yards away at the far eastern
end of the quarry.

He is sketching the quarry. Marking up a rudimentary map,
showing the roadway, the ramp to the lake, and approximate
depths of the water on the edge. At the far east end of his
map he marks up the underwater tunnel. He looks up, but the
mist has already thickened to obscure the rest of the quarry.
"Shit."

He uses his camera phone to take a still of the map, and
then a still of the carving on the piece of slate. He opens an
app on the phone. No signal. "Still no bloody signal Trace. I
can't upload nothin'."

"Leave that soft lad. Come upload with me you sexy
bastard." Tracey has got out of her wetsuit and is lying on
the inflatable mattress in the rear of the van. Dave puts the
slate face down on his notebook and gets into the back of the
van, slamming the door. Tracey screams and laughs.

The mist rolls in over the van. Robert moves silently down

the ramp to the side of the van. He slips on some loose slate, sending it clattering down the ramp.

Tracey's face pops up at the window. "What was that Dave?"

"Nothing babe."

"Is there someone outside?"

"Nah. You're safe with me girl."

"Yeah?"

"Promise."

Robert moves closer to the van.

The cooling fan on Laura's car is whirling madly as the car splutters down the track. The headlights shine through the gloom and light up a gateway. Beyond it is a large imposing Victorian slate house. Salhurst's house. Laura brings the car to a halt outside the gates.

Laura turns to Jimmy. "Have you got the map?"

Jimmy unfolds the map and studies it in the gloom. "Well this is where the map says we should be. It's a bit depressing innit? I can't read the writing. Hang on. Mort Lak? That's a bloody depressing name. Must be Welsh."

Laura looks hurt. She takes in the large slate house. No lights, but seemingly well kept. A painted name on the gatepost. Mortlake. She flicks the car lights onto full beam. The scale of the house becomes apparent. "Mortlake, Jimmy. It is the place. It's huge! I didn't expect this!"

Laura drives the car through the gateway and stops outside the house. She and Jimmy get out of the car. Laura looks up at the impressive building, and into the shiny black reflecting windows. No sign of life.

Laura walks towards the front door and picks up an envelope on the doorstep. The same black inked writing. 'Laura Salhurst.' "Look at this! They are expecting me!"

Laura opens the envelope. Inside is a key. No notes. Laura puts the key in the lock - it squeals as it turns. With a push the door opens. Laura excitedly steps inside. Jimmy follows.

The figure who has followed the car watches from the roadway. Her long black hair blowing in the rising wind. Unmistakably Becca. The occupant of the same house a century ago, dressed in a white homespun dress, slate amulet around her neck; Myfanwy's amulet. She has not aged a day since the quarry flooded. Her eyes are filling with tears, though she smiles to herself. "Welcome." A sound behind her makes her turn around in alarm.

Tom runs up the road towards her. "Becca!!!"

Becca puts a finger to her lips to hush him. "All is well, Tom. She's here. I know."

But Tom is looking upwards. Becca follows his stare. The sound of the Birds of Annwn flying overhead carries on the wind. Becca looks up at the birds weaving in the sky above. Her expression changes to terror.

Chapter 11: Out of the Dark Water

Laura and Jimmy are in the impressive entrance hall of
Salhurst's Victorian home. Colonial even. The large staircase
leads upwards passing family portraits to the darkness of the
first floor. Downstairs, rooms await discovery behind closed
oak panelled doors.

Laura stands open mouthed. "Wow."

Jimmy draws in breath between his teeth like a seasoned
builder about to quote for a job. "Bit grim innit?"

Laura is not paying attention. She opens the door and
enters the lounge. Laura reaches for a light switch, finding
none. She looks around the antique furniture. Everything
pristine. The room is large, high ceilinged, clean, tidy, with
a fireplace and a bookshelf stacked with books, as it was in
Salhurst's time. The photo of Salhurst in his Army uniform is
on the mantelpiece. Laura steps forward and looks at the image
from over a century ago. A family member she knows nothing of.
Who is this guy?

Jimmy leans on the door frame in disbelief. "This is like
being back in the 1980s. Where's the TV?"

Laura pushes by him wordlessly, leaving the room. She
opens the door opposite. Laura is in the large kitchen - a
cooking range, a pantry, a few cupboards, Welsh dressers with
crockery. On the table are fresh vegetables, and jars of
preserves. The jars are all labelled with the same black inked
handwriting. Laura picks a jar up. Gooseberries.

Jimmy looks over her shoulder. "Goose Berries. What the
hell are they?" He looks around the dim kitchen and reacts in
horror. "No microwave either!"

"I think that's called a range, we can cook on that."

"You can't cook without a microwave! Where's the fridge?
Jesus wept!"

Laura gives Jimmy another sideways look, irritation

rising.

She notices the back door. A solid oak door. A horseshoe nailed to the door. She hasn't seen that done since she went to an old pub in the countryside when she was a child. And bolts. How many bolts do you need? Surely not three. These bolts are huge.

Laura steps out of the kitchen back into the hallway. Laura wanders over to the stairs, looking up at the old pictures that line the wall by the oak staircase. Unfamiliar faces staring back at her in black and white.

Jimmy stands in the kitchen doorway. "Let's get the bags then." Laura seems lost in a daze. "Laura?"

Becca stands watching the birds swooping in the sky above. Tom is running back down the track to re-join Robert at the lake. He comes to a halt, stepping aside and nodding politely. Three women, all dressed in white emerge from the trees. Once Myfanwy's Morwynion, now her daughter's. Hannah, Mary and Rachel also look no older than at the day of the Quarry Disaster. They join Becca outside the house.

Becca watches the house. Not daring to look upwards. "The Birds of Annwn are back."

"When did they appear Becca?" Fear in Rachel's voice.

"Just when the girl arrived? Are you sure she is who you think she is?" Mary looks at the car parked outside the house with concern.

"I called her here. Do you doubt me, Mary?"

"No, but..."

"The Birds are flying. There will be a reason. I shall find the reason. We shall not sleep until the birds are gone." Becca's face hardening. Then it cracks as if about to cry.

Laura and Jimmy come out of the cottage.

Becca and the Morwynion move back as one into the treeline, unseen in the gloom.

Laura and Jimmy collect their bags from the car and head back into the house.

Becca whispers to her Morwynion. "That's her. Very well. You know what to do." Becca paces off up the track towards the village leaving the Morwynion outside the house. Tears are running down Becca's face.

Mary lets out a sigh. "But why is she here? Why is she special? Becca has the three of us!"

Rachel looks up at the birds in the sky. "Times are changing."

Hannah heads off the track following Becca. Rachel and Mary follow.

In the woods there is a rustle of dead leaves. Something emerges from a hiding place under thick leaves, behind a log. A blonde-haired girl shakes the dead leaves out of her hair and checks that all of the Morwynion have gone. She is in her mid-twenties. Unlike everyone else in this place she is dressed in contemporary clothing. A once white tracksuit. She brushes the dead leaves off herself and sneaks towards the house to get a better view. It's Sian, Gareth's sister. The missing girl who Gareth is looking for.

Sian watches the house intensely. She moves swiftly forward towards the house and approaches Laura's car. It is still hissing and ticking from overheating. Sian looks anxious and angry. She tries the car door. It's locked. Frustrated, she heads back out across the track and into the trees, disappearing in the gloom.

The lights from the quad bike light up the squat farmhouse at *Tyle Garw*. *The Wild Hill*. A fitting name for a sheep farm this remote. Sheltering in the little shade given by the hillside. Not even a real road leading to the door. But some settlement has stood out here on the desolate Snowdonia mountainside since Celtic times.

Gareth's quad roars into the farmyard. Wyn crosses the farmyard from the sheep pen. Itching for a confrontation.

"Where have you been?"

Gareth's heckles rise. "I'm back now. Is there more for me to do?"

"No. I've done it."

"So what's the problem?"

"You know. Why did you follow that young couple from away?"

Gareth attempts to play the innocent. "I didn't. I lost them."

Wyn is almost shouting now. "I saw you! You followed them! You won't find her. You never will. It's too late!"

"I'll find her! Just like I'll find Cwm Du!"

Wyn tuts, shaking his head. "No. They'll come to find *you* when the time is right."

"When you're dead."

"Aye. Until then, leave them alone. No good comes of them. They are lost for a reason. They have their place in everything around here, as do we."

"And mine is? To wait 'til you die?"

"Tend the bloody sheep. Try to make a living here."

"And what of Sian?"

The old man walks off to the farmhouse and slams the door.

Gareth starts the quad bike and roars out of the farmyard back down the track into the encroaching night. The quad's headlights are the only light on the mountainside under the black night sky.

Robert is standing at the water's edge watching the camper van rock nearby. Absorbed in the noises coming from the van. Forgetting the noises of the birds flying unseen above. The mist gets thicker and obscures the van momentarily.

The mist is really thick now, even dulling the sound from

the van. But there is another sound nearby. Behind him.
Something moving in the lake. Water being disturbed. Like
waves breaking on the shore. More now. Something is in the
lake. Maybe many things. Robert looks around suddenly alarmed.

Robert cocks the shotgun quietly pointing it towards the
lake. Shadows in the mist. People. They must be people,
surely? Figures approaching. Maybe more of these people from
the charabanc who have gone swimming in the lake before he
stood watch? He's seen a few of these swimmers in the last few
years. Usually seeing them coming to a bad end. So, this
wanton couple have friends, only emerging from the water now
night has fallen.

Robert backs off silently up the ramp, not wanting to be
caught. If they catch him, he only has two shells. Best to
beat a retreat, observe and report to Becca. Much more noise
from the lake now. How many of these beggars are there?

One of the shapes is moving in his direction. Suddenly
straight towards him. Lifting something. A spear. Robert's
insides turn to ice. A Gwyllion Warrior, lithe, athletic,
frightening, emerging from the water towards him. Robert last
saw one a hundred years ago. Apart from in his nightmares. He
dreams of them most nights. But this is no dream.

Pure terror grips him. Too scared to fire he backs off up
the ramp. Almost tripping, training his gun on the Gwyllion
figure who makes a strange clicking sound. Others join her.
Male and female. Dressed, if that's the term for it, in shards
of leather, with slate and bone breastplates as armour pieces.
Bare skinned. Bare footed. Bare toothed.

Robert turns and runs. Aware that the figures are not
following. They seem frightened of something. Working out a
means of following him. Returning into the lake.

Robert waits, too afraid to move. Suddenly he sees the
figures are moving up the cliffside on both sides of him in
the mist. They are climbing the cliff!

Robert runs up to the track. He must find Becca and the Morwynion! Then he realises he has been outflanked. The Gwyllion are on either side, blocking off the track. Their clicking sound fills the air. The creatures are speaking to each other. Robert runs into the trees.

Running through the mist, amongst the trees, tripping on tree roots, slipping in the slime. Aware of grey shapes on either side keeping pace with him, with some getting ahead. There is no cover in these trees. He has to get to somewhere he can defend. The old village, abandoned to the trees years ago.

It's so dark and misty. Where the hell is the village? Has he run the wrong way? Will he end up falling into the railway cut, breaking his neck before these beasts can reach him?

He falls over some rubble, rolling on the floor. The shapes of the derelict buildings of the deserted old village rolling around him, abandoned at the time of the quarry disaster.

The buildings made of stone, carried in from quarries up the coast, not the slate from the ground which his home was built from in Cwm Du.

The deserted buildings. The old village. No one comes here anymore. Apart from Huw the outcast. Everyone afraid of the ghosts from the disaster who come out of the lake to be here once more. Angry at those who lived. Angry and wanting their homes back. He has seen these angry ghosts, who were once friends. So angry at him and the others who got out of the quarry on that fateful day.

But this is the safest place he can be, ghosts or no ghosts. He knows it like the back of his hand, from childhood, twelve decades ago when he lived here as a child.

He runs for the old Vicarage. Overgrown with faded Victorian grandeur. The roof and first floor have fallen in, but there is a cellar. If he can lose his pursuers and get into the cellar they will never find him.

Shapes on either side now. Up ahead too, on top of the broken buildings. How many are there? No time to get to the Vicarage, he will have to make a stand at the old row of quarrymen's houses.

Robert turns sharp left for where he knows the row of houses are, but something is in his way. Gwyllion. Only one of them but he feels the others circling all around him as he stops. The Gwyllion moving towards him, holding a spear of some variety. For a moment he remembers his father's stories of the Zulu Wars.

He focusses. He fires the shotgun and the Gwyllion drops to the ground. Robert runs over the body towards the quarrymen's houses.

Everything freezes all around him. The Gwyllion still. Then moving cautiously once Robert has made it to the quarrymen's houses. He gets inside a house, setting up the shotgun pointing towards his pursuers through the window frame.

Movement in the mist, but not clear enough a target for another shot. His only other shot. Robert's heart racing. He has not felt such fear since Passchendaele. Waiting. Waiting for the wave of grey figures to come at him. He closes his eyes for a second. Thinking. What to do after he fires. No knife. No bayonet. Nothing to fight with but his bare hands. So be it. But he has to alert the others. He opens his eyes.

Atala the Gwyllion Witch standing over him. A powerful woman war-painted in shades of white, grey and black - partly for camouflage against the slate, partly for frightening effect.

Robert's eyes run over her body for a millisecond. What clothing she wears is old leather and bone. She carries a stone axe. Beneath her prominent almost Neanderthal-like forehead, her eyes aren't human and burn with hate. She clicks menacingly; nearby in the darkness her whisper is answered.

Robert raises the gun. A hand grabs it, pulling the gun away. A scream as the Gwyllion who has grabbed the gun rolls away in agony, hands burnt by exposure to the metal. Robert looks on in alarm.

Thud! Everything slowly goes black. His head falls forward with Atala's axe buried deep in his skull. Robert pulls the trigger. Bang!

The Gwyllion run for cover behind the buildings and debris of the abandoned village. Atala calls out in short hard phrases of clicks. "This is our enemy. Weak. Dead. Yes, their weapons hurt us. Yes. But we are many. We are strong."

The five other Gwyllion Warriors emerge from the mist.

Atala holds up Robert's head by the axe, allowing the weight to tear the head loose from the axe. Atala raises the axe once more.

Dave steps semi-dressed from the camper van with his diving torch in his hand. He sees the wall of mist, obliterating everything. He shines the torch around, but it just reflects back at him. He could be anywhere. Even under water.

Tracey calls out from inside the camper van. "What was that Dave?"

Dave looks around. "Must be someone out hunting babes..."

At the top of the ramp above him, Tom stands silently in absolute terror, not daring to move a muscle.

Chapter 12: Village of the Damned

Becca raises her head at the sound of the second gunshot. Annoyance crossing her face. A second shot? What a waste of ammunition! There are so few shotgun shells. Wyn Hughes of Tyle Garw has not been able to get them shotgun shells for over a year. Some cock and bull story about the police taking his gun away. He is just getting old. And unreliable.

Robert better bring back some rabbits to feed the people at the pub later. Something to show for using two shotgun shells in one night. She looks up into the sky. The Birds are still flying. What is going on? Someone moving behind her. Becca turns around. Mary, Rachel and Hannah are following her into the village. "Who is watching the girl?"

The three Morwynion exchange glances. Rachel turns on her heel and heads back down the track.

"Good. Come." Becca leads them on up the track. Ahead of her a towering black mountain. Not of natural rock but of slate waste. The waste from the flooded quarry and the other quarries all around the village. Teetering over the village below. Hanging as if suspended by someone's will alone.

The village of Cwm Du is dwarfed beneath. The largest building, the Chapel on the one Main Street off which a handful of little side streets exist. All of the buildings, bar it seems the Chapel are built of slate.

No signs of modern life. No electric light. No cars or other vehicles. No electricity or telephone cables. No satellite dishes. Nothing to mark time marching on in Cwm Du.

A black village under a black mountain under a moonless night sky black with birds.

Tom had thought of following the sound of gunshots into the trees but thought better of it. There is something wrong. Very wrong. Why would Robert leave the lake? Why would he fire? Why two shots? Ammunition is so scarce. Robert would never do that unless there was real danger. Something is definitely wrong. What if the people in the charabanc turned violent? Chased him? Attacked him?

Tom stands at the top of the ramp afraid to call out lest the people in the charabanc hear him. Movement in the trees in the direction of the abandoned village. Not one person. Many. So not Robert. Tom swallows hard and lies down in the ditch at the side of the track. Lying in the muddy water watching as shapes emerge through the trees.

Around half a dozen figures move swiftly towards the cliff edge. One hurt, nursing an injured hand. Two carrying a body. But it's not Robert. Too skinny. All of these figures are too skinny.

The others are carrying spears. Primitive weapons. One is carrying what looks like a coconut. Tom remembers coconuts from the fair when he was a child. Just after King George's coronation. He won a coconut. His brother won a coronation mug.

The figure stops momentarily to look all around. It's not human. Tom holds back a scream. Then the Gwyllion is gone. Joining the others running towards the cliff edge.

Tom moves off quickly into the woods and throws up.

The Gwyllion war party run headlong off the cliff edge falling into the black water below. Yards offshore Atala raises Robert's head and screams. The sound echoes around the lake.

The camper van door slams open. Tracey steps outside. "Dave? What the fuck was that?"

Tom moves stealthily through the trees, unable to see much in the thick fog. Fighting every instinct to run. Drawing on every ounce of courage to enter the abandoned village at night. He's heard the stories of the ghosts. And from the likes of Robert. Robert has no imagination. The ghosts must be real. Definitely. So where is Robert hiding?

He can make out the buildings up ahead. The old Vicarage. The quarrymen's cottages off to the left. A smell in the air. Familiar from a lifetime ago. Too familiar when he was a boy at the quarry. The smell of copper in the air. Blood. Tom swallows hard and heads for the cottages. Something catching what little light there is. A stick. No. Too uniform. Robert's gun. Tom whispers harshly, "Robert? Where are you?"

Tom rushes forward and picks up the gun. It's hot and wet. Tom looks at his hands, black in the pale moonlight. He smells it. The coppery smell again. Blood.

Tom drops the gun in shock and sits on a fallen log. The log is soft. It gives. Tom jumps to his feet in shock. It isn't a log. It's a body with no head. Robert's body.

Becca, Mary and Hannah walk silently down Cwm Du's main street, untouched by modernisation in a century. Passing the largest building in the village, the Chapel. Candlelight somewhere within the huge structure. This is one of the few points of light in the otherwise dark street around them.

They walk on passing the pub, The Quarryman's Arms with lamplight within, pooling outside the open door. Onwards passing the dark village shop and to the bridge over the stream that runs at the far end of the village.

Idris the Quarry Foreman is leaning against the bridge looking up at the massive flock of birds that are flying overhead. Becca joins him, the Morwynion keeping a respectful distance.

Idris draws on his cigarette, the light illuminating his features as he watches Becca from the corner of his eye. "The birds are flying. That can only be a bad omen."

Becca leans against the bridge beside him. "All will be

well. She's here."

Idris takes another puff on the cigarette. Looking at Becca questioningly. "So why the birds? Is she alone?"

"No. With a boy."

"What do we do with him?"

"Nothing. He will go in time. She will stay. All will be well."

"But if all is well Becca, why call her now?"

Becca turns from the birds to watch the stream flow beneath the bridge. Her long hair hiding her face from her Master at Arms. "Arwyn and the others are right. I'm getting old. Maybe I should ensure no one else comes into Cwm Du."

"You explained why the mad girl is here. She is from Tyle Garw. You need another to be our eyes and ears when Wyn dies. She will know what we need. No more mistakes by that old man."

"I'm making mistakes too."

"Everyone makes mistakes. How often do outsiders find the gateway? Maybe once a year or two. You should let me, and the lads see off outsiders if they get into Cwm Du. Let me deal with that."

"Robert and Tom can see that they leave in the morning. I promise." Becca sighs. "I'm getting too old for this Idris. It's all too much."

Idris tries to look into Becca's eyes. "You're younger than me."

"I've had a harder life..."

"Touché".

Rachel stands statuesque outside Mortlake, watching the dark house. No lights. No sign of life. The only thing out of the ordinary is the vehicle parked outside. Rachel has seldom seen a charabanc. Every year or so outsiders appear in them. Rachel would see them at a distance. When the outsiders who owned them arrived in Cwm Du, they became a problem. The

Morwynion's problem. A threat. When the threat was dealt with the blacksmith turned the charabancs into something more useful.

Those damn birds flying. Mary is right. They are a bad omen. A death portent. Last seen when Salhurst, the idiot who lived here in Mortlake, blew the Black Wall and drowned a thousand men. And now they are flying again.

Why is Becca not reacting? Is it because of some misguided love for her dead husband? The spirit of her dead husband and the decisions he made are what haunt Cwm Du to this day. Bad decisions which can't be undone.

Maybe Mary is right. Maybe Becca is losing her mind. Not getting any older, just like none of them are getting any older. But losing her good judgement. Driven by sentiment where she should be driven by her role to protect Cwm Du with her Morwynion, watching over this thin place.

Faltering steps on the road. Someone approaching in the darkness. It better not be Robert and Tom. Becca instructed them to watch the outsiders by the lake. If it is them, the outsiders better be gone.

Tom comes into view carrying a sack on his back. Tom is covered with black liquid as if the black water of the lake is pouring over his head. "Rachel! Help!"

Rachel shushes the lad. He never had any sense. As he stumbles closer she sees it's not a sack that he is carrying. That it's not black water, but black blood pouring over Tom. She rushes forward as the lad falls to his knees, spilling the body onto the track with a thud. She rushes forward. "What's happened?"

Tom looks her in the eye. "Gwyllion. They killed Robert."

Rachel stops thinking. Everything stands still. She looks at the sack. A sack, dressed in man's clothing, two arms, two legs, no head. She suppresses a shriek. She tries to think. "Where are they now?"

"They went back into the water."

Rachel looks up at the house. No sign of movement or life. "Are you sure?"

Tom nods.

Rachel lifts Robert's body over her shoulders and starts pacing towards the village. "Stay here. Watch the house."

Tom looks over his shoulder down the track into the darkness of the woods. He jogs up the road following her, watching as Rachel's white dress turns black with blood before his eyes.

A match flares and burns out in the near darkness. Laura is trying the light a fire the range. The matches aren't working. She tosses the matchbox to the floor in disgust. "Jimmy, I can't get the fire going."

Jimmy sits at the kitchen table looking on. "Let's go to the village and get something to eat. It's been a hard day." Laura looks up questioningly. "Come on. You're a woman of property now, Miss Laura Salhurst." He smiles.

"OK, let's explore my new domain."

Jimmy heads for the front door, pulling on his brightly coloured coat. Laura and Jimmy step out of the house. The mist drifts around. Laura locks the door, rattling it, checking that the door is secure.

Jimmy looks out into the impenetrable mist. "So where are we going?"

"Well there's no point going back the way we came. There's nothing down there except drunken Scousers. Let's go into Cwm Du. It's just up the road."

"And 'Just up the road' is how far in this country?"

"How do I know? A quarter mile maybe?"

"Are you driving?"

"I don't think the car is going anywhere until we find a mechanic."

"But we're going home on Sunday, right?"

Laura looks at Jimmy. Remembering the three-day proviso to owning this house. "I'm starving. Come on."
Laura takes Jimmy by the hand, and they set off up the track into the silent foggy darkness.

A figure steps into the road some way behind them following silently. Sian.

Idris and Becca are watching the black birds against the night sky. The birds are only visible now in the breaks in the mist which has rolled in over the village. The light from the Quarrymen's Arms up the road is the only illumination in the murk.

Idris reaches for another cigarette, then realises the pack is empty. "Wyn Hughes Tyle Garw wants so much for a packet of cigarettes now. Guineas! I'm smoking too much these days. Too much time on my hands."

Becca nods. "You'll have plenty to do when you help me teach this girl."

"Aye, but you need to break it to her gently Becca. Draw her in with kindness. Let her come to like you. To admire you. To love you. Then she's yours to do with what you will. You've never brought up children. They are sensitive things."

Becca swallows. "I miss Arthur every day, but now I get to bring his great grand-daughter back to Cwm Du, where she belongs."

"Why did you wait this long?"

"She's the first girl Idris. The first Salhurst girl in a hundred years."

Idris nods and turns to look up the road. A commotion. The Morwynion are already moving, protecting Becca instinctively. Someone is running down the street. A shock of red hair. Arwyn. Damn. What the hell does he want? Idris calls out, allowing the man to pass the Morwynion on guard. "Arwyn?

What's wrong?"

Arwyn breaks his stride, walking breathlessly passed Hannah and Mary. "Come!!! NOW!!!"

Huw is kneeling beside Robert's headless body. Praying over the body. Some of Robert's blood on Huw's faded red football shirt. As he prays blood pools on the pavement outside his chapel.

The other villagers standing there in shock, looking at the headless body, with Tom curled up on the road beside it, rolled into a ball like a hedgehog. Rachel standing over them, her once white dress now completely black with Robert's blood. Breathing heavily from the effort of carrying the body into the village.

Arwyn runs up the street, followed by Becca, Idris, Mary and Hannah. All of them slowing and stopping in shock as the villagers part to let them through.

Huw looks up, finishing his prayer, before stepping back, into the frontage of the chapel and vanishing through its door into the darkness. He is no longer the priest here.

Becca looks on in shock. "Is this Robert?"

Tom looks up. "They cut his head off Becca!!!"

Becca's face turns paler than her dress. Looking at the headless body. She whispers hoarsely. "Gwyllion?"

Tom nods. Murmurs from the villagers. Agitation. A few panicked faces.

Huw steps forward from the doorway of the chapel. He looks like a terrified child. "I knew this couldn't last. They have come back. They're going to kill us all."

Becca gives him a sharp look.

"This is God's judgement on you for following this pagan woman!!!"

Becca sees a few of the villagers silently nodding. Becca turns her stare on Huw.

Huw moves back into the shadows and disappears inside the Chapel.

Arwyn turns to Becca, angrily reciting the nursery rhyme Becca's mother taught them all.

"Behind the Black Wall do they wait,

Our world again they seek to take

To break the bonds that bind our fate"

Idris grabs him by the scruff of the neck and completes the rhyme, growling it in Arwyn's face.

"'While sisters stand to fight their hate'... It's Becca and the Morwynion who must face them. But our place is to stand and fight with them for this world. We must never forget that."

Arwyn is unbowed. "How could this have happened?"

Becca is thinking hard. Yes, how could they be out of The Otherworld, and out of the lake in Cwm Du? How? "They must have broken my mother's Knot in the lake."

Arwyn is becoming more agitated. "But how can that be? It's deep in the lake."

"The other Knots I have placed will hold them. Don't worry..."

Arwyn rounds on her angrily. "Don't worry is it? Robert is dead!!! They cut his damn head off!!!!"

Huw reappears at the chapel door. "Which one of us is next?"

Becca looks on worriedly at the frightened villagers milling around Robert's headless body. Rachel standing there, as if in a daze. Becca's stomach tightens in fear. "Rachel! Who is watching the girl?"

Chapter 13: The Quarryman's Arms

Absolute darkness. Echoes of small waves breaking. The sound of the Gwyllion scouting party wading through the black water of the narrow tunnel. Clicking. Finding their way along the tunnel cut from living rock. The echoes from the clicking changing now. Longer. More hollow. They are entering the cavern. The water getting shallower. To their knees now.

Continuing onward. Climbing over fallen rock which was once The Black Wall. That Black Wall placed by Druidesses before memories began, to keep them imprisoned within this rock. Within the darkness. Blind and forgotten. Until the Black Wall was destroyed. Which brought the waters which killed so many. But also set them free. If only for a day, generations ago.

Now she has walked free on the land above. The first of her kind in those generations. A land where those who banished them below have grown weak. Unable to fight them anymore. Atala feels the weight of the man's head in her hand. Her bare feet on the black slate floor. Darkness all around but movement. Atala screams. Clicking in response up ahead in the darkness. Then more. Soon a cacophony. Movement all around in the pitch darkness, but Atala's mind can see. The hundreds of Gwyllion, awaiting her return. Awaiting news from the world above. Atala screams again and the clicking stops. Atala raises Robert's head and screams. Screams from the hundreds of Gwyllion warriors. Weapons banging against each other, against the slate floor, against the slate walls of the place that has been their home and prison for millennia but shall not be any more.

Laura and Jimmy walk down the country road through the mist. Sian follows stealthily behind them at a distance. Sian kicks a piece of slate. Laura spins around, but Sian has already disappeared into the trees.

Jimmy looks around too. "What's the matter?"

"I thought someone was behind us".

"Out here? It's as quiet as the grave Laura. Come on let's find this village. It's spooky out here with no light."

"Don't worry, I'll look after you." Laura winks at Jimmy. They carry on up the track towards the black mountain of slate waste towering ahead like a black figure in the mist. Beneath it, Cwm Du is hidden in the murk.

Suddenly Cwm Du appears around them. Laura and Jimmy are in the village before they realise. The houses rising out of the mist on both sides. No lights in any of these houses.

Jimmy looks around at the dark buildings, and rising above them, the oppressive mountain of slate waste. "Jesus Laura. It's so dark. And that mountain is so... black!"

"That could be slate waste from the quarry. Apparently, most of the slate that was mined was no good. So they dumped it near the quarry."

"That's huge though! A mountain! So all this came out of that quarry that flooded?"

"I suppose. These quarries were busy for decades. Then the quarry flooded. Everybody died apparently."

"Is that why there's no one here? This is a ghost town Laura. Shall we go back? In the morning I mean?"

"No there must be people here. I've got relatives here. They sent me the letter and left the key at the house. They must be in the pub or something."

"But pubs are shut because of the virus."

Laura spins around, catching a glimpse of a figure moving into a doorway up the road behind them. "There's someone up there. There are people about. Don't worry."

They carry on walking along a street. The huge, dilapidated chapel towers above them. Its two massive windows looking down at them like sad, forlorn black eyes. They unknowingly walk through the pool of blood on the street.

"This has been abandoned for donkey's years. Aren't the Welsh big on chapels?"

Laura is looking around. "There are no cars. No TV aerials. Nothing. You're right. This is odd." She looks into the misty murk, spotting light up ahead. "There's a light down there. Come on."

They continue up the village street. Sian follows them, getting closer. Moving swiftly and silently behind them. Behind her there is another figure on the street too. Laura and Jimmy approach the pub. The sign outside reads 'The Quarryman's Arms'. Sian is right behind them. As Laura and Jimmy approach the light she reaches out, but someone pulls her back, arm around her and hand over her mouth. Sian struggles as she is pulled backwards into the darkness. Laura and Jimmy enter the pub oblivious.

Sian is thrust up against the wall. A hand on her throat. Rachel still covered with Robert's blood glares at Sian. "What are you doing?"

Sian cries out hoarsely. "Watching her for you."

Arwyn is on his feet, frightened and angry. "We have to do something Idris! The knot has been broken! And she has done nothing!" The hubbub from the villagers in the room rises in anger and fear.

Idris snarls at Arwyn. "There are plenty of knots! She has placed them all around us to protect us. Nothing can get through." Suddenly silence. Idris turns to the door.

Laura and Jimmy stand in the open door of the crowded pub. Wide eyed having walked into a conversation in a language which is not their own. A pub open. Full of people. No distancing between them. No one wearing masks.

But all eyes on them. The villagers watch them like hawks. Then as one, they return to eating small bowls of Cawl, lamb and vegetable broth, avoiding eye contact with the strangers.

Idris gets up from the table where he is eating. "Good evening. What can you get you madam?"

Jimmy looks around the room nervously at the startled villagers. He watches Idris open the hatch and go behind the bar. "Hi. Two pints of Stella please."

Idris looks perplexed. "Eh? Stella? Who's Stella?"

Jimmy realises there are no bottles of beer or spirits behind the bar. Just a big earthenware beer jug and some old wine bottles with handwritten labels. He is speechless.

Laura steps forward. "Hi, a pint of beer please for my friend, and a glass of water for me. Thanks very much. Are you serving food?"

Idris nods and starts pouring a pint of dark beer.

Behind them, unnoticed, Rachel bundles Sian into a seat at the corner of the bar by the door. Rachel is holding Sian in a painful wrist lock, not caring that she is still covered in Robert's blood.

Laura takes in the bar. The villagers less nervous now, watching them, particularly her, intently. They are all dressed in old, often patched up clothes, finishing their small bowls of Cawl nervously. Others are just staring at Jimmy and her.

Jimmy whispers in her ear with a snigger. "They must be all one family. Or maybe there is no lockdown in Wales. And I mean, look at this lot. They're all wearing charity shop clothes."

Laura is embarrassed. "Jimmy!" She notices a large old black and white photo behind the bar. Idris the Foreman at the quarry with a group of quarrymen, captioned 1918. She catches Idris' eye as he finishes ladling two bowls of Cawl. "Is that the quarry at work? Before the disaster?"

"Yes. An old family photograph."

"I think some of my family may have lived here in Cwm Du."

"Really? So what's your name?"

"Laura Salhurst."

A sudden hubbub of shock from the villagers. Talking in whispers amongst themselves. Arwyn stares at Laura furiously. A hubbub rises. Arwyn gets to his feet, ready to speak.

In walks Becca, with Hannah and Mary in tow. The villagers stop talking. Silent in their presence. Watching to see what happens next. Arwyn takes his seat.

Idris talks directly to Becca. "This is Laura Salhurst."

Becca breaks into a warm smile. "Welcome home Laura. Where are you staying? At your great grandmother's house?"

More hubbub from the villagers, astonishment and shock on their faces.

Arwyn mutters under his breath. "Mort Lake. Very apt name for the place."

Becca shoots him a warning look. The Morwynion watch the crowd of villagers threateningly.

Idris passes Jimmy the glass of beer and Laura a glass of dark, almost black, discoloured water. "Here you are Laura."

Laura looks at the glass of water aghast. Is it drinkable? "Er, thank you."

Idris passes two bowls of Cawl with spoons.

Laura smiles politely. "How much please?"

"No charge. We owe your family a great deal."

Arwyn growls from the corner. "We used to..."

Becca gives Arwyn another withering look.

Idris passes Becca and the Morwynion glasses of the dark water. Laura watches Becca and the Morwynion drink the water with one gulp. "So it's my great grandmother's house? What was her name?"

Becca seems distracted. She spots Rachel sitting by the door covered in blood. She nudges Mary who moves off in her direction. "I'm Becca. A pleasure to meet you, Laura." Becca draws Laura to one side leaving Jimmy alone at the bar momentarily, until in steps Hannah to talk to him.

Rachel slips out of the pub unnoticed while Mary sits threateningly beside Sian.

Jimmy hasn't noticed that Laura has been drawn away. He takes a sip of his dark beer and relaxes. "This beer is awesome..."

Hannah slides in beside him. "We think it is very good. It is brewed with local water. The very essence of life."

Jimmy backs away, trying to keep some distance from this very intense girl. "Really?"

Hannah smiles sweetly. "Really."

Becca takes Laura to a table. The villagers sitting there disperse to other tables. Becca motions for Laura to sit with her. Becca holds Laura's gaze intently. Uncomfortably. Laura glances down from Becca's eyes. Becca is wearing the slate amulet with the Celtic Knot.

"I like your pendant."

"Thank you. It's very old. It's local stone. It's been in my family for generations. It ties me here."

"What's the design? A Celtic Knot?"

"Yes. This knot is very special. It has no beginning and no end. It ties everything together. It should never be undone."

"It's familiar. I think it's the same one I saw earlier. Down by the flooded quarry."

Becca blanches. "By the quarry? What do you mean?"

"There was a diver there who had found it carved on a stone when he was diving in the lake."

Becca's head reels. "I'm feeling a little unwell. Excuse me." Becca gets up and leaves the pub.

Becca steps out of the pub into the darkness of Cwm Du. She sobs. How could this be happening? Now as Laura arrives so she can become her protege. She needs more time! Becca looks up into the night sky. The birds are circling overhead.

Chapter 14: Walking Abroad

Becca walks along the Main Street, her mind racing. Walking through the blood outside the Chapel and onwards out of the village. Walking quickly through the mist, deep in thought. Playing the same fears over and over in her mind.

Today she has failed. It is her role to be the protector against the things of The Otherworld. Cwm Du. Wales. Britain. Europe. The World. These places are her responsibility alone. As they were her mother's responsibility. This was the reason for her mother's sacrifice. She must ensure all is well tonight in Cwm Du so that the rest of the world remains safe.

The newly widowed Becca had time to think after the disaster at the quarry. Alone with no son to care for nor distract her thoughts. That was possibly part of Myfanwy's plan. She was so wise. She would never have made the mistake Becca has made today. Becca retches in fear.

It was Becca's idea a century ago to surround the village with carved Knots to ensure if this moment ever came that they would all be safe within Cwm Du. Safe from the Gwyllion. Forever. And her Knots would trap them if they did break through, so they could not go into the outside world which would never survive their return.

Now that moment has come. The Gwyllion have returned. Due to her weakness. She showed some leniency. Instructing that this English couple in their charabanc could leave Cwm Du in peace. Idris' request lest the arrival of Laura be dealt with in the usual way by his men or by the Maidens. As Idris ages, he values compassion. His memories of that distant war never fade. It makes him a good man.

This was her favour to Idris, to allow him and the men of the village to watch the strangers and make sure they leave causing no harm. She should have left the task to the Morwynion. That couple would've been dead and gone before they even went into the lake. Disposed of like all the others. Out of mind. No threat.

But they were not a threat! Surely? She never foresaw this! How could this have happened? What these two outsiders have done will change things here forever. But it is her weakness that has caused this. She can't blame those who do not understand.

But now that the couple have removed the Knot from the lake it threatens everything. The Gwyllion and other creatures of The Otherworld can enter the lake. And they can leave the lake. That endangers the entire world. Has she made enough knots? Becca's head spins. She stops to catch her breath. She has been running without realising it.

She is older. She is making mistakes. But when you have lived twice your natural lifespan you have so many decisions. There are bound to be bad ones. But that makes her no less responsible.

A century ago, Myfanwy placed one Knot to hold them at the entrance to the tunnel, and a pair of Knots the gateway to the outside world. Becca carved more Knots. She placed a Knot to hold them at the entrance to the village. Another knot to hold them at the far side of the quarry. Surely that is enough? Becca runs onwards through the mist.

She should have made more.

In the Quarrymen's Arms there is but a murmur. Most of the villagers silently watching Laura. Ignoring Jimmy.

Laura sits alone at the table eating the bowl of Cawl. It seems to be water and vegetables. Similar to Scouse she once had at a student party, which her friend Fiona told her was the same as Scotch Broth. Traditional food. The people around have finished theirs. Some still seem to be starving.

Laura smiles at the two girls of roughly her age by the door. One, a blonde, looking somewhat familiar, but that makes

no sense. She looks uncomfortable. The other, dressed in a
white dress, sitting very close to the blonde girl. Too close
somehow. She is watching everyone around Laura but avoiding
eye contact with her. Like a sentry on duty outside Buckingham
Palace.

Laura looks at the dirty water in her glass. It's the same
dark colour as the water in the lake. Is that where it's come
from? Is it drinkable? Others are drinking it. Glass after
glass. It looks really unhealthy. But she is parched. She
takes a sip. It tastes like clean water. Bottled water even.
She takes another sip. The girl dressed in white by the door
is now watching her intently. Smiling.

Becca reaches the old gateway on the narrow track. One
gatepost is a standing stone from time immemorial. One which
the quarrymen would not move on her mother's instruction,
despite her husband's insistence. The road had to be re-
routed. The other stone placed there to create a gateway to
control the flow of slate, before the railway arrived. This
was one of her mother's few victories in those days, helped by
Becca's protestations to her soon to be husband.

Becca touches the knot carved in the squat standing stone,
taking comfort. One knot may be gone. But this second one
remains. The knots at the gateway to the outside world can be
checked in the morning. They will be safe. So there is one
more to check so she can sleep this night. Ensuring Cwm Du can
sleep soundly.

Becca heads off along the edge of the quarry. Her feet
inches from the drop to the water a hundred feet below.
Beneath her the mist hides the water. Within the mist the
birds are flying.

Hannah has led Jimmy away from Laura to the other side of
the bar. There are photographs on this wall. Some framed. Some

tacked or even nailed to the old plastered wall. Some black and white faded pictures of the quarry at work, much like the picture behind the bar which Laura noticed. Jimmy notices some similarities in the faces in these old photos to the people in the bar. Family resemblances no doubt.

The more recent pictures are Polaroids. Faded to pale strange colours, but recognisably of the villagers in the pub now. So how old are these pictures? Jimmy feels someone moving up beside him. Assuming it's Laura.

"How old do you think these pictures are?"

"Not old at all. That's me."

Jimmy turns to see Hannah smiling sweetly at him.

She points to a picture that's very faded. She looks not a day younger. "These things, these photographs are a history of our village since..." Hannah stops talking. Lost for a moment.

"Since the quarry disaster?"

Hannah is obviously upset. She walks away leaving Jimmy alone at the wall of photographs. But not for long. Huw walks swiftly across the bar to join Jimmy taking him by the arm. "Where are you from? You do not belong here. Take your charabanc and get out while you can. The birds are flying. You have to go!"

Jimmy looks at Huw nervously. Especially as he doesn't seem drunk. Just mad. Fucking mad! "OK mate, I'll take my chara... char thing and leave in the morning. You don't need to tell me twice."

Huw is staring at one of the Polaroids. Faded and discoloured. But even so the shirt he is wearing in the picture is distinct and new. A new Liverpool football jersey from the 1960s. New in the photograph, now threadbare on Huw: who otherwise looks identical in the old photograph. Jimmy follows Huw's gaze. Huw is gone, like a frightened rabbit.

Jimmy watches him go and realises that someone else is coming towards him. Big. Drunk. Threatening. Bryn. He snarls at Jimmy. "I like your coat. Give it to me."

Suddenly Idris is walking towards them. Jimmy moves away
quickly, joining Laura at the table.

Idris squares up to Bryn, hissing at him angrily. "Sit
down. This girl is Becca's guest. We should not cause her any
complaint." Bryn nods and crosses to his seat, eyeing Jimmy
all the time.

Laura looks at Jimmy. "What's the matter?"

"Let's go. Just let's go, OK?"

"Why?"

"One of these nutters just tried to take my coat. And the
other says that birds are flying so we have to leave here."

Laura looks at Jimmy and smiles. "Seriously? They're
probably just drunk. Ignore them, Jimmy."

Becca stands on the cliff overlooking the flooded quarry
somewhere below in the mist. Behind her the tall structures of
slate tower upwards, disappearing into the gloom. Once these
structures held the cables which were used to lift the slate
from the depths of the quarry below. Now they stand as
mysterious as ancient pyramids, half visible, hinted at in the
mist which sits all around her.

Becca can hear the birds flying around the structures and
descending, down to her level. Seeming to know she is standing
there. Flying around her head. Faster and faster. Closer and
closer. Whooshing around her, their wings barely missing her
face. The mist clearing momentarily.

Becca looks at the water a hundred feet below. One step
away. One small step. She closes her eyes. She instinctively
grips the amulet around her neck and her eyes open with alarm.
What was she thinking?

She runs off, heading to an ornate tunnel running between
the massive slate structures towering over her. The birds
can't follow her here. She reaches the opening of the tunnel.

Her hand reaches out in the darkness to the knot she has carved here. Keeping any Gwyllion from entering the village from this side. Placed on the line of power in the earth. Beneath the water is the opening to the tunnel where her mother placed the knot which is gone. Out across the lake, at the end of the lane is another. The final one placed on the standing stone at the gateway is on another line of power running to this point.

The knots are safe. All will be well until morning. Becca walks back along the cliff edge ignoring the swirling birds. The final part of her lone task to atone for her mistake is next.

Huw watches the occupants of the bar from the corner by the door. Mindful of the Morwyn only feet away, but she is fully occupied looking after the mad girl. The one girl who has chosen to come into this hell from the paradise of the mountains outside. And who has stayed. Has been tolerated by Becca because her father is the man who is their envoy in the outside world.

Huw closes his eyes. He is surrounded by the madness which has befallen this village over the last hundred years. Once he led the village in the eyes of God. But the witch has gained prominence. Since the day of death, everyone has followed this witch and her Morwynion. They have turned their back on the one true God. Heathens every one of them!

Huw raises his voice, his clear, Biblical Welsh bringing the hushed voices in the bar to silence. "Brothers and sisters. You have forgotten the one true God. You have followed the ways of Satan and the witch who has led you to this. This night the creatures from Hell have returned to Cwm Du. The creatures have returned to punish you, in the name of God, to drag you back beneath the waters to the Hell that now awaits you all!"

Jimmy looks around the silent bar. Everyone staring at Huw. "What the hell is he saying Laura?"

Laura shakes her head and jumps out of her skin as a glass smashes against the wall beside Huw.

Hannah striding across the bar towards Huw. A harsh whisper. "Hannah!" Mary sits beside Sian looking at Laura. Hannah follows her glance. Taking a deep breath. She walks up to Huw. "Be a good boy. Run away home."

"You and your sisters are all going to die. ALL OF YOU ARE GOING TO DIE!!!" Huw walks quickly to the door of the pub.

Jimmy watches in disbelief. "Laura, what the fuck is this?"

Hannah shoots him a look and Jimmy shuts up. Terrified by the young woman's stare.

Arwyn gets to his feet. "Where are you going? Huw?"

Huw spits at Mary and slams the door as he heads off into the night.

Suddenly a hubbub from all around. Idris turns to Arwyn. "Go with him".

Arwyn looks terrified. "Out of the village? Tonight? No chance!"

Idris locks eyes with Hannah. "You can't let him go alone to the abandoned village!"

Hannah whispers with authority. "He is the priest of the false god. He was banished there for a reason."

The camper van is rocking once more. A figure walks silently through the mist towards it. Her hands search the pile of belongings beside the extinct fire.

The piece of slate. The knot visible in the darkness. Luminescent. This piece of stone taken from the Black Wall. Taken today from its place within the lake. Taken back from the thief. Becca moves swiftly and silently up the ramp and is swallowed in the mist.

Chapter 15: Emerging Into Darkness

Huw runs up the Main Street through the mist in the darkness of Cwm Du. In moments he is at his chapel. Large. Dark. Cold. Huw stands for a moment looking up at the building which used to be the centre of Cwm Du's life. Then he realises he is standing in Robert's blood. He jumps up onto the steps to the chapel and wiping his feet he walks inside the remains of the largest building in the village. The monument to the beliefs of the generations before. But no more.

The chapel is vast. The smell of damp and mildew fill the air. He can taste the decay. Huw coughs for a moment as he gets used to the smell of the dead air. He steps forward between the mouldy chapel pews. The floorboards bending underfoot as he walks towards the pulpit at the far end; the centre piece of the chapel practically invisible between the pair of full-length chapel windows which look out onto the black slate waste behind the building.

Huw steps into the area before the pulpit. *Y Set Fawr.* The Big Seat where the Deacons used to sit before they either died in the war, or at the quarry, or became followers of this witch. Huw is alone in a room built for a thousand worshippers. The thousand worshippers who attended services here three times a day back before the Great War. The War To End Wars. He had heard of more wars as the years went by, but those were rumours from the envoys from the outside world. Dishonest people who may have lied to line their own pockets. Why would God let another war happen after those horrors?

Huw apologises silently for his ungodly thought and turns to look at his addition to the chapel. One which God may disapprove but has not told him to remove from this holy place. The image Huw painted on the wall near the pulpit. The Son of God. On his Cross. Dying to take the sins of Mankind off their shoulders. Setting Mankind free. God's fallen

warrior, as he Huw is God's fallen warrior. A graven image
which should not exist in a place of worship. An image of
which the Deacons would have disapproved if they had not
abandoned Huw to this village of Pagans.

Huw reaches for the Bible, placed on the dusty and rotten
table at the foot of the pulpit. At least in this part of the
chapel the roof is sound, and the ground is mostly dry. He
opens the book to the Old Testament. The piece where God
speaks directly through the voices of the prophets, not
through the emissaries of his Son. Where God punishes the weak
for not following His ways. He realises it is too dark to
read. His candles are all used up. He has not even the word of
God to comfort him.

At the lake the sudden sound of waves breaking on the
shore. The sound of figures wading through the shallow water.
Looking for the sign of power Atala had told them was on the
lake shore, there to keep them away. Clicking sounds suddenly
fill the air. Clicking sounds which slowly die. The Knot has
gone. There is nothing to hold them.

There is no need to click. This new world of sight and
light opens up before him. He has heard of this sensation but
never conceived of it. His eyes have never seen light. The
chief elder talked of it. How it hurt him so much he went back
into the caves and avoided the water from within that killed
so many of his kind on the day the Black Wall fell.

Gol never tired of that story. And now he too sees. He
sees for the first time. It does not hurt like the elder said.
Yet everything is so... loud. Like the loudest of sounds
coming into his eyes.

Above him no rock. Above him space. And creatures in the
sky. Birds circling. The elder had been right about that. And
dark rock towering all around apart from here. Here he and his
twenty warriors can get from the water onto the land.

Ahead of him a shape. Moving rhythmically. Sound from within it flooding his ears. Cries and breathing like a battle. Like a war. A roar. Someone must have won.

Gol and his warriors surround the shape. Not daring to touch it as it shines so brightly. It seems to be that shining material the humans used to kill his kind, spoken of in the myths he was told as a child.

Gol is the leader now. Not a child listening to tales. He must not show fear. He steps forward towards the shining object. His foot kicks a piece of slate. It clatters and smashes against the shape. All of his warriors exchange glances.

Something moves within the shining object. An unfamiliar shape. A human.

Tracey pops up in the window, wipes the condensation and looks out. "There's someone out there Dave!"

"Nah, no one's out here babe."

"What if it's perverts! Dave, go and see! I hate perverts!"

Bang! Something hits the van again. Another piece of slate. Dave appears in the window. "What the fuck!" Bang! Another piece of slate hits the van. Dave pulls on his jeans and opens the van door. He looks outside. Just swirling mist. He steps out onto the cold wet slate. "Piss off. I got a gun!" Silence all around. "Go on! Do one!"

Tracey appears at the door wrapped in a towel. "Dave, who's there?"

Dave looks around. Shapes move in the mist. "Who the fuck is that? I'm serious, I've got me gun!" The shapes are moving everywhere Dave looks. Half a dozen people. More. Much more! What the hell do they want? Dave pushes Tracey back and picks up a spear gun.

Tracey looks at him in alarm. "Dave, don't! Call the

bizzies!"

Dave steps outside and closes the door behind him. He raises the spear gun. "I told you! Now do one!"

Dave realises the shapes are everywhere. Something moves towards him near the back of the van. He points the spear gun at the shape, unrecognisable even ten feet away in the thick mist. "Fair warning - piss off".

The figure moves forward again. Large. Low, rising up to full height. Becoming clearer in the mist.

Dave takes a breath. A Gwyllion Warrior moves out of the dark mist. Recognisably not human. Carrying some sort of club as a weapon. Its eyes shining in the near darkness. "Holy shit!" Dave tenses and the spear gun fires.

Thud! The Gwyllion Warrior screams and disappears back into the darkness. Screams of agony as the creature moves away up the ramp. The creature thuds to the ground. Then silence.

Dave stands terrified. Trying to take in what has just happened. "Oh Christ! What have I done?"

Tracey pulling on some clothes opens the van door. "Dave!!! What's going on?"

Dave whispering in fear. The figures in the mist have gone. "Trace. I shot someone!" Dave is sweating in fear and shock. "What if they come back with their mates? Or the bizzies? We gotta go!!!" Dave throws the spear gun into the van and climbs inside. He is about to slam the door.

The silence is broken. A clicking sound. Then another. Coming from all around. Suddenly a cacophony. Dave switches on the van headlights. Tracey screams in terror.

The Gwyllion War Party led by Gol, stand in the headlights. Screaming in the bright light. Blinded. Covering their newly opened eyes. Turning to face the lake to hide from the light. Their screams and clicking fill the air.

Dave climbs into the driver's seat and tries to start the

engine. He releases the handbrake. Tracey in the seat beside him, screaming.

The headlights fade as the van engine tries to start.

Gol turns around and throws his slate weapon at Dave. The slate weapon smashes through the van windscreen and hits Dave full in the face. The sound of the starter motor stops. Dave slumps forward.

Tracey screaming, shaking him furiously. She opens the van door and runs through the mist up the steep ramp.

The van rolls forward slowly towards the Gwyllion who part as it enters the water of the lake.

Tracey's screams filling the air as she runs in the darkness. A figure before her. Doubled up with the spear protruding from its belly. Tracey slips and falls beside the creature. It raises a club and brings it crashing down on Tracey's head. Silence.

Dave waking slowly. Tasting blood in his mouth. Cold. Very cold. And soaking wet. He opens his eyes. The lights of the van dying as water rises. He feels sick. Sick from the blow and sick as the van begins to tip. Water pouring into the van through the broken windscreen. Dave starts to think. Where's Tracey? The van is in the lake. Oh God! How far to the edge of the cliff?

Suddenly the van rolls off the submerged quarry edge. It tips nose first and the water rushes in further. Dave tries to open the door, but his hands won't work. The cold of the water freezing his brain. He starts to breathe in the black water of the lake. The van sinks to join the other remnants of the outside world which have come to Cwm Du to drown.

On the shore Gol watches the object sink under the waters of the lake. One of his warriors is carrying the other human's body to him. Atala was right. They are not a worthy enemy.

Becca stands in silence outside Mortlake. Convinced she heard a scream as she was about to slam the door. Her mind must be playing tricks on her. Not for the first time. But now there is a real danger out there. A danger she must face in the morning.

The mist is still so thick. It plays tricks on her senses. It hides what she should see and deafens her to what she should hear. But there is movement in the mist. She can hear shambling footsteps on the slate track. Something is coming. But from where?

Something is coming. If it is the Gwyllion, how could they have broken the Knot? This nightmare is getting darker. Maybe she should run. Fetch her Morwynion and the men. A coughing sound.

Huw wanders out of the mist. Drunk and morose. Huw doesn't even break his stride. "The plagues will be upon us. God will punish us all for your witchcraft Becca Salhurst! You're as dead as the rest of us." Huw staggers off into the night.

Becca watches Huw go from outside her former home. The man who would be her adversary returning to his nightly exile. Disappearing into the dark misty night as his power in Cwm Du has disappeared.

Chapter 16: The Old Village

Jimmy takes his phone out of his pocket. No signal. 5% battery left. And now the clock isn't working. Why the hell is the clock not working? Probably because the battery is going flat. Or no Internet. Who knows. Bollocks!

There is no electricity back at the house Laura has been given. No wonder she was given it if it doesn't even have bloody electricity. He has to charge the phone, or he'll be cut off from the world, in this place: the land that time forgot.

Then he realises. The pub is lit with old fashioned lamps. Flames within them. No fridges behind the bar, let alone any games machines. No bloody electricity here either!!! Jesus Christ, where has she brought him?

Jimmy walks around the walls of the pub looking desperately for an electrical socket to charge the phone. Nothing. He comes to Sian and Mary sitting by the door. The blonde girl is the only person he has seen here wearing normal clothes; what was once a white track suit. Her friend wearing a white dress that has seen better days.

Mary stares at Jimmy. "Go and sit down."

Jimmy looks at her in shock. "Excuse me?"

"Sit. There's a good boy."

Jimmy locks eyes with the girl. He stares into her cold eyes. She is not joking. And she looks fit. Not that kind of fit. Fighting fit. She doesn't break the stare. Doesn't blink. Jimmy crosses the bar and sits by Laura. "What the hell is wrong with these people?"

The sudden loud clanging of a bell. Jimmy jumps in shock.

Idris is turning off the lamps inside the pub. He calls out loudly in Welsh, "Closing time. Everybody out."

Silence. Frightened faces all around. No one is moving. Arwyn snarls quietly in Welsh. "No! Idris, I'm staying here."

A hubbub of agreement all around. "We're safer staying together. Here."

Idris continues with putting out the lamps. "Just go straight home, Arwyn. All will be well. Becca and the Morwynion will deal with this in the morning. We are safe enough."

Arwyn drunkenly rises to his feet. "They cut his bloody head off Idris!!!"

Idris glances at Laura and Jimmy who are watching, not understanding a word of what is being said. "Arwyn. You'll be fine. All of you will be fine. Go home." Idris moves through the bar and turns off the lamp over Laura and Jimmy's table. The villagers reluctantly begin to leave.

Jimmy finishes his beer. "I'd like another one of these please?"

Idris looks at him in surprise. "The bar is closed."

"Why? What time is it?"

"Time to close the bar."

"But isn't it a bit early?"

"No. Licensing laws. We close now. Drink up. Laura, lock your doors tonight."

Laura looks concerned. "OK. But why? Isn't it safe here?"

Idris frowns. He has said too much. He looks nervous, glancing around. He sees Mary lead Sian out of the pub. He whispers the word, afraid to be heard. "Gwyllion."

Laura looks confused. "Gwyllion? What's that?"

"The dark things in the night."

Huw quickens his step thinking of that witch somewhere behind him in the darkness. When he was a child he was told that her mother, Myfanwy, could fly. A hundred years later, maybe her bitch daughter may have learned the same trickery, as she seems to be everywhere at once. What if she's waiting for him up there ahead in the darkness. He knows she wants to be rid of him. Him, her reminder of the true Lord in this now damned place.

Huw can hardly see in front of him, but he has walked this road every night for the last seventy or so years since Becca banished him from living within the village. Keeping him from his flock. In this time those sheep have turned against him too, ignoring him and the Chapel, leaving him to live alone in the village they abandoned when the quarry flooded. That old village overlooking what was once their livelihood. The quarry. The place they seldom go any more as it reminds them of time spent in the sight of God.

Huw is an outcast. But that is a good thing. All of God's prophets are outcasts. He is being tried. God has a role for him still in this valley of the damned.

He passes through the gateway with that cursed sign, the Knot. Her mark of Satan cut into this ancient Pagan rock. Huw heads off towards the deserted village which is now his home.

"This place is fucking boring Laura. Let's go home in the morning."

Laura looks at Jimmy in genuine shock. "No! For the first time in my life, I've got something of my own!"

"Look at where you are! I got no phone signal, no Internet. Everyone will think we're dead. The sooner we get back to civilisation the better."

Laura can hardly see Jimmy in the gloom. He is feet away and the mist suddenly obscures him. For a second she is alone. But unafraid. Jimmy reappears. Laura lowers her voice, speaking calmly. "Remember the letter, Jimmy? I have to stay for three days. Otherwise I don't get the house. So we're staying. OK!" She walks off down the track through the mist.

Jimmy stands alone on the track. "Laura, wait for me!" He runs off following her in the mist.

Huw walks onwards through the mist, finding himself at the top of the ramp down to the water. Time to turn the other way, into the woods to find his way back home. He coughs in the chill night air. There are sounds out there somewhere. Mist confuses you. Something down by the water it seems. Movement, closer now. It must be those outsiders who that fool witch allowed to stay. No one should stay in this cursed place except for these villagers who so readily turned from the eyes of God.

What is that strange clicking sound? One moment it's behind him, the next in front. Huw turns and walks through the trees, along the little pathway his feet have worn away for decades. He knows every foot of the path. Every tree on either side. So what is that? Huw stops in his tracks.

A shape in the mist where there should not be a shape. Not a tree. Too large to be a man. But not dissimilar. More like the cave men he remembers from the books in school. Those books teaching that God did not create the world in seven days. Teaching the blasphemy that science can explain God's universe better than the word of God.

Huw steps towards the shape. It grabs him by the throat, lifting him off the ground. Huw stares into the shining eyes. More shapes appear in the mist around him. Gwyllion!!! Huw tries to scream but the grip around his throat is too tight.

Jimmy walks crestfallen alongside Laura. When did she decide what they were going to do? Fair enough they have come a long way, and the house is pretty substantial. But let's face it, who would buy it in this mad village? No proper road, no electric, no Internet. No nothing.

Laura is quietly fuming at Jimmy. She's seen a side of him tonight which she knows was there but had been funny in the past. Sarcastic with a big mouth. Yes, very funny and charming. But trying to get her to leave when she needs to be here to get that house! That beautiful house!

She can see light up in the gloom ahead. What could that be? There seemed to be no houses between Mortlake and the village. But she may have missed one in the gloom. Right now she can hardly see ten feet ahead of her. Then the house looms out of the mist. Laura swallows a scream. "There's a light on in the house Jimmy!"

Jimmy puts his arm on her shoulder. "I thought you locked up Laura!?!"

"I did!" They run to the house. The light is coming from the front window. The Parlour. The front door is ajar. "Oh God, the door is open!"

Jimmy moves to go inside.

"Jimmy! Wait! there could be someone in there."

"Great, let's have them." Jimmy pushes his way inside.

Laura follows. They rush through the dark hallway into the parlour. An oil lamp is alight at the window.

"Is anything missing?"

"I wouldn't know Jimmy. Oh God, do you think someone is still here?"

"I'll check upstairs. See if our bags are still there." Jimmy heads out of the room.

Laura scans the room. The painting and photographs of her newly found family stare back at her through time. Suddenly Laura's jaw drops. On the mantelpiece is the slate with the Celtic Knot which the divers had at the lake.

Huw's head smashes against the stones of a fallen down house in the village. For a moment his vision blurs. Then he sees the creatures from Hell gathering around him. Creatures he saw in the waters coming from deep underground when the quarry flooded. How could he not have foreseen this? The demon drink! It has robbed him of his faculties!!! He knew they were back. Poor Robert lost his head to them. As he will lose his head to them. Any moment now.

He has faced death before. But not for around a century. He'd forgotten the feeling paralysing his body. The readiness for meeting his saviour. His saviour who always redeemed him. Kept him on this mortal coil to serve him. To have a purpose in the madness.

Then he understands. All creatures of the world are God's creatures. These creatures are sent by God to test him. As the witch has been sent to test him. These creatures may come from Hell, but they are the tools in the hands of God. Sent to destroy the witch. After a century of blasphemy God has acted. This enemy of his enemy must be his friend.

Like the missionaries who went out across the world from Wales, it is his role to teach these heathens about the ways of God. Like the missionaries who those savages tortured, he is merely misunderstood. Soon they will love him and understand the love of God. Huw smiles at the faces all around him. "Welcome."

Gol looks down at the human. Smiling and laughing. Sounds he recognises from when the darkness takes the minds of the older members of his people deep underground. The lack of light. The lack of camaraderie. The lack. His people call it The Lack when the mind fails, when the old ones walk away deep underground to die in the darkness alone. In the places of the dead. Away from the walking dead humans and their mindless actions. The places of serenity. And at last, death.

Gol bends down putting his face in front of this human Lack. Listening intently. The Lack is laughing and making sounds. Communicating to him. Thinking that it can talk to a leader like Gol. Only those with power talk to Gol. But this one is not afraid. Why not? Maybe he once held power and that power has gone. Like the older ones: the Lack. This is a human Lack. Gol pulls away to think.

The Lack helped Gol become the leader years ago. Killing the old leader before they walked away to die. Maybe this Lack can help him too. Gol pushes his sharp slate knife into the Lack's arm. It screams in pain. Gol removes the knife and the Lack laughs. Gol pushes the knife deeper. It screams again. Soon it will worship him for his power to give and take away pain. Soon this human will obey his wishes as the Lack did.

Laura looks at the Celtic Knot, studying it properly for the first time. The pattern is getting familiar now. It is definitely the same one that the woman in the village, Becca, had around her neck. That's a coincidence. But who would have brought it here? The divers? Couldn't be. They don't know where she lives. And how could they have got in?

Who would break into a house and leave stuff behind? That makes no sense. Maybe it's a housewarming gift. That must be it. But from who?

Jimmy enters the parlour. "Everything's there. Nothing's been touched."

Silence for a moment. Laura thinking. A distant sound distracts her. "Can you hear that?"

"What? I can't..."

"Ssshhh! Listen!"

The sound of Huw's screams carry on the wind. Laura heads out of the parlour. The front door is still open. She steps outside. The mist hangs heavy. Somewhere out there is the sound of screaming. Not too far away, but where, she can't tell. Jimmy joins her. "Hear it now?"

"Yes. Must be kids mucking about."

"It sounds like someone in trouble Jimmy."

"Nah. Kids. Those Gw...Gw... the things in the night. Someone's fucking with us. That's all. Come back inside."

Laura and Jimmy step inside Mortlake and shut the door against the night.

Chapter 17: The Long Dark Night

Becca screwing up her eyes tight shut. Wishing she could do the same to her ears. Her fingers in them, pushed in so tight they hurt. But that doesn't keep out the screams.

The screams of dying men are what haunts her dreams at night. The screams in the cavern where her husband died at the hands of the Gwyllion. The screams of her childhood friends and neighbours dying in the black water flooding the quarry. The screams of those who wandered into Cwm Du by mistake.

Now somewhere out there in the mist Huw is dying. Dying at the hands of those creatures.

And it's her fault. She should have shown the mad old fool some compassion, but as usual he was drunk and playing the great man of religion. Treating her like some sort of devil. The same religious prejudice which caused so many wars back before that war to end all wars.

Right now, not too far away, this man is dying. What can she do alone? With her Morwynion she could drive these Gwyllion back to the lake. Keep them in the water until she could carve a Knot to hold them in the lake once more. And on a dark night, she could swim out and place a new Knot where her mother had once placed the Knot. Remaking the seal between worlds. Keeping these creatures in The Otherworld, in Hell where they belong.

It would be simpler if she had not given the Knot to Laura. She didn't think... she doesn't think these days. Then she realises. By taking the Knot from the water's edge and giving it to Laura, she has opened Cwm Du to the Gwyllion.

Laura lies there looking around the bedroom. Wired. It's been such a long day and she can't sleep. Jimmy asleep like a baby beside her. He must have drunk more than he realised. He is comatose.

Laura studies the room in the low lamp light. It seems hardly changed in say a century. No signs of the modern world. No radio. No alarm clock. Nothing like that. It's like time is not important here.

It has the feel of one of those haunted houses you see in horror films. Frozen in time. A time long ago. But clean. So clean. Fresh. Lived in. But by who?

She has been too afraid to turn out the lamp. Not that she knows how. There are a few knobs and levers, but no obvious off switch. Now she's happy for the light.

That screaming hasn't stopped all night. Hours must have gone by, but she can't sleep. That screaming must be part of the reason why. If that is kids, surely they would have gone home to bed by now?

A click from downstairs. Was that a door closing? What did that barman say? Lock the door! Did she lock the door? She can't remember. She was half awake. But not anymore.

Laura gets out of bed and walks to the window. The mist is still thick outside though there is a hint of light in the sky now. Dawn. It will be good to see this place in daylight. Hopefully those bloody kids will have stopped screaming by then.

Laura needs the bathroom. Jimmy said it was at the back of the house near the kitchen. Laura picks up the lamp and leaves the bedroom.

Laura heads off down the stairs, passing paintings and photographs lining the walls as she goes. Unnoticed when she was going to bed. Now those faces are watching her through time as she tip toes down the stairs.

One photograph stops her in her tracks. An old faded black and white photograph of the man in the painting in the parlour. His cold stare enough to make Laura pause. It is a picture of him with his wife and child. A boy. The mother not smiling. Not happy it seems. Her face is familiar. Very familiar. The woman she met in the pub who ran out. Becca? No. It can't be. Some writing on the bottom of the picture. 1915. This picture is over one hundred years old. But she looks exactly the same as the woman in the pub.

This is what happens when you don't sleep. Confusion. Mad ideas. Laura feels like a duvet is being pulled over her brain. Softening everything. She better find the toilet and get back to bed. Get some sleep before the morning.

She heads for the front door, bolting it securely. Realising the key must be upstairs in her trouser pocket. Damn she's tired to have forgotten to lock it in the first place. It's OK, no one is able to get through that door with that bolt locked. It's huge. This place is like a fortress. There is a lady's scarf hanging from the coat peg at the back of the door. It falls to the floor revealing a horseshoe nailed to the door. Just like the one on back door in the kitchen.

Laura finds herself walking into the parlour. Why? Jimmy said the toilet was near the kitchen. She is about to head out but ends up looking at the Celtic Knot on the mantlepiece.

The slate is shining in the lamplight. Like a black mirror. Laura crosses the room and looks at it closely. Examining it. Running her finger along the cut in the slate. No joins. One line crossing and interlocking to form the Knot. No beginning. No end. Fascinating. Laura picks up the Knot in her free hand and heads out to the corridor and off towards the rear of the house.

In the parlour, two figures emerge from the shadows.

The screaming is far less regular now, but Becca is still in tears. Every nerve frayed. Where are the Morwynion? They should be here. She told them to watch Laura, keep the village safe, but surely they would know to come out here to find her? To work out a plan of attack? Where are they?!?

Becca steps away from the gatepost with the Knot on it.

The Knot is all that gives her comfort right now. No Gwyllion can pass the Knot. There should be no doubt that the Knot will hold these creatures back. But at this moment she is nothing but doubt.

Yesterday the world was a safe place, but outsiders somehow found her mother's Knot under the black waters of the lake, removed it and brought it here. They opened the gates of Hell. How could she have foreseen that?

No doubt she has made an error. She allowed these outsiders to stay. That's why she needs this young girl here in Cwm Du. But is this girl ready? Is Laura another of her mistakes?

She needs her Morwynion. Here, where they can assist her. War is coming.

She moves through the mist. The darkness still hurting her eyes as it is so bright. Everything so loud. Those things in front of her now she is away from the lake. Living things. Not moving. Solid. She moves her hands along the rough surface of the thing. Unmoving. Hard. Sharp. But not as hard and sharp as rock.

But there is so much that is not solid in this place. Above her no rock. Beside her no rock. She has freedom to move.

Her two warriors have stopped clicking now. Not using sound. Using that new sense as she does. Seeing each other for the first time.

She remembers the tales of those insane old ones, the Lack. Told to her as a scared child. Telling her about the fall of The Black Wall and entering a world of light. This world.

And now there is sound. Cries of pain. That is a human cry. Gol is nearby. Gol will tear something apart to make it do his bidding. But he is not as effective as she, the Warrior

Queen. She understands. Thinks. Gol does not think.

She does not want to be in Gol's presence. Not when he is creating pain. He takes pleasure from this and then believes himself superior to his true station.

She needs to explore this place. Find the ways. The entrances. The places to pass from one chamber to another. To explore this new world as she did as a child in the darkness, when she would explore new places in her underground world. Places which now hold the human dead.

She hates dead humans so much. Husks. They stink. Dangerous to her kind. Her brother killed by them when he wandered too far away from her as a child. She will never forget his death, nor the anger of her mother, nor the scars she left on Atala's back.

More loudness up ahead. Something searing Atala's eyes. Her warriors click wildly. They wish to run. Atala will not run. Atala has never run.

She leads her two warriors towards the loudness ahead. Not a great distance away. Before her a low layer of stone. Not natural. Even. Long. Stretching out as far as she can see. A break in the layer. Beside this break is the loudness. Dangerous. Remembered from the stories of the Lack. The shape cut into the living stone. The line with no beginning and no end. The line that kills her kind.

And something more. Something beyond. In the break between the rocks. A human shape. Not like the human she killed earlier. A loudness burning dimly within her human form. She has found what she fears. A human leader. Those the Lack called Druidess.

The Gwyllion warriors are no longer beside her. They are behind her. Showing terror. Atala turns to them and roars.

Becca freezes. She sees them. Yards away as the mist swirls. Creatures she has not seen for a century except in every dream in every night of her long life. Preparing to attack. But fearful. They see the Knot. Becca hisses. Her words cutting through the night. "You're not welcome in this world."

Atala hears the sound. Alien, but the meaning is clear. She is hearing the enemy of her kind. An enemy from across the millennia. Endless time unmarked by those beneath the ground where the daily sun cannot be seen or felt. Where time has no meaning. Atala clicks angrily and loudly in response. "I have come to drive you into the darkness and lead my people into this light."

Beside her, a warrior roars, emboldened by his Queen's words. Rising up to full height. Huge. One of Gol's family. Like him, unused to thought. The warrior rushes forward, throwing his slate weapon at Becca.

Becca dodges the object flying towards her, but the edge of the slate cuts her forehead before embedding itself in a tree. Becca drops to her knees in pain holding her head. She watches helpless as the Gwyllion runs and bounds towards her keeping low to the ground as it has done in countless battles beneath the earth.

The warrior burns as it passes the Knot. Bounding through the gateway on fire. Unsure of what is happening. Until the pain begins. It drops feet away from Becca who crawls backwards into the trees. Away from its flaying arms. Out of sight. Terrified.

The Gwyllion roars in pain, rolling on the ground as its flesh burns. Atala roaring in anger beyond the gateway. In a moment the Gwyllion lies dead. Flames rising from its still body.

Becca uses the slate weapon embedded in the tree to struggle to her feet. She rips the weapon free and walks forward. The sound of things moving fast through the mist.

Beyond the gateway more Gwyllion join the two who faced

her. One huge. Scarred, brutal, threatening. Holding a body by its neck. Huw. Bloodied and unconscious. Seemingly dead.

Becca lets out a yelp. A half scream. She walks forward to the burning Gwyllion body. She slams the sharp slate weapon down on the Gwyllion's neck. And again. And again. With each blow regaining her strength and composure. Grabbing the Gwyllion's severed head and raising it free of its body. Holding it high above her head. Its black blood pouring down over her.

The Gwyllion roar in anger. Watching her from a safe distance beyond the Knot which they know is holding them back by promising them a fiery death. Just like the Lacks had said. Madness proving to be the only truth in this world of light. They back away into the mist leaving only Atala and Gol facing Becca.

She steps forward holding the slate weapon and the warrior's head. "I'll drive you back into the lake. I'll remake the Knot. I'll keep you in Annwn."

Atala clicks angrily and turns away into the night. Gol stands facing Becca. Watching her. Remembering her face. He smiles. He holds Huw's body by the throat. The mist swirls. Huw screams. Then he and Gol are gone.

Becca stands alone, illuminated and kept warm by the burning body on the ground beside her. Becca wipes the blood from her eyes. Her blood and the blood of the Gwyllion Warrior. The same colour. Black.

Silence falls. Silence except for the sound of the Birds of Annwn flying in the darkness above.

Chapter 18: The Morning After

Silence in the bedroom except for Jimmy's snoring. Laura
asleep at last, face into the pillow. The light from the lamp
flickering as the oil begins to run out. Shadows moving across
the room.

The lamp light shining on the black slate with the Knot
carved into it. The piece of the Black Wall. Millennia old.
Like a black mirror. Her face reflected in it. Hannah replaces
it silently on the bedside table beside Laura's head.

Laura tosses in her sleep. Hannah and Mary exchange
glances and disappear back into the shadows in the corners of
the bedroom.

Laura looks down. She is dressed in white. An old dress.
Not her own, but hers now. Comfortable. But it's cold here.
Very cold.

She looks around. She is alone. The place is dark, but she
can see. She is in a cavern. Black. Pure black stone strewn
all around, like that piece of slate the diver found. But
shattered into shards on the ground all around, turned to dust
like black snow. Sparkling with whatever light is here in the
darkness.

Up ahead of her the cavern wall is broken. A great hole
where there was once a solid wall. Laura walks towards the
hole in the wall.

Hands reaching up through the black snow at her feet.
Skeletal hands. Long dead. Her dress brushes the ground
revealing the remains of white dresses on the skeletons in the
black dust. Laura feels a hint of panic.

She reaches the broken wall and gazes beyond. Wind blowing
in her face. Getting stronger. Black dust flying around her
suddenly. The howl of the wind with a clicking sound cutting
through it.

The dust clears, the darkness lightens. Laura gazes on a vast plain stretching off before her. A black bird flutters overhead. Then there are more. One lands beside Laura, turning to look at her. It crawks, but it sounds like the bird has spoken a word. "Annwn."

Laura looks back out across the plain and sees distant figures moving in the swirling dust. A few become a thousand. Become tens of thousands. Become a horde.

The horde is moving towards Laura across the plain. Quickly. Getting closer. Moving faster. Raising dust which the wind drives into her eyes. The clicking sound is becoming deafening. Laura's face turning black with the dust. Water flying in the wind like black rain. The black liquid covering her face. Running into her mouth. Tasting of blood.

Laura wipes the black blood from her mouth and eyes. The birds fly away. She is alone. She looks around the cavern behind her. Down at the ground by her feet. Something is moving. Atala appears from out of the dust, teeth bared.

Laura snaps awake. Looking directly at the Celtic Knot by her bed. Dawn light creeping into the room. The lamp has gone out. A click downstairs. Laura swings out of bed, rushing down the stairs, towards the back of the house. She bursts into the toilet, just in time. Throwing up.

Hannah and Mary move quickly away from Mortlake and onto the slate track outside. A figure walks towards them through the pre-dawn mist.

Her once white dress is black. Black with her own blood and that of the Gwyllion warrior, whose head she is carrying. "Where have you been?"

Hannah points at the house. "Keeping her safe as you asked." She can't take her eyes from the decapitated head dripping blood onto the track.

Becca frowns. "And Rachel?"

Mary is likewise transfixed by the Gwyllion head. "She is due to meet with Wyn at the gate."

Becca's mind swirling. Rachel is alone!

Rachel stands in the tunnel overlooking the lake stretching out below in the half light. The Birds of Annwn are soaring over the lake. She steps outside the tunnel passing the Knot Becca made to protect this end of Cwm Du. Rachel is exposed now, beyond the protection of the Knot. She shivers in the cold pre-dawn air.

She has spent the night cleaning Robert's blood from her dress. The still wet, newly washed dress clings to her body. Its cold grip making her shiver at this ungodly time of the morning.

Rachel shivers again, looking at the path she must walk along the edge of the quarry, down near where the Gwyllion emerged to kill Robert, whose blood is still in her hair.

The Gwyllion will probably not come out in daylight as they are creatures of the darkness. But right now the sun has not risen. And her dress is white against the grey-black slate. And the Birds have seen her and are circling over her head. And if those creatures from Hell can see her, the Gwyllion would see her coming from a distance.

Rachel takes a deep breath, shoulders the heavy bag of bottles to trade and sets off along the path at the edge of the quarry.

Trying not to look down at the black water below. She has never been afraid of heights. She was taught if she ever fell into the lake she could swim to the ramp where the slate used to be pulled out when this pit was still a quarry. That's the only way out. But that was with no Gwyllion in the water. Thank the gods that they bottled the water ready to trade yesterday. She does not want to go near that water until Becca has sealed the lake against the Gwyllion. Made their world safe once more.

A bird swoops near her head. Rachel slips sending loose slate falling into the water over a hundred feet below. More birds swoop at her. She has to get off this narrow path.

Rachel runs in the half light, tripping momentarily, catching herself and keeping on going as the birds swoop. She is off the narrow path and onto open ground. No matter what the birds do now she is safe from falling. But up ahead are the woods. And whatever lies within them.

Rachel runs now, the bottles in the bag clanking loudly. The sky is lightening as the sun gets ready to appear over the mountains on the other side of the lake. She can't be late.

She runs along the path, taking a short cut through the trees onto the main track. Passing the ramp which leads down to the water. The abandoned village off through the trees on her right. Where Huw lives. Huw? Is he safe there with Gwyllion abroad? Is she safe right now? The sound of her heart beating is deafening but is nothing compared to the clanking of the bottles and the pounding of her feet on the rocky ground.

She runs on up the track, trees on one side, a tall wall between her and the quarry. Between her and the rising sun.

Up ahead is the gateway opening out onto open mountainside. There is still time. Rachel sprints, coming to a halt at the gateway.

She looks out onto the pre-dawn mountain. Vast and empty. She closes her eyes and catches her breath.

Rachel opens her eyes. Ahead of her is the crossroads and a kind of charabanc she has not seen before. The man sitting on it is not Wyn. A much younger man. Slouched. Seemingly asleep.

Rachel steps through the gateway and approaches the man. Yes, he is asleep. Rachel circles. No sign of the goods Wyn had promised to trade. So this man must be nothing to do with Wyn. A traveller maybe. Best left alone.

Rachel returns through the gateway as the sun rises hurting her eyes. She turns around. Open countryside once more beyond the gateway. The crossroads has gone until sunset. She continues off down the track back to Cwm Du.

Wyn sits in his Land Rover. Still seething. Having woken well before dawn to drive here to trade with the Morwynion. Seeing Gareth sitting on the quad bike waiting for dawn. Having beaten him to the gateway. Wrecking his chance to trade today. Why does he do this? Why rush to be a man when you are still no more than a child? He will have to spend his later years rising in the dark of night, packing materials to trade. Day after day after day after day without end. Seeing his own face in the mirror grow old before his eyes, looking older than his own father as the women he meets remain unchanged. Gareth has this all to come. Why rush it? Why do his children run to Cwm Du when the place is hell on earth? Then he remembers that when he was a child Cwm Du seemed a heaven where he would never grow old and die. Now death is all he has to look forward to.

Gareth snaps awake. So tired. He sits on the quad bike at the crossroads. The sun is up. Nothing but open country in front of him. He has missed that golden moment when Cwm Du opens to the outside world. He stayed awake all night here for that golden moment. And he's missed it. Gareth roars in frustration.

Rachel continues down the slate track back towards Cwm Du. The sun rising quickly creating a darkness behind the wall between the track and the quarry below. Rachel stops. Senses on edge. Something is wrong. She moves into the shadows behind the wall, gently putting down the bag of bottles so they don't make a sound.

Further up the track a dozen Gwyllion step out of the trees. Blinded and disorientated by the rising sun. Crying out as the sun hurts their eyes. An argument of some kind between a huge male and a powerful female. The male leading the others away down the ramp, leaving the female and another warrior on the track. She screams after the others. A warrior returns and throws something down onto the track. A body. Wearing a red shirt. Huw!!!!

Rachel holds back a gasp. Rachel pulls back into the shadows, closing her eyes in terror.

A few moments later Rachel peers back down the track. The Gwyllion are gone. So is Huw. She gets to her feet, moving as quietly as possible through the shadows along the wall. Hidden in darkness and hidden behind trees. Emerging at the top of the ramp. Below the dozen or more Gwyllion are walking into the water of the lake. One is pulling a bloody body. Is it a woman? No, only Huw would be out here. It must be Huw! The lake swallows the Gwyllion. They disappear beneath the still blackness and are gone from view.

Rachel moves silently up the track towards the village, the only sound the gentle clinking of the bottles she is carrying. She continues up the track to the gateway. She can smell bacon for the first time in months, since Wyn last traded pig's meat with them. She loves that smell. But where is it coming from?

Something is lying on the track the other side of the gateway. Black. The shape of a man. But burnt beyond recognition. Rachel remembers the story of how the Knot would cause a Gwyllion to burn if it passes by. So it's true. This Gwyllion must have gone by the Knot in the darkness and met its doom.

Rachel runs up the track towards Cwm Du. Bottles clinking

frantically. Passing Mortlake. Entering the village. Joining the villagers congregating outside the shop. Joining the other Morwynion and Becca who turns angrily to meet her.

Laura watches Jimmy. Still fast asleep despite the dawn light streaming through the window. Laura shrugs, pulling on track suit bottoms from her bag, and a pair of running shoes. She tip toes out of the bedroom.

She opens the front door and breathes in the cold morning air. The mist has pretty much gone but has left a chill in the air. At least that screaming has stopped. Laura closes the door. Turning left for the lake she jogs off down the track.

The only sound is those damned birds still circling overhead. Laura jogs on taking in the woodlands at dawn as she runs. Building up the start of a sweat. Heart pounding now. Thoughts whizzing through her head.

She rounds a corner and sees a gateway up ahead and a large bag lying in the road. Black. Smouldering. As she gets closer, she realises the bag is very large and smelling as well as smouldering. She runs around it telling her mind not to play tricks on her. Of course those aren't arms and legs. If that was a body, there would be a head. Red blood, not a black sticky tar. She runs off through the gateway.

Laura runs on into the shadows of the forest track. The gloaming swallows her.

Rachel tries to avoid Becca's scowl. This is a new thing. In the last few years. Becca never scowled years ago. Too grateful for the wisdom and skills of the Morwynion her mother held so dear. But there has been a different Becca in these recent years. She used to mourn her husband and son. Now she is angry. And this morning Rachel can feel the Druidess' anger.

"Where did you go last night?"

"I prepared to trade with Wyn, like I always do." Rachel looks into Becca's angry eyes. What has she forgotten? What has caused this anger?

"I needed you last night. Gwyllion were outside the gateway. I was alone. I could have been hurt."

Rachel swallows hard. She hadn't thought to look to her mistress. And there was an enemy at the gate. Rachel swallows hard. She needs to let her know what she has seen. "They are gone."

"Gone? How do you know?"

"I went to the border. Wyn was not there. There was a younger man. He was asleep. He had nothing to trade..."

"And? There were Gwyllion there?"

"By the ramp. Around a dozen. They had Huw. They went into the lake. They are gone."

"They took Huw?"

"Yes. They pulled his body beneath the waters."

Becca scowls. Nodding to herself. "That's for the best. We need to bury Robert. Come."

Laura reaches the top of the ramp. She can see the ruts in the pathway where her car struggled its way onto the track before getting her that last half mile to her house. Yes. Her house.

The same narrow tyre marks coming from further down the track, when she drove in last night. No new tyre marks. So those divers should be down by the lake. Yes, that makes sense. Back in the city she could never notice anything like that.

Laura looks through the branches of the trees. She can just see the water's edge, but there is no sign of the camper van. OK, they must have gone. They did say they would be heading off. Good. She will have the lake to herself this morning. No divers. No Jimmy. Just herself. Alone for the first time in a long time.

Laura moves quickly down the muddy ramp. Her footsteps melding with the footprints there. A lot of barefoot footprints in the mud. That must be the villagers going fishing or something. Whatever country people do. At least there is no one here now.

Laura arrives at the water's edge. The vast lake becoming visible in the dawn light. The sun directly in her eyes. Reflecting on the black water surrounded by the near black cliffs which border the lake. Not a ripple on the water.

Laura looks up at the hundreds of birds still circling in the sky. Like a massive black cloud, swirling and weaving patterns, moving around and around. Reminding her of the pattern of the Celtic Knot which was left at her house. It's like the birds are mimicking the pattern as they fly.

Laura crouches down. Looking over the flat surface of the water. Something is floating out on the surface of the water, a couple of hundred feet away. Another of those bags, like the burnt one on the track by the gateway. Laura glances around for a moment. When she looks back again the bag has disappeared in the light mist which is forming.

Tracey's body descends into the darkness of the cold water.

Chapter 19: A Funeral

Robert has been wrapped in a white cloth like an ancient
mummy. His headless body covered to hide the wounds inflicted
by his killers. He has been laid on a door as a makeshift
briar, which is carried by Idris, Arwyn and others, all
dressed in their finest funeral black.

They are following Becca, Rachel, Mary and Hannah, dressed
in white. The Druidess, carrying a flaming torch walking ahead
of the Morwynion; the body, bearers and the mourners follow.
The entire village dressed in black, following the white clad
Morwynion across the dark slate wasteland. Following the flame
held high in the morning mist.

Sian walks alone, around a hundred feet behind the others.
Dressed in her only clothes, her dirty white track suit.
Ignored by all the villagers. Not a member of this community.
Literally an outsider who has walked into this world. Only
tolerated as her family are their link to the outside world.

The funeral party is dwarfed by the thousand feet high
mound of waste slate which hangs over Cwm Du. The single
burning torch leading the way through the morning mist. Becca
and the Morwynion lead the villagers down onto a railway
cutting to a cave into the mountainside.

They reach the entrance to the cave, like a dark mouth
running deep into the mountain. The Morwynion are carrying
unlit torches, which Becca lights from her own. Becca sees
Sian stepping forward and ignores her. Becca leads the
Morwynion and the bearers with Robert's body into the cave.

Daylight is dead in here. Gone. Forgotten. Robert's
shrouded body is laid amongst slate cairns within. A cemetery.
The cave of the dead. A place where the dead lie before waking
to dig through the hard earth beneath them, deep beneath them
to walk the darkness of The Otherworld below for eternity.
Becoming Husks of their former selves: the mindless Dead.

The white shroud shines in the flaming torch light. Each of the villagers stand expectantly outside in the dawn light, each picking up a piece of slate before entering the tunnel, one by one, forming an orderly procession.

Sian struggles to see within the darkness. Momentarily she can see what is going on, before the villagers close ranks in front of her and she sees no more.

Becca speaks quietly as one by one the villagers lay their slates over the body, until all have left the cave and Robert has become another slate cairn alongside the others within the mountain.

Sian picks up a piece of slate and steps forward. Rachel grabs her arm, twisting it. Sian drops the slate and Rachel leads her back outside. Sian walks away, nursing her bruised arm, watching Becca join her Morwynion at the entrance to the tunnel. Sian walks back to the village, following the other villagers. Kept at a distance, by everyone.

Becca takes Rachel aside. "You and I need to speak. Walk the bounds with me."

Rachel nods.

"Hannah, Mary, watch over Laura. Keep her out of harm's way." The two Morwynion walk off across the slate waste back towards the village, their white dresses merging with the mist, then shine like white sails in the rising sun on the sea of black slate.

Rachel walks silently beside Becca, dwarfed beneath the mountain of slate waste towering over them. They walk along another railway track towards the massive slate structures which tower like ancient Babylonian Ziggurats above the far side of the village.

Here the railway track has rusted away, and they are walking on bare slate towards the tunnel which leads through the huge slate structures ahead.

Rachel watches Becca walk wordlessly, becoming more frightened of what Becca is thinking. Becca's silence becoming deafening. Her face unreadable. Their footsteps clacking rhythmically on the loose slate waste.

The only other sound now the Birds of Annwn flying over the lake beyond the massive slate bastion between them and the quarry beyond.

Becca and Rachel walk into the slate tunnel, into the blinding light beyond. Light mottled by the swirling black birds.

Becca steps out of the tunnel onto the cliff top overlooking the lake. The mist has lifted, and the Birds swirl forming patterns in the sky. Becca turns to Rachel. Her speech prepared.

Rachel feels her eyes close as Becca prepares to admonish her. But there is not a sound.

Rachel opens her eyes. Becca is staring in disbelief at something behind her. Rachel turns around. Where this morning there was the Celtic Knot, now there is no Knot. It is smashed. Gone. Rachel's heart skips a beat. The protection of this route into the village is destroyed. She looks at Becca in terror. "It was here not an hour ago!"

"You're sure?"

"Yes. This must be the work of the Gwyllion."

"But you saw them leave. Under the waters?"

"Yes."

Becca roars. "Who did this?!?!? The Gwyllion cannot come near the Knot. This is the work of men!!! Who did this!!!!!!!!"

Rachel's face shows pure terror. She has never seen Becca like this in the hundred years since the day The Black Wall fell.

Laura is alone at the water's edge. The sound of shouting is echoing around the quarry. Where is it coming from? Someone is very angry. She can't understand the words. Welsh maybe. It puts her on edge that there is so much anger in this beautiful place.

Her senses heightened now. Fear rising. She senses something, no someone, moving up above in the trees. A few people in fact, moving fast, struggling. Perhaps those kids from last night?

Suddenly Laura feels very alone. Something telling her to keep quiet. To hide. She moves lithely into the shadow of the cliff at the water's edge below the path. Out of sight. In a moment the kids, or whoever they are passing by above, have gone. But Laura stays in the shadows for a minute or two. Frightened.

There has been no sound or movement for a while. Laura walks up the ramp. At the top of the ramp she turns for her house but thinks better of it. Still nervous after hearing those shouts, and with those kids are probably still around here somewhere.

Suddenly THWAK! An impact. Almost like a gunshot, coming from somewhere back towards the village. Laura turns and heads the other way, away from Cwm Du. Not wanting to come across those kids. No way.

As she walks there is another impact. She winces at the sound. It's the sound of destruction. It comes again. And again. Laura walks faster now along the track, away from that sound that rattles her mind.

Becca sits on the ground crying as Rachel looks on, helpless. Rachel looks at the smashed Knot in terror. Trying to remember if the Knot was made when she was there this morning. Yes it was. Definitely. This is really recent. The debris of the smashed slate is still on the ground.

So what did she see this morning? The Gwyllion went under the waters of the lake, taking Huw with them. So who could have done this? Who would help the Gwyllion? Threaten their very lives? The outsider girl, Sian? The other outsiders with their charabanc at the lake are gone. So who? Laura??? Rachel closes her eyes. That would be an existential betrayal of Becca's kindness.

Something cuts through the sound of the Druidess' tears and the swirling of the birds overhead. Like distant gunshots. Regular. Rachel looks around.

Becca gets to her feet and exchanges glances with Rachel. "What's that?"

They both step out towards the edge of the cliff and try to work out where the sound is coming from. Becca's eyes widen in fear. "The Knot at the Gateway! Someone is breaking it!" Becca runs off along the narrow cliff top path, birds swooping all around her. Rachel swallows hard and follows.

Laura sees the gate up ahead and the sunshine on the mountainside beyond it. As she gets closer she realises that the road seems to have disappeared beyond the gate. Now there is just open mountain. And wasn't there a crossroads here when they arrived last night? Where is it? Where the fuck is the road that they arrived on!?!

Laura goes cold. Is this a different road? No it can't be. This is the track that she drove along. The one which they drove off to go down the ramp to get water for the car. The one that went on to her house.

So why is there no road, and no crossroads outside the gate? What the fuck is going on? Is she losing her mind? Laura leans on the gatepost. Her head reeling. What did the divers say? That they couldn't find the road out! Oh fuck! This is insane!

Laura leans on the gatepost made of slate and sees another

Celtic Knot carved onto it. What the hell is going on here?

Becca runs through the trees. The impacts getting louder now, louder than her feet slamming on the slate waste. Filling her ears. Filling her heart with terror. She knows. She just knows! She reaches the wall which protects the village. The gateway through it is yards ahead.

Becca runs out onto the track to the gateway and stops. In seconds Rachel has joined her. Both speechless. Both look on in horror. THWAK!

Huw is on his knees, using a piece of slate to smash the Celtic Knot carved on the gatepost. His face is badly bruised, his shirt bloody, his eyes dead to the world. THWAK! He mindlessly smashes the Celtic Knot again. He coughs wildly.

Becca rushes forward. "What have you done!?!?!"

Huw turns to her in fear. Fear turning to anger. Anger to pure hatred. "Destroying your magic, witch!"

Becca wells up with tears. "This is what protects our people, Huw. *Our* village. *Our* world from what lies within The Otherworld".

"NO!!! That is the role of the Lord Our Saviour. You aren't our saviour, witch! These creatures are the creatures of God. Sent by God to rid this place of your evil ways. Restoring the will of God to this world."

"Huw! Listen to yourself! Why would you let these animals kill our people? The Knots will protect you. We will save you!"

"Last night you drove me away. Banished me into their arms. Last night you wanted me dead. Not saved. So this is my gift to you all. Deliverance from your sins."

Becca has tears running down her face. She never thought of this. She had tolerated this man, with his outdated religion, merely sending him outside the village to live, as he had done to her mother all that time ago. She should have banished him outside Cwm Du, or let Rachel kill him that night he raised a gun to threaten her. Then she sees that Huw is still bleeding. Shivering in pain. Coughing again. Sick. The sickness that the Gwyllion bring! "What have they done to you?!? Let me help you."

THWAK! The last vestige of the Knot carved into the gatepost has gone. Huw struggles to his feet.

Rachel whispers in Becca's ear. "Behind us..."

Behind them two Gwyllion Warriors emerge from their camouflage in the trees and approach threateningly.

Becca and Rachel turn to face their foes. Rachel spins back around punching Huw who has raised the stone to bring it down on Becca's head. Huw falls to the ground and crawls away.

The first Gwyllion Warrior thrusts his spear at Rachel who grabs it, pulling the Warrior forward off balance. She hits the Warrior in the face, knocking him to the ground. Rachel kicks the Warrior in the head, knocking him unconscious. Rachel stands facing the other Warrior, spear in hand, a fierce glare on her face.

The second Warrior stops and backs away into the trees. Rachel takes the spear and drives it viciously into the fallen Warrior's body. Driving the spear into the body again and again, its black blood spraying onto her white dress.

The second Gwyllion Warrior looks on in terror. He runs off into the trees.

Blood soaked, Rachel returns to Becca's side. She looks around for Huw. "Where did Huw go?"

Becca stands as if in a trance. Shocked by what has happened. Shocked at how this man could turn on his own people to threaten Cwm Du. And threaten the world. "They're breaking the Knots... there is only one more."

"But you can remake the Knot? Make all well again."

Becca crouches by the defaced stone and sobs.

Laura walks back down the track towards Cwm Du. Still confused by the road back to civilization not being outside the gate. That is so fucking mad. At least those gunshots have stopped. If only those birds would go away. Still circling over the lake creating a din worse than rush hour traffic.

Something tells her to stop. Something tells her to hide. She moves off the track into the trees. Heart racing. What is the matter with her? She's been like a frightened cat all morning. Then she sees someone running along the track. A man carrying a spear. But is it a man? Different. Very thin, but very powerful. The same kind of shape as that bag lying on the track earlier.

The man runs down the ramp towards the lake. Laura moves quickly along the track and looks down the ramp. The man is standing by the water. And she can hear him, even above those damn birds. He is making loud clicking noises. Angry. As if screaming out across the water.

His shape silhouetted against the black mirror of the water. That shape. Dream like. Nightmarish. Familiar.

Laura begins to shiver in fear. Half remembering the nightmare that woke her. She heads off quickly along the track back towards Cwm Du. Back towards the house. Safety.
She starts to run but there is another figure coming down the track to meet her. A man. Limping. Holding himself like he is in a lot of pain.

Laura watches intrigued. The old man limps towards her. Bloody. Hurt. Not noticing her, as if in a trance. Laura steps aside to let him pass. "Hello? Are you OK? What the hell is going on here?"

Huw stops. He had not seen her. He turns to her. "To me belongeth vengeance and recompense; for the day of their calamity is at hand, and the things that shall come upon them make haste." Huw limps away down the track coughing wildly until he is out of sight.

Chapter 20: Trying to Comprehend

Laura watches the crazy old man limp off down the track and into the woods. His coughing now drowned out by the birds swirling overhead somewhere in the mist.

Laura shivers. What the hell is going on here? She turns towards the village and continues down the track. What did the old man say? It sounded Biblical. Like some sort of prophesy.

Laura turns a corner in the track. The gateway to Cwm Du is up ahead. A figure is lying on the roadway by the gate. Dressed in white, like a ghost. Long black hair. Looking like a character from one of those Japanese horror films Jimmy has been watching since lockdown.

The figure raises her head, looking through her long black hair at Laura. Rising rapidly to her feet. White dress covered in mud. It's Becca. The woman she was talking to in the pub last night. The woman who ran out like a crazy thing. Walking towards her now with arms outstretched. Tears flowing. Gasping and muttering.

Laura backs away. "Becca?"

"Laura. Why aren't you in Mortlake? It's not safe, Laura. It's not safe! Go home!"

Laura continues to back away. "Go home?"

"Go to Mortlake. That's your home. We need you home. I need you home."

Laura turns to run. But there is another figure coming out of the morning mist. Rachel appears from the trees, her white dress also covered in mud. Or is it mud? If it were red, it could be blood. It smells like copper even from this distance. Just like blood. Black sprayed all over her dress, her face, her hands. Her eyes wide, teeth bared in her blackened face. The face of a mad woman.

Laura turns back to Becca. "What's going on here? Are you alright?"

Becca points to a gatepost. "They're undoing the Knots. Remember what I told you? The Knot is endless, and binds everything together. The world as we know it unravels as the Knot unravels. It breaks and we're undone with it." Becca drops to her knees and picks up the shards of slate, holding them up to Laura. "See? Do you see?"

Laura steps forward and examines the damage from a safe distance, aware of Rachel closing behind her. "Who did this? That old man down there? Or that dark man? The man with the spear?"

Rachel grabs her by the shoulder. "Where is he? The dark one?"

Laura backs away in shock. No one should be this close to someone they don't know. There's a pandemic. Doesn't she know that? Laura composes herself. "He was by the lake." Laura turns to Becca. "So who is that dark man?"

"They used to live here a very long time ago. Now they're back. They've come to kill us all."

Laura reaches for her phone. But there is no signal. "Call the Police."

Becca looks at her askance. "I protect this place. I will drive them back... They should fear me... They should fear you, Laura."

"Fear me?" Laura thinks about the figure she saw. Athletic. Armed with primitive weapons. Not speaking. Clicking like an animal. Just like those figures in her dreams. Thousands of them. Coming for her. Coming for her alone!

Becca grabs her. "But they will fear you. This is your inheritance."

Rachel moves towards Laura. Face to face with her. Intense. "They're savages, from our ancient history... We learned their story from Myfanwy, Becca's mother. The story of The Black Wall."

Becca takes Laura's face in her hands and sings to her as

she would a child. Her child. Her family.

"Gods of days gone by

Inside the mountain lie

Behind the Black Wall do they wait

Their world to take and seal our fate

While sisters stand to fight their hate."

Laura breaks free of Becca's grasp. "What has this got to do with me?"

Becca follows her. Fierce. "You're here for a reason Laura."

Rachel cutting off her route back down the track. Like a sheep dog, moving Laura towards the gateway. Towards Cwm Du. Towards Mortlake. "You're our sister." Rachel steps forward to embrace Laura who jumps backwards in alarm.

Laura looks at the two women, intense, angry. Covered in mud, or is it blood? Laura runs through the gateway, stepping on the shards of smashed slate.

Rachel moves to chase after Laura, but Becca grabs her arm. Becca cries out. "Laura! Come back. Please!" Becca and Rachel watch Laura disappear through the gateway.

Becca turns to Rachel. "She will be fine. Hannah and Mary will watch over her. You find Huw. Stop him destroying the final Knot. Take him across the boundary."

Rachel looks concerned. "But he is sick!" Becca is looking at the broken shards of the Knot on the ground. Rachel runs off up the track then turns into the trees, heading for the deserted village.

Laura runs quickly along the track, terrified. Looking behind her, watching for those two crazy women who seemed a little strange last night. In the cold light of day are certifiably insane. Don't they know there's a pandemic? What the hell is going on here? Laura falls over something in the track.

She hits the slate ground hard. Right beside what she thought was a bag. Blackened. Burnt. Smelling like bacon. Sort of human shape, if it had a head. Because it has arms. Legs. Torso. Oh fuck!!!!

Laura is at Mortlake before she realises she is on her feet. Breathless. Frantic.

Jimmy is looking under the bonnet of the car. Tinkering, with no idea what he is doing. Looking busy. He looks up at Laura. She rushes passing him, slamming the front door behind her.

Laura is sweating in fear. She heads towards the back of the house. The sound of Laura being sick in the bathroom echoes around the empty building.

Rachel moves swiftly through the woods as she has done for over a century. Senses heightened as they only can be for one of the Morwynion. The Birds of Annwn up there in the clearing sky hiding the sound of movement, so she must use her eyes. Her nose. She can taste blood. And fear. Up ahead. In the village where her grandparents lived when she was a child. In more innocent times. Her grandmother so proud that Myfanwy had taken an interest in the young Rachel. The girl who used to beat the boys in races, in fights, and in school. Rachel would be a pioneer. Apparently, women would be permitted to vote soon. She would enter a different world. But then came the Great War. And in Cwm Du time stopped.

Rachel sees some red between rocks in the distance. Her eyesight like a seagull. Seeing for miles. Here, fifty yards through foliage and rubble. That's where the old man is hiding.

Rachel moves like a fox for a hen. Through the trees, but the hen has seen the fox.

Huw runs off, sweeping around, making his way for the track. Rachel moves to cut him off, but slips, falling,

banging her head. For a second blackness. Then just pain. She
sees the red shirt run back towards the track. Rachel shakily
gets to her feet.

Becca walks down the ramp to the lakeside. The black water
glistening as the sun breaks through. Sunlight and the shadows
of the thousands of the Birds of Annwn flying overhead. The
Birds seeing her now. Swooping around her. Enfolding her in
their world. Warning her. Making sure she knows. Making sure
she knows that The Otherworld is at one with Cwm Du. Letting
her know if she does not fulfil her role, as her mother did,
as all of her foremothers did, that soon The Otherworld will
be as one with all of this World above. And far more lives
will be lost than were ever lost in that trivial Great War
that Becca and the people of Cwm Du remember.

Becca moves slowly as the Birds swirl around her
protectively. She picks up a piece of slate. Split a century
or more before, to be discarded with the millions of tons of
poor slate blown from the ground beneath; the mighty quarry
before her that is now the lake.

Becca takes her amulet from around her neck. Becca sits on
a rock by the water's edge and starts to move the amulet's
sharp edge across the slate. Tracing a pattern she knows. A
pattern woven in air by the birds around her.

A pattern she is forgetting. How does it go? The amulet
leaves a scratch on the stone where there should be a mark.
But it is not marking the slate. And the pattern is not
unified. Not one continuous line. Becca has forgotten the
pattern of the Knot. She drops the amulet and howls in rage.

Laura is sitting on the Victorian toilet. Tears flowing
down her face. Staring at her phone. At the screen which says
"No Signal". She is alone. In what should be her dream home in
a village which is turning into a nightmare. She throws the

phone against the wall, rolls into a ball on the bathroom
floor and sobs.

Huw has reached the track. Standing on the top of the ramp
down to the quarry. Down to the water. To where God's
Creatures are waiting to purge the Witch and her followers
from Cwm Du.

Huw takes a step onto the ramp, towards his new masters.
His torturers. And stops. Thousands of birds swooping and
circling at the water's edge. Amongst them a shape at the
water's edge. He strains his eyes. The Witch herself.

Huw remembers. The Gwyllion want him to smash the Knots.
There is only the pair of remaining Knots. The barrier between
Cwm Du and the outside world. He has to hurry. The she-hound
is on his tail. Rachel. A girl he taught in Sunday school and
who was one of his flock until that witch Myfanwy took her
away into the darkness.

Where did the she-hound go? She means to kill him. At
times of trouble and doubt his sanctuary has been Capel Mawr.
The Big Chapel. Where he is in the sight of God. The only
place for Huw to go. The safety of the house of God. Back to
Cwm Du. Back to his chapel. Huw turns and limps the best he
can back for Cwm Du. Through the gateway. Passing the Knot he
smashed. Coughing like a dying old man.

The body of one of the Creatures on the road. A Christian
village would have buried it. Not left it to the rats. But he
has no time to give the Creature the Last Rights. Huw limps on
towards Cwm Du.

Towards Salhurst's house. The Witch House outside of the
village. An outsider is working on a charabanc. At least the
boy has the sense to leave this cursed place.

Huw limps on passing Mortlake. Quiet, not wanting the
outsider to know he was there. Moving as swiftly as he can.
Feeling the effect of every blow, every cut, every scar

inflicted upon him for the sins of men in Cwm Du. Nothing can make up for the sins of these women. These witches.

Suddenly they are on him. Hannah and Mary grabbing him, pulling him to the ground. Beating him. Then there are three. Rachel pulls him to his feet, grabbing his hair and leading him away. Away from Cwm Du. Away from Capel Mawr. Away from this mortal coil. He knows where she is taking him. A swift death would have been a kinder punishment than this. Huw cries and screams as he is pulled along the track.

Jimmy is still examining the car. The pipes and metal are a total mystery to him. But he needs to get out of here. Get this piece of shit working. Get back to the real world. He shrugs in despair. "Fuck knows..."

Suddenly a noise at the gate behind him. Jimmy looks around.

One of the women in white from the pub last night is passing the gateway. Her white dress is covered in something. Is it blood? Why would it be blood? Her face black. Her wild white eyes and teeth shining in the morning sun.

She is struggling with something. Trying to drag it along the track

Jimmy walks towards her. "My days!!! Are you OK?"

Rachel drags Huw's body up the track.

Jimmy stops dead. "Fuck!!!!"

Rachel glares at him as she pulls Huw off up the track out of sight.

Jimmy stands dumbstruck then rushes back into the house. "Laura!!!!"

No reply. The house is silent.

"Laura where are you?"

Jimmy looks in the parlour. In the kitchen. Nothing. Not a sound. "This place is fucked! We're fucked! There's a girl out there! From the pub last night. Covered in blood. Pulling an old guy up the road."

Silence. "Laura?" Jimmy climbs the stairs. "I'm off! With
or without you!" Jimmy charges into the bedroom. He grabs his
bag and heads out. He runs down the stairs. "Laura! We're
leaving. Come on! Where are you?"

Silence.

Jimmy heads out through the front door, slamming it behind
him. He stands outside the house. "Laura? Where the fuck are
you? We have to get out of here!"

Rachel drags Huw up the slate track. His boots
occasionally digging in. A vain attempt to stop the
inevitable. Huw crying like a child who is going to be thrown
out of the house for bad behaviour. His previous warning got
him banished to the old village by the quarry. Alone with the
ghosts of forgotten quarrymen. But they are ghosts of Men of
God who wouldn't hurt him.

For so many nights he wished those ghosts would keep him
company in Capel Mawr. There he was so alone. He had grown
used to being alone for decades.

Huw catches sight of Rachel every now and again as she
drags him by the hair down the track. Determined. Angry. There
will be no reasoning with her. She will banish him beyond Cwm
Du. Beyond the pale. Beyond the veil of death. He has lived
twice the time God promised him on this earth. His three score
years and ten have past for a second time, so maybe it's right
that his time is coming.

Huw can reconcile this so long as the time is up for
everyone in Cwm Du. Those who turned their back on God. On
Capel Mawr. On him.

Huw sees the tall wall on one side of the track now. The
approach to the gateway. To the boundary with a world he once
knew. That was over a century ago. He knows that once outside
Cwm Du, his hours will be numbered. Numbered down to maybe

minutes. Maybe seconds. Huw is about to die. Coughing wildly
which he knows is a sign that he has caught the pestilence
carried by the Gwyllion, which only drinking water from the
lake can cure. The essence of the sickness of The Otherworld
in the water acting as an antidote.

His head smashes against the Celtic Knot carved on the
gatepost. This time the Knot does not smash. He is dropped to
the floor. He looks upwards.

Rachel stands above him, looking downwards with hatred in
her eyes. She uncaps her bottle of water and pours most of the
black water onto the ground.

Huw tries to catch the falling water in his mouth, but
Rachel puts the cap back on the water.

"This will not last long. Nor will you. Becca should have
let me kill you. I suppose this is the same thing."

Huw realises forgiveness is a Christian concept. And he is
not to be forgiven by these witches.

Rachel drags Huw to his feet. She puts the near empty
bottle of water in Huw's hand and pushes him through the
gateway. "Goodbye Huw."

Huw passes out as he falls. Falling into nothingness. Like
falling from the top of the cliff into the quarry below.
Falling into hell. He is as Judas, torn by pain. Falling.
Remembering the fate of Judas. Falling and his body bursting
covering a field in his blood.

Huw falls hard. Knocking the breath out of him. He lies
for moments coughing, trying to catch his breath. But he is
intact. His body has not burst onto the mountain gorse. He
looks around to admonish Rachel, but he is on the open
mountain. A place he does not recognise. No sign of the road
to lead him to civilisation and Christian souls. No sign of
Rachel, nor the gate, nor of Cwm Du.

Huw is alone on the open mountain.

Chapter 21: Within the Woods

This new sense. Revealing this world beyond her darkness.
Beyond the water which surrounds her. She sees beyond the
water now. The movement of creatures. Moving fast. Around and
around a shape. A shape glowing with faint power. One of those
who sent them back beneath the water on the day the Black Wall
fell. A Druidess.

Danger. She descends back into the dark water to safety.

Becca is alone on the shore of the lake which is now the
medium between her world and The Otherworld. A doorway she is
trying to close. But she is not succeeding. She has forgotten
how to carve the Knot. The only thing which will hold back The
Otherworld in her absence. And she has forgotten!

Becca gets to her feet, the Birds of Annwn swirling around
her as she moves up the ramp back towards the road to the
village. The Birds flying higher, above the trees over her
head.

From the lake, newly opened eyes watch her leave.

Huw walks across the mountain. Knowing he won't find the
gateway again. It's gone. At least until sunset. Chances are
he will not live that long. He is finding it hard to breathe.
Hard to think clearly. There is little water in the bottle
Rachel gave him. The water that could save him from the
pestilence gripping him. When she poured away the contents of
the bottle, she poured away his life. Without the water he
won't live long. It's the water which has given him twice his
three score years and ten. God promised less. It is that witch
which has allowed him more time. Now he has left her thrall he
understands this. What if he was wrong about her?

Huw drops to his knees, as if in prayer, but not in
prayer. He knows prayer is futile. He can feel his body ache.

Pain in every limb. The work of decades now felt in every muscle. And his mind is clouding. As is his sight. And his hearing. He can hear a strange sound in the distance getting closer. Like a distant cow crying out in birth. A moan. Unfamiliar and wrong. In the distance his clouding eyes see a charabanc approaching across the open mountain.

Jimmy jogs down the track, keeping an eye out for that crazy girl. The one dragging an old man up the same road by the hair. So hang on, what is he doing going the same way? Because it's the way out. The only way he knows! He needs to get out of here to get help.

There's no one to help him here in this village of the crazies. Or is there? Those Scousers! The divers! They are probably still by the lake. That bloke, Dave. He could look after himself. They could go back to find Laura and then get the hell out of here!

Jimmy rounds a bend and sees a burnt sack in the road. The noise of the birds overhead filling his head. He can't think. He runs around the bag, whatever it is. He keeps running, through a gateway out into the trees. Then he stops dead. Someone on the track coming towards him. A woman dressed in a dirty white dress. Shit!

But it's not the same girl. It's another one. She walks by him, preoccupied. Not noticing him. Carrying on up the road towards the village. It's the woman who was talking to Laura last night in the pub and who just walked off. She seems as mad as a crack head. No sign of that other girl. The one dragging the body. Thank fuck!

Jimmy runs onwards. To his left, he sees the ramp down to the lake. To the divers. Jimmy runs down it, losing control, struggling to keep his feet on the slippery surface. His legs go from under him. He lands on his back, as the world spins and he rolls down the ramp.

Everything hurts. Jimmy lies there for a second, checking to see if he can still move. Yes he can, but it fucking hurts. Where are the Scousers? "Help!"

No response. Jimmy tries to sit up, fighting the pain in his head. Sounds from the water. People moving. They're coming back to shore. They must have been diving. "Hey! Over here."

Faster footsteps. Bare feet on the slate waste which forms the beach here.

Jimmy sits up. It is not the divers who have come out of the lake. "Who the fuck are you?!?"

Laura leaves the toilet. Jimmy has long gone. Why would he leave without her? Laura walks to the front door and considers looking for him. No, he'll be back as soon as he realises that Google Maps doesn't work here. He's a city boy. He'll be lost.

She walks into the parlour and looks at the pictures of the family she did not know she had. And at the pictures of the woman who looks so much like Becca, the woman she met in the pub last night, who is a total psycho.

Mortlake. Her home for so long. For well over a century. Since before the quarry flooded. Since the days her mother held all of this responsibility she now holds. And held it so well. Banished from the village by Huw and the deacons of the chapels, but still holding the love and respect of everyone. Everyone: the thousand and more men who worked in the quarry at its height, and the hundreds who died on that day when her own husband nearly ended the world.

That day her mother passed all of her cares to Becca. And she now has to let that go. This burden of responsibility for Cwm Du and for the world outside. And Mortlake. She has to let Mortlake go. It was her home a century ago when there was a family here. There has not been family since that day when Arthur went off onto the mountain and her husband died beneath it.

But now Mortlake will be a home once more. For Laura and her new family. With or without that boy who was running away down the track. What did Laura see in him? What does Laura see in her? An ageing woman losing her mind. Losing her memory. Not fit to hold her responsibilities anymore. Desperately trying to pass them on. But now the Gwyllion are back, maybe there is no time to teach Laura what responsibility means.

Becca looks down at her mud covered dress and walks on.

It hangs from the tree. Pinned to it by its own weapon with which Rachel had killed it. Black blood on grey skin, punctured deep. Just because it was not human does not mean that it did not bleed. It did not die painlessly. This creature suffered. That makes her smile.

Sian runs her hands over the creature's face. She has never seen one before. It's a bit like when she went on the school trip to the zoo. They wouldn't let her play with the animals. They said it was dangerous. And it was; for the animals. She just wanted to make them scream, to see what sounds they would make. Like she did to the lambs when Dad and Gareth were out in the fields.

She wants to kill one of these. Cut its head off to keep her company for when those bastards in Cwm Du won't talk to her.

She pushes her finger into one of the wounds and pulls it out. She smears the blood on her face just like one of the savages in those cowboy films her Dad used to watch. She stops. There is movement behind her. It must be Rachel coming back.

Sian moves behind the tree, covering herself in moss and dead leaves to hide her white tracksuit.

Someone crying out in pain. Maybe Rachel has caught another one. Sian peers out from her hiding place. It's not

Rachel. It's that boy from the pub last night. The good looking one who came from outside. With loads of those creatures.

Jimmy is thrown to the ground. He looks up. Fuck me. A dead one of these things that have dragged him up from the lake. Pinned to a tree! Jimmy feels one of those stone spears in his back. "I didn't do this! It's not me!!!" The big man, creature, whatever, stamps on his back, knocking the air out of Jimmy. He coughs and splutters. He feels sick.

Gol pushes the base of his foot deeper into Jimmy's back, inflicting pain. Learning the sound this new thing makes when it screams. He is thrown backwards.

Atala snarls at Gol. Moving between the human and the large male. Reminding Gol who is in charge. Gol has strength but no cunning. No thinking power. He must be reminded of his place!

That she creature, the one called the Druidess may have made many Knots to hold them back. Only one of these creatures can destroy those Knots to clear a path for Atala's war party. She needs this weak creature to be kept alive. She must stop Gol from killing this one in revenge for the loss of one of their own. They are legion. The death of one warrior is not a matter of concern.

Atala pulls up the human by his hair and drags him away through the trees. Gol watches her go. Trying to understand what Atala is thinking. He follows, the twenty or so Gwyllion War Party following him.

All bar one. Looking at his brother pinned to the tree. Dead. Killed by these creatures. He will be avenged. The blood of a thousand of these puny creatures will flow for his death. Now that he and Gol and all can see in this new world, this will be inevitable.

The Warrior steps forward to touch his dead brother. He

closes his eyes. Returning to the darkness that has been his existence, and the existence of his kind for what feels like all time.

Then blackness of a different kind. Silence. Nothing.

The Warrior is dead before he hits the ground. Sian has driven her knife into its head, like she saw her father killing sheep. She has longed to do that to a person. So this is good practice.

Sian smiles.

Chapter 22: On the Mountainside

The sun is shining out here. Such a rare thing back within Cwm Du. The air is so much clearer outside that God forsaken place. Huw remembers times walking these mountains as a child. Almost a century and a half ago. Sheep. Foxes. Birds of prey. No birds flying here today. Not like the thousands of birds over Cwm Du. A clear sky. Huw smiles.

The last time he was here there were no charabancs. None of these contraptions like the one approaching. Stopping beside him.

Boots, legs. An old man's walk. Shaky. Like his own should be. But now Huw can't stand. He can't sit up. He can hardly breathe. The figure looks down at him.

Speaking in English. But with the harsh local accent. Like hammer on slate. "Are you ok?"

Huw wonders what this means? 'Aw kay.' "Help me". That is all the English Huw remembers at this moment. Dropping back into Welsh, repeating over and over. "Helpwch fi."

The figure crouching down over him. Speaking Welsh now. "Where have you come from?"

"Cwm Du. I'm the Reverend Huw Huws." Expecting the assistance his calling deserves from the populace. The very word Parchedig means 'respected'. But there is no acknowledgement.

The figure stands up and returns to the charabanc, returning in seconds with a shotgun. Wyn looks down at Huw, putting the shells into both barrels. "You have no place out here. She would not let you leave of your own free will. You're an abomination on this Earth. As a man of God, I'll do you the courtesy of sending you to your Lord."

"I'm not well. Help me!"

Wyn puts the gun to Huw's head and pulls the trigger. Blood scatters across the whitened poor grass and echoes around the high mountains. This poor grassland Wyn cannot put his sheep onto any more as the poison spreads from Cwm Du.

Wyn returns to the Land Rover, putting away the gun and bringing over his petrol can. His neighbours laugh at him. The man with the petrol Land Rover. Paying a fortune to fuel the vehicle, but it is the machine that works when the frosts come down and turn diesel to jelly. And petrol is handy at times like this.

Wyn removes the bottle of water from Huw's hand, wiping the blood from it on Huw's clothes. He pours petrol onto the body, returning the can and the water bottle to the Land Rover.

Wyn lights a cigarette and stares out across the mountainside. How did this man get out of Cwm Du? Why would he leave if he did not have a death wish? Maybe there is a sickness in Cwm Du too? Best do what he is doing.

Wyn looks up into the clear blue sky. So peaceful. Just the sound of the rushing wind through the mountains. No sound to tell you that this is the twenty first century. He long ago gave up on looking at news in newspapers or on the television. He long since left that world behind to stand between the two worlds. Between the legends around Cwm Du and the reality he learned about the outside world in school.

He smashed the television on the day when Sian had killed a lamb. Nothing could be the same after that. He could not let the girl out of his sight. But months later she was gone. Ran away one night. The worst thing she could have done is go into Cwm Du. Not that she knew how to get there unless she followed him. Cwm Du would be a fate worse than death. Hopefully she is in Liverpool or London and still alive.

At least he has his son to keep contact with Cwm Du. Like his father and grandfather before him. A job best done by men. And the only way to make a living up here on the mountain.

Wyn tosses his cigarette onto the faceless corpse, walking

quickly away as it burns. Waiting quietly until it has burnt up. He will come back later to dispose of it at the farm. With the others.

A distant gunshot carried by the wind. Lost in the whistle of the wind around the side of the chapel. He stands alone on the narrow mountain road. A rudimentary car park opposite, cleared by farmers and covered by slate waste carried from one of the countless slate tips on the mountainside. A car park with one vehicle. A quad bike.

The cold wind stinging his eyes. Both creating and hiding the tears as Gareth looks at his mother's gravestone. The newest one here. This chapel hasn't seen a service in years. Forgotten. Too far out of any village or town. Not even within sight of his home. Just nearby. A convenient place to bury his mother. He is the only one who comes here, now Sian has gone. The women in the family always leave.

Gareth wipes away the tears, clearing his eyes. Reading the Welsh language inscription. Shorter than the others on nearby graves. Because his father did not believe in Biblical quotations.

Margaret, beloved wife of Wyn. Mother of Gareth and Sian of Tyle Garw. 1968 - 1999.

Beloved. Right. Enough said about a short hard life. Gareth turns and leaves.

Laura is sitting in the lounge. Her lounge. In the silent company of the faces of family she didn't know she had a few short days ago. Faces looking at her through time. Laura realises there is no clock here. No parlour clock to mark the passing of time. No clocks in the entire house. Like time wasn't important. Maybe it's not so important here. Time seems to be measured by the day, not the hour.

The front door opens and slams. Laura jumps out of her

chair. "Jimmy? Thank God!"

Light footsteps. Becca enters the lounge, carrying a basket, closing the door behind herself.

Laura jumps out of her skin. Seeing the dark hair matted over Becca's face. The once white dress covered in black mud. The undeniable smell of blood. And Becca's wild eyes.

"My apologies for earlier." Becca takes a seat opposite Laura, looking at the floor. Distracted. Cradling the basket.

Laura composes herself. "And I'm sorry about running away like that."

"I understand. Rachel and I were.... Upset."

Laura takes her seat again. Not knowing what to do when someone walks into your house as if they live there.

"Here are a few things for you for the next few days." Becca puts the basket onto the floor between them. Some vegetables, bread and some bottles of dirty water.

The same dirty water she was drinking last night. Is that the reason she is feeling so off colour? "Thanks, but I have to leave. Jimmy's gone."

Becca's face emerges through her matted hair. "Laura, you have to stay for three days! Otherwise you don't inherit this house! And I need your help! Laura this is so important. These savages are..."

Years of diversity lessons in school kick in. Laura interrupts. "Savages? It sounds like they have a right to be here. You just need to talk to them surely? Work something out?"

A deep frown crosses Becca's face. This girl has so much to learn. "They want us dead! They want us huddled around fires watching their eyes in the night as they kill. Us! Everyone! Everywhere!! They are not people. They are not human. They are a plague!!!"

Laura hadn't expected the venom in Becca's voice. She gets to her feet. "Look, whatever this is about, it has nothing to do with me!"

"It has everything to do with you. And me. Both of us!"

"Look, I don't understand. You don't understand. I have to get back..."

Becca raises a finger to silence Laura. Eyes narrowing. "Back to what Laura? What's there for you in that city? You're penniless. You have nothing there. You are nothing there!"

Laura is stung and rushes out of the room. Becca follows her to the staircase. Laura points to the Polaroid of Becca in the Lounge, mounted on the stairway wall. "Is this you? Why is it in my great grandmother's house? Are we related? Who are you?"

Becca smiles. Trying to appear calm when inside she is bursting. "We need you here in Cwm Du. We need a new generation. You and your little one."

Laura freezes. Something gripping her deep inside. "What?"

Becca puts her hand on Laura's belly. "It's a little girl. It's what we need here. My little boy, your great grandfather..."

Laura's head is spinning. Confusion. She is not listening anymore. "No, I'm just sick in the morning, that's all..."

"Your little one. She will be a very special girl, just like you..." Becca tries to embrace Laura who pushes her aside.

Laura rushes out through the front door.

Becca looks defeated. She sighs deeply, Rachel emerges out of another room. Becca resumes her usual demeanour. "Rachel. Follow her. Keep her safe."

Rachel follows in Laura's footsteps through the front door, closing it behind her.

Becca looks at the Polaroid photograph taken almost half a century ago. Faded, but unmistakably her. Unchanged on the outside, though inside she is now dying. Becca puts her head in her hands.

Soft singing somewhere in the trees. Carrying on the wind.

Hannah and Mary are walking swiftly along the track towards the lake from Cwm Du. They stop. Listening intensely. The sound of an almost forgotten Welsh folk song bringing back memories. The two Morwynion exchange glances, heading off into the trees. Fanning out. Moving quickly, but with practiced steps, making no sound.

Sian is sitting on the ground, with the dead Gwyllion Warrior's head cradled in her lap. She looks up at the Morwynion and laughs. "See! I told you I was like you! See!"

Chapter 23: The Mothers of Time

Laura's head is spinning as she runs down the rough slate
track. The trees on either side whizzing by. Blurring like her
thoughts. The world going out of focus.

A baby. Could she be pregnant? She had not had time to
realise or consider it with so much going on since that
envelope arrived. When was that? Only a couple of days ago?

What would she be able to offer the baby? Nothing. Until
now. But now she has a new house. A new place to live. No more
of that dirty northern town. But is there a doctor here? A
hospital? And is there a Jimmy? Would he do the right thing
and look after her? But does she need him? Where the hell has
he gone? The bastard just left her. Ran away. But not from
this. He doesn't know. She has to find Jimmy. Where would he
have gone?

Laura runs down the road, avoiding that thing on the
track, whatever it is. Not wanting to look at it.

Maybe she should keep running. Maybe Jimmy has just kept
running down the track. But there is nothing at the end of it.
Nothing out there. But perhaps she made a mistake. Maybe she
should run up the track and get the hell out of here
regardless. Sell the house. Fix the car. Go home to her mum.

She runs through the gateway on the track. Her feet are
dragged from under her and she falls heavily onto the ground,
twisting herself to protect her stomach. No, not her stomach.
Her baby.

As she twists something heavy smashes into the ground by
her head. Laura rolls away and sees one of those dark figures.
Wild eyed. Female, wielding a kind of spear made of... stone.
She rolls away from another blow, getting to her feet. Facing
the creature.

Becca was right. It isn't a person. It is a creature.
Human-like. Muscular but short. Too short. Head too small. But

very quick.

An intelligence in those eyes. Poking the spear at her. Laura narrowly avoids the tip, which whips back for another blow at her belly. Laura realises what the creature is doing and screams in terror for her unborn child.

Another jab with the spear at her belly, missing her and splintering the stone wall she is now backed up against. The jabs driving her away from the gateway, away from the track, into the woods. Into the semi-darkness. The creature seeming to see better here. Her blows getting more accurate.

Laura is suddenly trapped by a tree which is growing out of the wall. The next jab drives the stone spear into the tree. Laura is trapped between the wall, the tree and the spear.

The she creature screams in triumph, trying to pull the spear free from the tree, for the final strike. Bang. The she creature is knocked into a heap. Someone grabs the spear, trying to prise it free. The girl who was with Becca, also with that black liquid covering her white dress. Thank God!!!!

Laura moves quickly back towards the track. Exchanging glances with this girl. Not much older than her. But fierce. Face still covered in black blood. Teeth bared. Whispering in a harsh but frightened voice. "Laura. Go home. Run!"

Laura turns and runs back to the track. Standing there panting. Looking back into the woods but they are so dark she can't see the two fighters. But she can hear them. She looks back towards the house. Towards Cwm Du. Then down the track towards the outside world. But all of those trees. Anything could be in those trees. She crouches, hugging herself.

Rachel kicks Atala again. The thing screams and mutters what can only be words in a language Rachel can't understand. Spitting. Cursing at her even. This is the Gwyllion's leader. Their Warrior Queen as Becca is her Druidess. If this spear came free from the tree, Rachel could kill it. Cut the head off this snake. Leaving this bitch's followers leaderless. Out of their element. At the mercy of Rachel, Mary and Hannah. They would all be dead by sunset. Becca would remake the Knots and the world would be safe from these creatures once more. Rachel tears free the slate spear.

The bitch creature runs off into the woods. It is fast! Jumping between the trees. Obviously able to see now. Rachel thought the Gwyllion were mostly blind. Killing that warrior had been easy. It could hardly see her. But now things are different. They must be learning how to see.

Rachel runs after Atala into the woods, following her into the gloom. Realising that the deeper she goes into the trees, the darker it is getting. The early summer leaves are thick here, the shadows beneath them pitch black here, where the trees have been allowed to grow free outside the boundaries of the village.

She is going deeper into the woods now, not into the abandoned old village which Rachel remembers from childhood, rather off towards the workings at the north side of the village. Into the shadow of the mountain of slate waste which casts its oppression over Cwm Du.

Laura is shaking with fear. Crouched like a ball in the middle of the track. The sound of the girl and that creature have disappeared into the darkness of the woods. Now the sounds of the birds circling over the lake nearby drown out everything else. For a moment she feels safe. Watched over.

What is she going to do? She can't go further down the track, not with those creatures out there. She was so shaken up by what Becca had told her, she totally forgot about them. Maybe the best thing to do is stay at home.

Suddenly Becca is beside her. "What's wrong Laura?"

Laura jumps out of her skin. She spins around ready to run

away. "Oh God! It attacked me!"

Becca grabs her by the arms. "Who attacked you? I sent Rachel to guard you."

"She did. Your friend... she fought it off and chased it into the woods."

Becca scans the woods. There is no sign of Rachel nor the Gwyllion. "Rachel will kill it. You see? They are just savages. We need to send them back to whence they came."

"Why did it attack me? What have I done? I just got here!"

"Laura. They know who you are. Like they know who I am."

Laura looks at Becca. Dark hair matted on her face. Covered in what looks like blood. Talking about killing creatures from another world. All of this is real. Too real. It is all too much. "Leave me alone. Please, you're scaring me." Laura runs back up the track towards the safety of Mortlake.

Becca watches her go. What does she have to do to convince this girl of her place here? Becca looks down onto the track in despair. Into a pool of rainwater. Reflecting like a mirror. More than a mirror. For the first time in her life she looks like an old woman. Like her mother in many ways. But she can never be what her mother was. On that day when she was tested. When the Black Wall fell, and she saved the world. Can she save the world like Myfanwy did? And can this slip of a girl, Laura? Becca holds back a sob as tears fill her eyes.

She remembers her mother, well over a century ago, sitting here on this wall by this gateway, waiting for her after school with berries picked from the forest for her tea. Becca showing her school history book to Myfanwy, her mother who was never taught to read.

"Does it have pictures?" Myfanwy pushing through the pages of the book. Page after page of writing which she doesn't understand. "Is it in Welsh? Do you understand it? Read it to me."

Becca turns to the chapter she has to read for homework. Home, here on the edge of the quarry as the siren sounds for a detonation pending. "It is in English. All of the books are in English, except for the Bible."

Myfanwy winces. Her mother had told her no good came from books. Power comes from memory. It is important never to forget. Her mother telling her exactly what her mother had told her; tales told across millennia on these then unchanging mountains. But now these mountains are changing as the slate is ripped from them. So she remembers the stories. Remembers the histories. Telling her daughter and the villagers these tales. Because the histories taught today are just stories told by those who won wars. Conquerors and Christians.

Becca clears her throat, putting on her best speaking voice. "Chapter Six. The History of Wales. After 1362 Wales became a part of Great Britain, with Scotland and Ireland soon to follow. Castles were built to govern this wild and lawless land, which had not seen order, nor peace since the days of the Romans. Lords were..."

Myfanwy shuts the book. "I don't understand all of those English words. But what I do understand is that this is lies, Becca. The history of these islands stretches back through time. Our role, my role, your role in the days to come, is to guard our people. We don't need castles. They need castles. We are safe in the arms of our mothers, keeping us warm, and safe from the dark things in the night. Keeping us safe from the bears, the wolves, the Gwyllion and all that used to walk the land well before those castles were built. Some day they will need us again."

"Mam. Parchedig Huw came to class to tell us how Jesus saves us, and when I said that you would save us from the Gwyllion everyone laughed."

Myfanwy flushes. "Becca, I'll tell you of how our mothers

saved this land, and this world well before even the Romans killed what they thought was the last of us just across the water in Mona." Myfanwy takes Becca's book. "Their books don't tell the truth."

Myfanwy gets to her feet and walks to the top of the ramp to the busy quarry below. The bustle of men a hundred feet below moving safe from the blasting area just across the quarry. She points out across the quarry, across the huge slate towers which house the cables to drag the slate up from the belly of the earth to the rail line.

"Here, somewhere on this mountain, three thousand years ago the Mother and her Morwynion built a camp. The women brought their able men together under the leadership of the Mother. They were not making war on each other anymore. Now they would make war on our common enemy. The Gwyllion. Creatures which walked the night, bringing sickness and death, taking their animals, then taking their children. Everyone was now here on the open mountain, it seemed unprotected at the places beside where those creatures would emerge from Annwn. They seemed like rabbits on the open mountain ignoring the eagles above."

Becca joins her mother looking out over the lip of the quarry at the as yet unspoilt mountains, where down below, closer to the sea, the land is black with the waste slate from the quarries which were easier to reach years ago.

"And the Gwyllion were bold like rats. Not fearful of the daylight as their prey was so weak. So near. Helpless. They ran from a cave down to the village. Killing. Holding old men's heads in triumph. But as they came to the huts they found the Mother and her Morwynion ready. The Mother drove them like rats back to their cave where they thought they were safe. Safe in the darkness of Annwn. But the Morwynion had seen where they ran."

Becca's eyes are enthralled. She has not heard this story

before.

"The Mother and her Morwynion took weapons of iron and Knots they had carved in the slate with them into the darkness. As they listened to the sound of the Gwyllion clicking in the darkness they could hear Annwn open around them. The Mother had dreamt of a slab of pure slate in the cave, and if she could find it, it would seal Annwn forever, and keep the Gwyllion in the darkness for all time."

Myfawny leads Becca back from the top of the ramp. The quarrymen below are ready for the blasting.

"The Mother found the place in the cave in the darkness deep within the mountain. A place where she felt power in the ground. The power which runs through the standing stones which mark the land above. So below within this cave, lay the gateway to Annwn, The Otherworld. This was a place on lines of great power. The Mother screamed. The sound echoed around the cave and around The Otherworld. From above dropped a wall of solid slate. The Black Wall. It fell closing the gateway to The Otherworld. Though she was dying, she carved the Knot on the wall. That sealed the Black Wall. She died to save the world."

A huge explosion echoes around the quarry. Tons of slate loosen from the cliff wall, dust fills the air as the sound dies.

"Only one of her Morwynion emerged into the light outside the cave. She became the next Mother. She sat at the entrance to the cave for the rest of her life making sure the Gwyllion did not return. Over years we have forgotten where the cave is. But it is here on this mountain. So I wait here, as you will wait here to ensure the Gwyllion never return."

Chapter 24: Lost Lamb

Becca stares into space, looking at the place where she and
her mother spoke those decades ago. The day she learnt the
true role of the Druidess. What she has to teach Laura at this
time of crisis. But it would take years to teach Laura what
Myfanwy had taught her. And now there may be no time. So many
decisions to make. And some may be wrong. She realises Idris
and Arwyn are standing beside her waiting. "You need to speak
to me?"

Idris, respectful. Holding his massive work sledgehammer.
Trying to broach the subject. "We can't find Huw."

Arwyn, sharper, still smarting from the argument at The
Quarrymen's Arms last night. Smacking the iron slate chisel in
his hands impatiently. Sensing Becca is losing control. "Huw
wouldn't have missed a funeral. They are the only fun he has.
He is the minister after all. Even if you don't let him
speak."

Idris swings his hammer. Nervously explaining to Becca
what feels he needs to do. "We are going to check his home in
the old village. The Gwyllion could have taken him in the
night."

But Becca is not paying attention. Looking wildly into the
woods. She screams, "Noooo!!!!!"

She has lost the bitch in the trees. It is as if no one
has walked here in decades. The trees are thick, low hanging.
The undergrowth tangling around her legs. And there are no
tracks to follow. Rachel has lost her.

Then a sound a little further ahead. A branch snapping.
Rachel sees a movement. Atala running quickly and lithely
along the overgrown slate wall. Rachel follows with the
creature's spear in hand.

Rachel trying to run in the undergrowth, her legs being

caught in the weeds. Tripping. Falling onto a low stone wall hidden in the weeds with a thud.

Beyond her a ten-foot drop onto the old railway which carried the slate down the black valley to the port and the outside world. To places she has never seen. Rachel shakes her head. Shaking off the effect of the blow to her head. Feeling blood in her mouth where her face has hit the wall.

Atala appears on the railway track beneath her. Standing at the edge of the track. Seemingly scared by something. Penned in. Locking eyes with Rachel and screaming in anger.

Rachel scrambles to her feet and looks for a way down. When she was a child, she couldn't climb down these walls. Even the boys who were stronger than her at that time, could not climb down. But now she is a Morwyn. She swings her legs over the side of the wall. Her old boots finding footholds in the stacked slate as she descends. Stealing glances at her prey, who is backing away nervously. Rachel reaches the ground. She turns to the bitch creature and moves forward, using the slate spear to push back the creature.

The creature seems afraid. Moving backwards in a straight line. Staying on the slate at the side of the track, sometimes stepping on the old wooden sleepers, but then jumping back to the edge of the track.

Rachel realises. The railway track may be brown and rusted, but it is iron. The creature cannot cross iron. Iron is fatal to it. Rachel has the creature trapped.

The creature seems to sense that Rachel knows this and runs off down the track. Moving swiftly. Heading along the track towards the tunnel ahead.

Rachel has it cornered. That tunnel collapsed years ago. Rachel now sprinting down the track. Eyes focussed on her prey. Closing fast on the creature as it enters the tunnel, only a few feet ahead of her.

Rachel runs into the darkness. She can't see. Where did it

go? She stops, trying to work out where the creature went.

There is a figure in the middle of the track. Across the iron rails. Human. Not Gwyllion. The little light catching the bright clothing. Rachel steps forward, pointing the slate spear at the figure. Total silence in the tunnel except for whoever it is breathing. Could it be one of the villagers?

A shaky voice. Not local. Speaking in English. "Help me." The English boy from The Quarryman's Arms last night. Laura's boyfriend. Coughing hoarsely.

"Come here. It is dangerous. Come to me." Rachel watches Jimmy emerge in light. Looking pale and sick. Face bloody. Hands bound. His eyes looking to his side.

Rachel follows his stare. Something moving in the darkness. Whoosh! Smashing into her.

Rachel knocked off her feet by the slate club. Landing on her back across the iron rail. Broken nose, smashed face. Her own black blood on her white dress in the half light. Gurgling on the blood in her mouth.

The sound of Laura's boyfriend crying in pain. Her eyesight comes back into focus. Gol standing over her, a massive slate club in his huge hands. Atala and the Gwyllion War Party emerging from the gloom behind Gol.

Gol brings the club down hard on Rachel's head.

"Becca? Becca!!! What's wrong?" Idris resisting the urge to shake her. You should never touch the Druidess.

Becca looks at him. Deathly pale. Sweating. Feeling the loss of her Morwyn. "Something's happened."

Arwyn looking concerned. "To Huw?"

Becca distracted, trying to focus as she feels Rachel's pain. Coming back to herself. "No... Oh, Huw? I banished him."

Idris and Arwyn exchange glances. Arwyn's jaw slacks open in shock. "What!?!". But Becca is walking away.

Idris watches her go. Letting the word sink in. Banished!

No one has been banished in the century Becca has led them. Becca sent the children away to have lives in the outside world when she realised they were becoming dependent on the black water from the Otherworld. As are they all. She let the children leave as she had let her son leave. It was a humane decision.

People are so scarce in Cwm Du now. Over the years a few people have died, usually by accident, but no one has ever been banished! Away from the black water which now gives them life, banishment is a death sentence. And Huw does not deserve death. Living in the old village away from Cwm Du has been punishment enough. Huw needs to be brought back. Idris takes a deep breath. Questioning Becca is new to him. "How long ago was this? Which way did you send him?"

"Why?" Arwyn following Becca, reaching out to grab her and then stopping. Remembering Idris at this shoulder. That hammer ready to strike if Becca is threatened.

"This morning. He broke the Knots. He betrayed us all."

Idris and Arwyn exchange glances again. "Why did he do that?"

"He helped the Gwyllion. I couldn't forgive him. He is gone. So is she."

Idris pales. Huw a traitor? What is she saying? Who else has gone? Idris is trying to make sense of what Becca is saying. This has become more common. And the reason she brought this girl Laura to Cwm Du. And it may all be too late now. He puts his arm around Arwyn, whispering in his ear. "He can't come back. He is a threat to us all."

"So she says. How do we know?" Tears in Arwyn's eyes.

Idris leads Arwyn to the Knot in the gatepost. Both look shocked at the smashed rock where there was once a Knot. Idris breathes heavily. Fear rising. The defences are down. "Becca. Remake the Knot." He turns around. Becca has gone. The sound of her making her way into the woods through the heavy undergrowth, following in Rachel's footsteps.

Arwyn looks at Idris. "Come with me to the gateway. If Huw is outside, we can bring him back at sunset."

Idris looks into the trees. Becca has disappeared. The sound of the Birds of Annwn is deafening. He nods. "Come on."

Idris and Arwyn stand at the gateway, watching the mid-afternoon sun dropping towards the horizon behind the mountains. Knowing that they are seeing is a different place to what is actually beyond Cwm Du. Myfanwy's magic still at work a century on.

Arwyn sound enough of mind to remember the crossroads and the road which leads down to the coast and to the towns. Places he can never see again in his existence. Just as Huw is never to be seen again. But at least now they can tell the villagers that they have tried. Tried to find Huw. Tried to bring him home. But it's too late.

It has been too late for Huw for a hundred years. One day his chapel is full of the families of the area, glad to be in the light of God. Overnight they knew that all that can save them is the daughter of the old woman of the mountain, who married the Quarry Manager. She has now become the old woman, at least on the inside. Old with the weight of the world on her shoulders. Is it any wonder after a hundred years that she has become the Mistress of Life and Death. Especially now that the Gwyllion are back.

Idris and Arwyn exchange glances and return down the slate track towards Cwm Du.

Gareth rides his quad bike across the open mountain towards the small plume of smoke rising in the cloudless afternoon sky. A fire up here at this time of year could get out of hand. Before you know it, the entire mountain may burn. And so might his sheep and the grass that sustains them.

Gareth rides across the open ground crossing heavy vehicle tracks leading to and from the area of the fire. Who has been up here? Only his father would have any business on their land.

Gareth stops the quad. Something is burning on the gorse up ahead, and beyond it dead white grass stretching out into the distance; the polluted land as his father calls it. Gareth walks over to kick earth over whatever is burning. Then he stops. It is a man's body. Unrecognisable. Burnt to a crisp.

There is the smell of petrol in the air. The body seems to have collapsed on itself. He has never seen a man burnt to death before but it shouldn't look like this. This can't be right, surely? A little like a *Dracula* film he saw on the television when he was a kid, when his dad was asleep. Dracula turning to ash in the sunlight. It is like this body has turned to ash. Bodies don't turn to ash. He knows that. There should be bones.

Gareth sees something shining on the blackened ground. Small. Some round. Others flattened out like solid shiny silver. Melted lead pellets. Someone shot this man before setting him on fire. Who would do that? He reaches for his phone, to call the police. But something else catches his eye. Nearby is a clump of burnt paper. It is a Bible. An old one. He opens the cover. 'Parch. Huw Huws. Cwm Du.'

He puts the phone back in his pocket. No need for the police. This person is from Cwm Du. And Cwm Du is just a legend. Gareth registers the heavy vehicle tracks nearby. His father's Land Rover. His father has shot this fugitive from Cwm Du and burnt the body. Keeping Cwm Du a secret as he has always done. Even from him.

Gareth looks at the white grass stretching out beyond the body into the distance. Dying ground. This is what his father calls polluted land. Never saying what was polluting the ground. There is nothing up here, so that nothing can only be

Cwm Du. Now Cwm Du is contaminating the outside world he has to do something too. He has to get Sian out of there.

Gareth lets the fire burn, consuming the evidence of what his father has done. He throws the Bible onto the body to burn. There can be no trace of this man.

Gareth climbs onto his quad, checking his shotgun and shells, before driving off across the open country. A short cut across the open mountain to the crossroads where Cwm Du will appear to him in around an hour.

Becca follows the lines in the undergrowth. Rachel has not been careful to hide her tracks. Too concerned with following the Gwyllion. Not thinking of the danger to herself. Becca knows she is dead. Rachel, Hannah and Mary have been her Morwynion, inherited from Myfanwy. Now she feels an emptiness. She knows Rachel is dead. Knowing the truth used to be her talent. But lately this has not always been the case. So she must try to find her. In case she is wrong.

Shapes in the trees up ahead, moving towards her from deep in the woods. Heading directly for her. But human. Not Gwyllion. At least she thinks so. Becca stops, realising she is unarmed. Why did she venture out here on her own?

The shapes step into a break in the trees. Hannah, Mary and Wyn's daughter. The strange girl. Sian. The girl is covered in black blood. Rachel's blood?

Hannah speaks, her voice fighting the wind in the trees and the Birds of Annwn above. "This girl killed a Gwyllion Warrior."

Sian stands in the light. Her white modern outside world clothing covered in black blood. She holds up the Gwyllion Warrior's head. "I want to belong. Please!"

Hannah continues. "We can't find Rachel. We both felt her leave us. We need this girl. There must be three... we need three."

Becca is transfixed by the severed head in Sian's hands. "We need to find Laura."

Sian's face crumples. "I was here first. Why not me? Why her? I was born to be a Morwyn!!!" She tears herself free of Hannah's grasp. She throws the Gwyllion's head at Becca and runs off into the woods.

Becca watches her go.

Hannah picks up the Gwyllion head from Becca's feet. "Rachel is gone. You have to decide who will be the Morwyn in place of her. Laura or Sian."

Becca looks at the Gwyllion head, staring into its dead eyes.

Idris and Arwyn stand on the slate track. They have seen war. Industrial. Brutal. But nothing like this. Rachel's dead body is pinned to a tree. Her face hardly recognisable. Her dress is torn open to expose a gaping bloody mess. Her heart has been torn out

Chapter 25: A Family Madness

The front door of Mortlake is flung open. Laura rushes out carrying her bag. She unlocks the driver's door of her car, throwing the bag onto the passenger seat.

She climbs in and shuts the door, locking it behind her. Checking the passenger door is locked too. Panting. Panicking. Pushing at the ignition key. Praying that after a rest the car will work fine. It has to. She needs to get the hell out of here. To hell with her inheritance. To hell with this house. She is in fact, in hell here, and she needs to get out.

Finally, the key slots into the ignition and she turns the engine. She knows little about cars, but she knows this is not good. The engine grinding rather than turning over, not firing but whining like a beaten dog. Laura willing the car to start running. Then remembering. Water. She didn't give the car more water. She switches off the ignition.

She pops the bonnet and runs back into the house to the kitchen in the back. Looking around desperately. There is no tap! She runs to the parlour, picking up the bottle of dirty water Becca had left her.

She runs out of the house and stops in her tracks. A girl in a filthy once-white track suit is looking under the bonnet of the car. Wasn't she at the pub last night? She turns around. A manic smile Laura remembers from some of her more colourful care in the community customers in her job at the supermarket. The smile beneath the eyes. The eyes not smiling but staring directly at her. "Your car has seized. It's going nowhere. What are you doing with that?" The girl watching the bottle of dirty water.

"I was going to put it in the car."

"That's a waste. Give it to me." The girl launches herself at Laura, grabbing the bottle of water.

Laura backs away. "Who are you?"

"Sian. Obviously. Becca sent me to look after you."

"Thank you, but if you can't fix the car, I can look after myself." Laura takes in what Sian is wearing. The white track suit covered in dark stains. Just like Becca and her friend's white dresses were covered in black. Blood. Black blood. Yes, she must be another of Becca's crazy friends no doubt. Oh Christ! She is never going to get out of here! Laura lets out a sigh.

"What's wrong? I'm here to look after you."

"What would be wrong? My boyfriend has disappeared. My car won't work. And I'm fucking pregnant!"

Sian listens. Taking this information in. "What you need is a friend. Let's go inside your house and have a chat. I'm sure your boyfriend will come back soon. I'll wait for him with you. Stay here with me."

Laura starts to tear up. This is all getting too much. "If I stay, I inherit this lovely house. In a little village in the middle of nowhere. Full of freaks... No offence."

Sian moves towards her. "It's not that bad. I came a long way to live here."

The wind rushes fiercely through the trees. Laura glances around. The wind shaking the trees opposite the house. "I've been attacked."

"Who attacked you?"

"They're in the woods... I've seen them. We've got to leave! Right now!"

"We'll be safer indoors. Come inside where you're safe with me." Sian takes Laura by the hand.

The smell of blood is overpowering. "Your clothes..."

Sian gently pushes Laura ahead of her, still smiling. Whispering under her breath. "Oh don't worry. This blood isn't mine."

The door to Mortlake closes the door behind them.

Idris leads Becca, Hannah and Mary along the track. Up
ahead stands Arwyn, holding his iron chisel like a rifle. He
is nervously watching the woods, just as he did on watch in
the trenches a couple of lifetimes ago. They join him near
Rachel's body, still pinned to the tree. Stark. Bloody.

Becca's eyes fill with tears. "Take her down and take her
to the shop. I shall deal with her funeral preparations
there." Hannah and Mary reluctantly step forward.

Idris whispers. "What are you going to do?" He watches
Hannah and Mary helping Arwyn take Rachel's body down from the
tree. "Will you take Wyn's daughter as a Morwyn?"

Becca stands silently considering. Unable to decide. Even
with no other options, unable to decide. "There must be three.
Or all is lost. There is no time to wait for another to
appear. I just hope that the girl is... trustworthy..."

Becca and Idris exchange worried glances. Idris looks at
the sky. Beyond the Birds of Annwn, the sun is skirting the
mountain side. In a short time it will descend into the sea
beyond the veil of unreality which hides Cwm Du from the
world, and vice versa. Darkness will fall.

Idris takes a deep breath. The worried sergeant coming to
the surface. "Soon they will be familiar with the ground. They
can operate better than us in darkness. The sun is setting.
Soon they will mount an attack. Becca, you need your third
Morwyn. We need to be ready!"

Gareth rides his quad towards the crossroads. Open
mountain ahead as far as the eye can see. He stops his quad on
this apparent road to nowhere. Silence. His shadow reaching
out lengthening visibly towards where he knows the gateway to
the slate track to Cwm Du will be revealed. The sun is yet to
set. He has made it in time. He is not going to let this
opportunity pass. He must step inside that lost world, find
his sister, and bring her out to safety at dawn.

And if he is to take over from his father in the passing
of time, a knowledge of Cwm Du will be useful. Entering Cwm Du
is something his father has been too afraid to do in the half
century he has been the go-between. Just like his father
before, too afraid of Becca Salhurst and her Morwynion.

Gareth gets off the quad, shouldering his shotgun. Wishing
he had the time to get back to the farm, pack some food and
water, and something to keep Sian quiet. Doubtless she will
not come willingly.

The bare mountain landscape is bathed in the various reds
of the setting sun. He turns around to check how long before
the sun will actually set. It is gone! He turns around in
panic, seeing the gateway to the lost world of Cwm Du. The
gateway clearly visible only yards away in the half light.

Gareth sprints forward through the gate and onto the slate
track beyond. It feels strange. Like the air has changed.
Colder here. Wind through the trees off to his left. And
another incessant noise. He slows and stops and looks behind
him. The gateway is there with a Celtic Knot carved on each
slate gatepost. But beyond it the crossroads has gone. Where
it should be there is open mountain. No sign of the quad bike.

Gareth swallows hard. At last, he is here, in Cwm Du. A
place even his friends at school said did not exist. He lets
out a laugh and heads off down the track bordered by trees and
a high slate wall. In the sky above him a thousand black birds
are circling, squawking incessantly. In seconds Gareth is lost
in the gloaming and the cacophony of wind through trees and
anxious bird cries.

Laura stands by the parlour window quietly checking the
lock on the sash window. Very aware of Sian idly pacing the
parlour behind her. Every step. Every move, even though she
can't see her. But is it idle? Laura feels that Sian is
keeping herself between Laura and the door.

The lock on the sash window is not going to move. As if someone never intended the window to open. A bar of iron is locking the window shut. She has never seen that before. It reminds her of the heavy bolts across the front and back doors of the house. Too heavy really for domestic use. Making the house a fortress. A fortress currently keeping her indoors with her unstable new friend.

"So who is this man?" Sian has picked up the picture of Salhurst in First World War uniform.

"I don't know. He is a relative of mine."

Sian stops in her tracks. "You're a Salhurst?"

"Yes. I've inherited the house."

"From Becca?"

"No..." Laura leans against the window. Thoughts suddenly swirling in her head. Would that be why Becca is looking out for her? Entering the house as if she owned it? Because she does own it? What the hell is going on here?

"How are you related to Becca?" Sian staring at her again. Not in a friendly way. The pretence of a smile gone. "Why are you here? Are you here to take my place?"

"Sorry, you've lost me." Laura tries to move away from the window, towards the door.

Sian blocking the route in her deliberate random way. Sian picks up a piece of paper Laura had forgotten she had placed on the sideboard. Oh God, the flyer about the missing girl! So much has been going on, Laura forgot about the flyer the farmer had given her when he fixed her car. No wonder this girl looks familiar.

Sian holds the flyer with her picture. "What is this? Why have you got a picture of me!?! Who gave that to you? Was it the police?" Sian is getting highly agitated.

"No. I met your brother Gareth. He's looking for you."

"Really? Well, he'll never find me here. No one will find me here. We are not in the real world anymore."

Laura is getting more and more frightened. Sian is breathing heavily. The stare stronger. The smile long gone. "You should get in touch with your brother, he's worried about you. His phone number..."

"Phone? There are no phones here. Haven't you noticed? We're not in Wales anymore." Sian starts to cry in anger.

"Are you OK?"

"You can't say that. 'Are you OK?' 'Are you OK' is what I'm supposed to say to you!!!"

"Sian, why don't you sit down. Everything is fine."

"Yes. I'm here in Becca's house at last. She needs me now. She needs me to look after you. I belong here. I'm one of the Morwynion now."

Laura desperate as Sian closes in. "I don't understand."

"The stories we were told are true. The Druidess and her Morwynion hold back The Otherworld. And the water keeps you young." Sian takes a mouthful of dirty water from the jar.

"How does that water keep you young? You're not making sense Sian. Please..."

"The lake water comes straight from The Otherworld. It keeps everyone here young... I'll be young forever, just like Becca and the others."

"That's crazy."

"Don't you dare say that!!!! You don't believe me? That man in the photo is Becca's husband! He was the Quarry Manager who blew up the Black Wall and let out the Otherworld over a hundred years ago!"

"Now you're talking nonsense!"

Sian is increasingly manic. "Everyone here except you and me are over a hundred years old. Can't you tell? How they dress? How they talk?"

"Sian, please, calm down."

"Don't you tell me to calm down!!! I'm not mad! Gareth. He's the mad one! I'm a good girl!"

Chapter 26: Brother and Sister in Blood

The birds are deafening as they fly out over the lake. He can just see them through the trees to his right in the gloaming. He can just make out that they are making patterns in the sky. Or the same pattern maybe. Gareth doesn't notice the blood on the tree on the other side of the track as he tries to find a vantage point to look out over the lake.

The vista opens up before him. The wind roaring in his face. The sound of the birds louder than ever. A steep ramp leading down from the track to the lakeside. The lake stretches out before him, black and dead. Gareth has seen lakes at every time of day, morning and night, whether caring for his sheep or fishing. Lakes always reflect the sky but this lake is black, not reflecting the reds and purples of the sunset he left behind.

Gareth walks down the ramp towards the lake. The thousands of black birds flying over it are not reflected either. The lake is a body of dead black water.

He reaches the water's edge. He can now see the expanse of the lake and the cliffs of slate surrounding it on all sides. As far as he can see this little beach is the only place where the water meets the land. The cliffs tower in the falling light, and above them at the far end of the quarry from the way he entered, stand tall towers of slate. They remind him of pictures of pyramids and other old buildings from the ancient world he has seen in school picture books.

The birds are deafening here. They drown out the sound of everything else as Gareth takes in the vista of the lake, the cliffs, the towers of slate and the hint of a mountain of slate waste beyond. So Cwm Du is not unlike many places he has visited in the area, where entire villages huddle at the feet of mountains of waste slate. Billions of tons of industrial waste, over a century old, scaring this land forever.

Gareth crouches and looks at the water. Not clear. Not even the brown he has seen in other lakes. The water isn't clear enough to show the slate beneath, the water itself is black. It shines like oil in places. He puts his hand into the water. It disappears from sight in the dark water. Gone. He snatches his hand away in fright.

His dad had said that Cwm Du was lost because The Otherworld was let out when there was an explosion. The barrier between this world and the next got blown away. So the local druidess created a barrier around Cwm Du to save the world. Is this water from The Otherworld? Does he really need to ask that question after only being able to get here when a roadway appeared at sunset? His dad used to say some mad things. The maddest thing though is that he was right.

Gareth smells his hand. No smell from any kind of pollution to explain the blackness.

He looks out across the lakes and sees ripples in the water. Something is moving beneath the surface towards him. Probably a fish. Maybe a big fish. OK, something bigger. Gareth stands up and backs away from the water's edge, shotgun at the ready.

Whatever it is moving beneath the water is still coming. The top of a head. A diver maybe. No the shape of the head is not human. It breaks the surface. The eyes not seeing him immediately. The creature gasping for breath. The face looking around as if trying to see. Almost like it is being born. Not a human face. Nor a human body. Grey, scrawny but muscular. Naked. Wearing a necklace of bones. And carrying a weapon.

Gareth swallows hard. Another of his father's mad tales taking form before his eyes. The creature from the stories his father told him and Sian to keep them at home at night, now coming at him through the water. 'Beware of the dark things in the night', his father had said. This is that dark thing. A Gwyllion.

It has seen him. It tries to run towards him but is impeded by the water. Gareth backs away. It makes a strange clicking noise. It raises the stone weapon it is carrying. Gareth instinctively fires the shotgun. Black blood sprays from the creature's head and it falls back into the water. Swallowed immediately by the black water. Dead. A pool of blackness on the surface of the dark lake. And it is gone.

Gareth pants hard. Has he killed a man, or something else? Now he really is following in his father's footsteps. Be careful what you wish for. Fuck!

More ripples beneath the water heading towards the shore. Gareth turns and runs off up the ramp into the semi-darkness.

Laura moves along the wall, trying to put the parlour table between herself and Sian. Watching the obviously deranged girl. The girl who for some reason thinks that Laura is here to take her inheritance, whatever that is. It clearly isn't the house, so what the hell is she afraid of losing?

Laura trying to make sense of what Sian has been saying and realising that she won't understand it, because it is madness. She needs to get the hell out of here. But outside the house it is getting dark. She has no choice but to make a run for it, into the darkness where there are worse monsters waiting.

Sian is drinking the water from the jar and stares into space for a moment. Calmer it seems from drinking the dark water. Not watching Laura now. In her own little world which Laura guesses is not a good place to be. "I just want to belong. I don't want to be the crazy girl who lives up on the mountain anymore. I want to be a part of Cwm Du. I want to be a Morwyn. But now YOU are here." Sian is not staring into space anymore, looking directly at Laura. Putting down the jar of water. Re-energised in her madness.

Laura keeps moving slowly, hands on one of the dining

chairs. Wishing there was some cutlery or something with which to frighten the girl. "Look Sian, I don't really understand. I'm going off to look for Jimmy, OK?"

Sian lunges forward. "No!!!!" She tries to cut around the head of the table, but Laura is quicker.

Laura gets through the parlour door and slams it on Sian. Sian drags on the handle from the other side. Laura realises there is no key. Shit! She lets go of the handle and runs for the front door, opening it and running into the gloom outside. The sound of running feet behind her.

Laura sprints from Mortlake onto the track heading for the way out. The way she came here what feels like a lifetime ago.

The woods darkening around her and the clacking sound of running feet on loose slate getting closer behind her. Laura glances over her shoulder to see Sian only feet behind her. Teeth bared in fury. But Sian coming to a halt. A look of horror on her face. Laura runs straight into a figure on the track. She screams and is thrown to the ground with a thump.

Sian sees everything unravel. The moment that she kills her competitor for role of Morwyn is turning into the moment when she is taken back to her former life. What kind of life was that? There on the mountain with him and her father. Mother long gone, killing herself one night in the barn. She felt so betrayed that her mother had escaped. So alone. It took years for her to escape here to a world where she won't grow old and never die. But now he is here to take her back to that living hell. She snarls. "Gareth!!!"

"She's your sister, isn't she?"

Gareth's eyes are dragged away from his sister who he hasn't seen in two years. At his feet is the English girl whose car he fixed only a day or so ago. He ignores her.

Sian. Unchanged from the day he last saw her. Isn't time

supposed to pass at a different speed inside the fairy realm? Sian. Wild eyed, covered in blood. Nothing has changed in however long it is in Sian's world. "Sian. Come home."

Sian stands there like a rabbit caught in headlights. Her head spinning. Rage turning to terror. How the hell did Gareth get here? Did Laura tell him that she was here? So he could take her away? So Laura could be the next Morwyn? Sian pulls her knife out from behind her back. "No!"

"Call the police. Does your phone work?"

Gareth doesn't even look at Laura on the ground at his feet. "Call the police? And say what?"

Laura pauses. Suddenly afraid of this man. "Anything! That my boyfriend is missing!"

Gareth laughs, mocking her. "We are in Cwm Du. It doesn't exist. People who go into Cwm Du are never seen again. Cwm Du is a legend to scare bad children like us. It is not real. Everyone knows that."

Laura desperate. "Please!"

Gareth fishes in his pocket and takes out his phone. He passes it to Laura, not taking his eyes off his sister. "Go ahead. Call them."

Sian starts backing away down the track. Gareth follows her. "Sian, we're leaving. Now! Come on!"

"I want to stay!"

"Sian, there are Gwyllion. They're coming out of the lake. We need to go!!!"

Sian shakes her head, still backing away. "Gwyllion don't scare me."

Laura is trying to unlock Gareth's phone but realises there is no signal. Exactly like she and Jimmy have had no signal since they arrived last night. "It's dead."

Gareth glances back at the scared girl holding his phone. "You will be too unless you get to somewhere safe. Get out of here. Go!"

But it is Sian who runs off down the track back towards
Cwm Du. Gareth follows, sprinting to catch her.

Laura left alone, still trying to make Gareth's phone
work. The sound of the birds overhead is deafening, but there
is something else. A sound somewhere behind her in the rush of
the wind in the trees. That clicking sound. Those creatures
are somewhere nearby. Laura runs back towards Mortlake.

Sian runs full tilt towards Mortlake, rushing through the
open door, closing it but Gareth is already there. Tight
behind her. Keeping the door from closing. Grabbing Sian by
the hair. Pulling her back out of the house. Sian screaming in
anger. "Leave me alone!!!" She slashes at Gareth's arm with
her knife.

Gareth lets Sian go and she falls forward across the
hallway onto the foot of the stairs. Gareth comes through the
door, standing over her. "Come on Sian! No arguments!"

Sian looks up at her brother. Someone she hoped never to
see again. Someone who would keep her at Tyle Garw. Tied to
the outer periphery of life while she wants to be at the
centre of it. Not on that farm. Not in one of those far off
English cities. Here in Cwm Du.

She followed her father for months on the open mountain,
learning how not to be seen. Invisibly watching him at dawn
trading with the white clad women of Cwm Du. Asking him who
they were when he was blind drunk. He told her of The
Morwynion. They were all she dreamt of. She knew her destiny
was to become one. She had to get to Cwm Du.

Now her brother, just like her father, standing over her
with a shotgun telling her how to live her life. But it is her
life and she only has one chance to live it. "I'm not going
anywhere. I'm staying here to look after Laura. That's my job.
Let me stay and do my job."

Gareth's eyes narrow. Same old Sian. Dreaming. Well this

dream is over. He steps forward and the door slams behind him. He looks around.

Laura leans against the door, panting. Locking the iron bolts across the door. Turning around and realising that Gareth and Sian are an even more pressing problem.

Gareth raising his shotgun to Laura. "Why are you making my sister stay?"

"I'm not..."

"See? Sian, we need to go."

Sian shaking her head manically. "I'm not going anywhere without Laura."

"OK, so you're both coming with me. At dawn."

Laura blanches. "Excuse me?"

Gareth turns to her, menacing. "This is not a debate. We are leaving at dawn."

"I'm not going anywhere without Jimmy."

Gareth rounds on Laura, raising the gun. He is knocked flying by Sian, who tries to stab at him.

Laura watches the shotgun slide away across the floor. She thinks better of going for it. God knows what these two are capable of.

Gareth grabs Sian's arms, closing his eyes as she tries to bite at his face. He rolls her onto her back and head-butts her with a sick thud. Sian falls back unconscious.

Gareth picks up the shotgun and points it at Laura. "Got any rope?"

Chapter 27: Tied Down

Becca stands in the shop she runs for of the village. The shop
has not used money since the Black Wall fell. The purpose of
the shop is to distribute food from what little fertile land
that they have in Cwm Du. Everything is shared by the village.
An idea Idris talked of when he came back from the war. This
sounded like the best way to run society when the quarry
company and the outside world went away.

For her part, Becca and her Morwynion gathered food and
clothes from any outsiders who found a way into this black
valley. Those they killed because they would spread the word
that Cwm Du exists, and so risk the outside world breaking in.
Breaching the Knots she and her mother had placed to protect
that outside world from what was beyond the lake.

She buried their bodies on the waste ground outside the
village where no one ever walked. At night she saw their
ghosts walk the slate wastelands. By the morning they were
gone.

She tolerated only the family of Tyle Garw, the nearest
farm outside the boundary. They knew to visit the gateway only
at dawn or dusk. And she needed to trade, otherwise her people
would starve. Besides, the men of Tyle Garw were too afraid to
enter. She allowed their mad daughter to live on the edges of
Cwm Du, lest she become a useful bargaining chip in the case
of any disputes.

Otherwise, no one who entered lived. A simple rule which
she broke only a couple of days ago. A young couple. Innocent.
Looking for pleasure as opposed to riches. Or so she thought.
What a mistake to make! They were not so innocent. They caused
The Otherworld to return. But it is her fault for breaking her
own rules. She should have let the Morwynion deal with them in
the usual way.

She was distracted and made that terrible mistake. With

Laura arriving imminently, she thought an order to let
outsiders live would prevent any mistakes and Laura being hurt
by accident. An important order to give, in light of the
former soldiers who make up so much of her population. Trigger
happy to a point of using up all of their ammunition. She has
had to keep these men informed. Keep them obedient. Keep them
alive. But above all, she had to bring Laura here and keep her
alive.

But this decision to spare the young couple has resulted
in the return of the Gwyllion, for which her soldiers are
unprepared. For which even her Morwynion are unprepared.

She looks down at Rachel. Unrecognisable. A clever village
girl. One who could have got out of Cwm Du. Been educated.
Taught children elsewhere in North Wales. Had a normal life.
But Rachel decided to take a higher calling and serve her
Druidesses. First Myfanwy and later Becca. But when this next
crisis happened, despite a century of keeping order, Rachel
has been trapped and killed by these primitive creatures. This
Morwyn became weak. The way Becca herself has become weak. It
is time for new blood.

Becca realises what is happening. Her powers of
understanding may be dimming but they are not gone. A hundred
years ago the Gwyllion took a momentary opportunity to escape
The Otherworld. They were doubtless unprepared and so were
defeated. Now they have another chance. And this time they are
ready. A hundred years of preparation. It is now the Druidess
and the Morwynion who are unprepared.

Becca looks out of the shop window into the failing light
and sees the eyes of the entire village staring back at her.
Sad. Scared. Expectant. Becca looks away. She cannot face
them.

Becca looks at the two figures in the semi darkness of the
shop. Their white dresses and pale faces making them look like
the ghosts she sees in the night. "Hannah. Bring the girl from

Tyle Garw. We need her. Mary, come with me."

Gareth tightens the twine tying Sian to the dining chair.
An antique chair but strong, built to last. It will hold Sian
secure. He starts to tie her legs, working quickly, knowing
these knots since he was a young boy. Keeping the knots out of
reach of prying hands or mouth. Tying down his sister so she
can create no problems until dawn when he has to get her back
through the gateway, back to reality.

This English girl is docile enough now. Standing looking
out of the window into the gloaming as if expecting her
boyfriend to return. That streak of piss would not be able to
hold his own against one of those creatures, let alone many.
In fact, no one should be out alone at night in this place.
Including himself.

The knots are done. Gareth gets to his feet. Time to
decide what to do with this English girl.

Laura glances around and sees that Gareth has finished
tying up Sian. One danger diminished, but should she believe
Sian that Gareth is as crazy as she is? "I need to find Jimmy.
He's been gone for hours. He was trying to get out of here. Do
you think he's gone far?"

"No. He can't have gone far. There's no way out of Cwm Du
unless you know how. The gate only opens at sunrise and
sunset. And I didn't find him out on the mountain. Unless he
was carrying a Bible."

Laura looks confused. "Jimmy was definitely not the
religious type."

"So he's out there in the night somewhere. God help him."

"Will you help me look for him?"

Gareth looks at Laura askance. "Why would I do that? All I
want is Sian back home. Your boyfriend can go to hell."

Laura tears up. "Please. We're going to have a baby. I

need him to help look after me. And I need to be at home."

"Don't think this is your home you bitch!" Sian is awake. Straining at the bonds. "I'm the one who should stay here. You should leave! Make her go Gareth!"

Gareth watches Sian askance. "What does she mean Laura? Why would this be your home?"

"I've inherited this house."

Gareth goes white. "I've seen old photographs. This is the Quarry Manager's house. You're a Salhurst?"

Laura nods.

Gareth shakes his head. "She will never let you leave! God knows, you are probably going to be her next Morwyn!"

Laura looks at Gareth. He is as crazy as his sister. What the hell is a 'Morwyn'? Why would she want to be one?

Sian furiously pulls at the bonds which hold her to the chair. "No!!! It should be me! Me! Me!!!"

"Gareth please! Help me find him!" Laura looking desperate.

Gareth thinks fast. "OK, I'll help you. In a few years I'll have to trade with the Morwynion, like my father does now. Like my grandfather did before him. If you are one of them, I want to be fairly treated. Never threatened. Treated with respect."

Laura nods her head trying to placate him. "Gareth, I have no idea why I was brought here. But what the hell. If that is what I need to promise you to get you to help me, yes I'll treat you well."

Gareth nods in agreement. "Does your car work now?"

"The car is seized. You can't take me anywhere in that!!!" Sian railing in her seat.

Gareth turns to Laura. "We'll take one look around the village. I need to see this place. This is the only chance I'll ever get. You're a Salhurst, the people there won't hurt you, so I should be safe with you. I hope we find your boyfriend. If we do or if we don't, we come back for Sian. Whatever happens, I leave with Sian by dawn."

"OK. We'll all leave together. Thank you." Laura hands the phone back to Gareth.

Sian roars. "Don't you leave with him Laura! Laura!!! He's not sane!!! He's dangerous!!! Come back!!!"

Gareth loads his shotgun, removing the spent shell he used on the Gwyllion warrior. He leads Laura by the arm out of the room. Sian struggles against her bonds screaming in frustration as the front door slams shut.

Idris looks on in exasperation as the hubbub from the villagers rises. Anger, confusion, fear. All emotions rising around him. How is he going to control this situation?

"I can't believe you didn't tell us the girl is pregnant!!!" One of the village women is in tears. "There have been no children here since you sent them away. We need children!"

Arwyn is furious. "What is wrong with you? Letting people into Cwm Du. You know what happens if outsiders come here. It is happening again. Now the Gwyllion have returned, and it is all because you've lost control!"

Becca steps forward and in one motion slaps Arwyn before he can even think of defending himself. "I deserve your respect. After all I've done for you! All these years!!! The sacrifices I've made!!!"

The villagers back away as Mary steps forward beside Becca, ready to defend her.

Idris hasn't backed away. "Becca, this is a time of crisis. The enemy are here, and you are taking no action. Your time is ending. It is the way of things. You need to move aside for the next generation. I know that is why you brought Laura here. It is a part of your plan. You're not at fault! But we need you to lead us in one last battle, so she inherits a free land. As you inherited a free land from your mother. Or this will be a wasteland. Worse, the Gwyllion will enter the outside world and the whole world will be a wasteland."

Becca is in tears. "Find her Idris. She should be at Mortlake. Locked up and safe."

Idris smiles kindly. "Then she will be safe enough in Mortlake. We'll find her and bring her to you, but once this fight is won. We must arm ourselves the best we can. We must go to the shore of the lake and defend our land!" Idris walks up the street, followed by the men, carrying their quarry tools as weapons. Hammers, chisels, the occasional gun. They disappear into the failing light.

Becca looks at the village women surrounding her. Frightened faces, some already heading home. Becca puts her head in her hands and in a moment she is left alone with Mary outside the shop, as the village women disappear into their homes. "Everything is unravelling Mary."

The calm black surface of the water breaking up as if a shoal of fish are feeding. The heads of Gwyllion Warriors break the surface of the lake. Gasping for breath, then clicking wildly as they search around in the near darkness for others. Clicking in response ahead of them, on the shore and in the woods.

Gwyllion emerging from between the trees and along the cut slate edges of the beach. The new arrivals emerge from the water and join Gol on the shore. The clicking and the cries of the birds overhead merge into a wall of sound in the darkness.

Laura and Gareth walk as quietly as possible up the track towards Cwm Du. Both are looking around nervously. Laura stops for a moment.

"What's wrong?" Gareth follows her gaze into the trees. "Can you see something?"

"Not exactly. I think there is something or someone over there." She points into the darkness.

Gareth cocks the shotgun, aiming it in the direction that Laura is looking.

"Stop that!" Laura pushes down the shotgun.

"If you think there is something there, I believe you. You're a descendant of Myfanwy."

"Who the hell is Myfanwy?" She looks back into the trees. "Whatever it was has gone." Laura heads on up the road towards Cwm Du.

For a moment Gareth holds the shotgun on the trees. Then he uncocks the gun and follows Laura towards the mountain of slate waste, beneath which Cwm Du hides in the darkness.

A few yards behind him, a figure drops onto the track and heads off into the darkness in the direction of the lake.

Sian has struggled with these bonds for what seems like hours. But Gareth's knots are good. They are tied in places her hands and mouth can't reach. Whatever she does, she is still tied to the chair. The chair is so stable she has not even been able to tip it over in the hope of breaking it. She is tied into a Victorian master of the house's chair, which won't let her go. By her brother who has never let her go.

Suddenly Sian gets the overwhelming feeling of being watched. Sian looks out of the window. It is dark outside now. Not even moonlight. No one to be seen. But something is out there. After years of living in the woodland, she knows when something is watching her.

The something crosses the window. The front door creaks open. The sound of those birds comes in with the something, drowning any sound it may make. Hiding the sound of footfalls on the slate floor. Sian senses the movement behind her. Nearby. A warrior of some kind. Only a warrior would not make a sound in an empty house.

And here she is tied to a chair. Unable to move. Unable to defend herself. Will it end like this? This life which has led her into a new world only to be slaughtered like a bound sheep on the farm where she was born?

The something has gone into the other rooms. The hint of movement on the stairs. A floorboard squeaks upstairs, just over her head. Now descending the stairs. She closes her eyes and holds her breath. A six-year-old girl again, hiding in the darkness hoping she won't be found.

Then a familiar smell. Female. A figure moving behind her in the periphery of her vision. Then into view. Hannah. The Morwyn. Knife in hand. "Where is she?"

"I haven't hurt her. I've been looking after her. But it should be me. I should be the new Morwyn. I've been here for so long. It should be me!"

"The girl is Becca's heiress. You will serve her, honour her and obey her, as you will serve honour and obey Becca."

Sian's eyes widen. Laura is here to succeed Becca? Elation. "So there is a place for me? As Morwyn?"

Hannah nods. She puts her knife over Sian's bonds. "I ask you again. Where is she?"

"My brother took her."

Hannah puts her knife to Sian's neck.

Sian swallows hard. "She'll be back."

"How do you know?"

Sian smiles slyly. "He won't leave without me."

Chapter 28: The Bonds Unravelling

Gareth looks around him as he and Laura walk into the village of Cwm Du. Not really knowing what he should be expecting as he walks into what has been until tonight a mythical place in his mind.

What he sees is not so unfamiliar. Or is it? Long rows of quarrymen's cottages made of slate on either side of the road. Looking like other villages in the area in old photographs he has seen, before someone got the contract of covering all the traditional cottages in North West Wales with twentieth century pebbledash.

There is nothing modern here. No lights. No cars. No double glazing. No satellite dishes. No electrical wires. It is like being in a museum. A living museum. He is now getting the sense of being watched by eyes unseen.

He looks at Laura, as nervous as a cat, glancing around herself quickly, looking into windows and reacting as if she is seeing faces looking back at her from the darkness within.

If he and Laura had looked behind them, they would have seen Idris and a dozen men, armed with quarry tools watching them walk towards the centre of the village. Idris stands in the middle of the road, signalling to the others, leading them as they all follow Laura and Gareth silently into Cwm Du.

The humans up the track are moving away from them. A moment ago they were going to wait for Gol and the others to join them. To create a larger force. There were too many humans carrying that cold hard rock that kills. Iron.

The humans are returning to their caves no doubt. Afraid of the dark. Afraid of them. They are gone. Leaving the place undefended.

The Gwyllion scouting party move swiftly into the settlement, eager to make the most of their enemy's weakness.

Coming to the entrances to the humans' caves. But there is
iron everywhere. Across every entrance. Iron making each
entrance inaccessible. Keeping those inside safe from the
revenge upon them which has been millennia in planning. Safe
only for now.

Gareth takes in the huge chapel, once dominating, now
broken and decayed. Towering above it is what has dominated
village life even more than the chapel. The mountain of slate
waste.

He follows Laura as they walk onwards down the street,
passing the dark and silent Quarryman's Arms. Laura stops in
her tracks, Gareth bumping into her in the half light. Laura
whispers. "Someone's down there." She points down the street,
down to the building nearest the river bridge. Becca is
sitting huddled and alone outside the shop.

"Who is it?"

"It's OK. I know her. Come on." Laura heads off down the
street towards the shop. As she approaches Laura slows. She is
able to look in through the darkened shop window. She can just
see a white clothed figure wrapping what appears to be a body
on the shop counter. Laura knows that the body is Rachel. She
can feel the pain, the loss, the loneliness in Becca as she
sits looking back at her. Laura speaks gently to Becca. "Are
you OK?"

Becca is smiling through her tears. "I knew you would
come." She gets to her feet and notices Gareth, shotgun in
hand standing in the half light.

Laura gestures to Gareth to keep back. "I'm looking for my
boyfriend Jimmy. Have you seen him?"

Becca opens the shop door. "Laura, come inside."

Laura remains frozen to the spot. Afraid for a moment as
Mary comes to the door. Mary's hands covered in blood which is
not her own. "No, I need to find Jimmy and leave."

Becca smiles sweetly. "That's not possible."

"Not possible?"

Becca reaches out trying to take Laura's hand, but she steps backwards. Becca's eyes harden. Charm is not working. Maybe instruction will. "You must stay here. You're the last of my family!!! You're the last Salhurst. We need you here, to lead us."

Gareth steps forward, gun in hand. "It was Salhurst who blew the Black Wall and caused all this!"

Becca snarls at him. "And a Salhurst is always the cure. She will be the next Druidess. In my place."

Gareth takes a breath, realising now who he is talking to. "You're Becca Salhurst!!!"

Laura takes a deep breath. "So are you my cousin or something?"

"Laura, I'm your great, great grandmother. You must stay here with me."

Laura looks at the woman, who can't be more than two or three years older than her. "That's insane!!! You can't be! That would make you over a hundred years old!"

Becca thinks for a minute. "I was born in 1890. What year is it now?" She takes Laura by the hand. "The water of The Otherworld has kept my body young. As it will keep you young. In Cwm Du everyone lives forever."

Laura's head reels. The gold sovereign. The house. The old Polaroid photograph on the stairway. The way Becca let herself into the house. HER house. But this is insane. As insane as Sian and Gareth's stories. But they are the same story. A history. A testament. Laura tears herself free from Becca's grasp. She feels Gareth's arm around her.

Gareth talks to Becca, over Laura's head. "This is all coming to an end. The dark things are here. I saw them come out of the lake. You're not going to survive this night. Laura, let's go."

Laura tears herself free. "Not without Jimmy!" She looks beyond Gareth into the gloaming and her face falls.
Idris and the villagers are standing behind Laura and Gareth, the men holding old rusting Quarrymen's tools.

Gareth follows Laura's gaze, letting her go and pointing the shotgun at Idris. "Laura, come with me. We're getting Sian and getting out."

Idris stares into Gareth's eyes. "You are not going anywhere." Behind him the Villagers move forward threateningly.

Gareth grabs Laura and puts the shotgun to her head.

Laura cries out in shock. "Gareth!?!"

Becca drops to her knees. "Don't you hurt her! Please!!!!"

Gareth pushes Laura towards Idris and the villagers, the shotgun still to her temple. "Let us go and she won't be hurt."

Becca growls at Gareth in Welsh. "You will stay here!"

Gareth replies, whispering angrily. "No I won't! You have made my father and grandfather's lives hell. Serving you. At your beck and call. You aren't talking to them: you are talking to me." Gareth pushes Laura struggling at gunpoint through the crowd of villagers.

"Laura come here!!! Please!!!!!" Becca screams. Gareth staggers for a moment, and the villagers step backwards in shock.

Gareth composes himself. Whispering in Welsh to the Druidess who is on her knees. Tears of blood running down her face. Her Morwyn Mary emerging from the shop beside her, with murder in her eyes. "Keep back or I'll shoot her." Gareth pushes Laura up the street, half running into the gloaming.

Becca has her head in her hands, hiding the blood running from her eyes.

Idris takes charge. "The girl is the next druidess. We can't lose her! Come on!" He hurries up the street followed by the village men.

At last an entrance with no iron. An open entrance into a large space. Decayed. Damp. Like a giant cave. The scouting party moves quickly in the darkness. No humans here.

The scouts move around the great space, looking for any hidden humans, or entrances into other spaces.

One warrior looks up at the wall. An image, like some of the Lacks make to communicate a message to their descendants in the caves of home. It looks like his dead brother who he saw earlier. Pinned up on a tree. Eviscerated. Dead but looking down at him. Understandable to the warrior even in its human form. A dead warrior defeated.

A sound behind them. The party gather quickly to defend themselves and move towards the entrance of this large cave.

Gareth turns the gun away from Laura as he drags her up the road out of the village.

Laura glances behind her and sees Gwyllion emerging from the Chapel. Weapons at the ready but ignoring her and Gareth. Facing their pursuers, Idris and the villagers. "Gareth! Stop! There are creatures!"

"Yes, the Gwyllion are here! They're everywhere. We have to get back to Sian!"

"What about Jimmy?"

"He is probably dead already!" Gareth drags Laura away into the darkness at the edge of Cwm Du. Into the dark moonless night. Their footfalls and the rising sound of the birds up ahead meaning they are running deaf as well as blind.

Idris leads the men walking briskly up the road following Laura and the outsider boy out of the village. Despite the fact that she is unwilling, the boy has managed to drag her out of sight. "They are getting away!!! She's the future. We can't let her get away from us!!!!"

Arwyn runs ahead, not wounded like many of these war veterans who returned to the quarries when they were discharged from the Army. Then he stops in his tracks, turning in alarm. "They're here!!!"

The Gwyllion scouting party emerge from the entrance to the chapel. Maybe three of them, but who knows how many more are inside.

Tom steps forward with his pistol. Arwyn pushes the weapon down. "Save your bullets, we shall need them later." He raises his iron chisel. "Idris. Go! Get the Salhurst girl. I'll stay and send these creatures back to the hell they came from."

Another three Gwyllion appear at the chapel entrance. Idris and the other Villagers exchange glances. "Form a line. Draw them out. We can't fight them in the dark!"

The clicking of the Gwyllion rises to a cacophony of snarls and war cries. They fan out across the frontage of the chapel. High on the chapel walls, towering over the villagers below.

Arwyn rushes forward, ducking a blow from a Gwyllion warrior. He drives his quarryman's chisel deep into a Gwyllion warrior's belly. The warrior falls forward, dropping onto the ground, his blood joining Robert's blood which still stains the pavement. The creature burns as Arwyn snatches back his chisel.

The Gwyllion jump down and attack the villagers, stabbing and swinging with their slate weapons. A clash of weapons: slate being shattered by iron. Shards of slate shattering on the floor, leaving the warriors undefended.

Gwyllion warriors falling under blows from the Villagers' hammers, chisels and cutting tools. The smell of burning flesh fills the air, as the Gwyllion burn.

Tom is driven backwards, the Gwyllion warrior stabbing him with his slate spear. The villager fires his pistol.

The sound of gunfire drowned out by Gareth and Laura's feet hammering on the slate track as they rush headlong into the darkness.

Laura glancing around watching for any movement on the track or in the trees nearby as they run into a cacophony of sound of the Birds of Annwn who are somewhere overhead in the swirling darkness.

Chapter 29: No Return

Idris looks down at the dead Gwyllion bodies, still burning outside the chapel in the night. Nearby Tom lies bleeding with his wife and others tending to him tearfully.

Idris' band of warriors stand looking at him expectantly. Local boys he grew up with on these mountains, went to Sunday School with him in the building before them, worked together in the slate quarry before volunteering with him to go and fight a war which they had only read about in the London newspapers.

The Great War. A period of time which shaped them all as men. Friends together, as the remainder of their regiment in Flanders were also childhood friends from places of which he had seldom heard. Those young men of entire towns and villages wiped out in a single morning under a leaden sky, in the mud of what used to be farms.

Returning home damaged cogs in the machine. Returning to a dying quarry in a part-dead village. Returning to face these creatures now burning at his feet. Creatures which haunted his nightmares even more than the ghosts of his friends who never returned from Flanders to Cwm Du.

Idris used to fear these creatures far more than the Hun, though he had not seen one in a century. The wrenching fear deep in his guts when he saw them return, has turned to anger and hatred again. And now he knows they can be defeated. He has watched them fall within a minute of fighting. He may have no ammunition as that lazy swine Wyn had not traded bullets with Becca for years, blaming some or other law of the land. But the way to kill Gwyllion is iron on flesh. Face to face combat. He never realised that.

"See how their bodies burn? See how iron kills them? Just like Myfanwy's stories when we were children. They are men of stone. We are men of iron. Forward! Let's find Myfanwy's heiress and drive the Gwyllion back to Hell!!!"

Idris marches off up the track, out of the village, followed by a handful of the men who followed him to the recruiting meeting in Caernarfon over a century before.

Footfalls in the near darkness. Laura and Gareth running down the slate track towards Mortlake. The house dark in the night ahead of them. Running together through the gateway. Mortlake's door open like a black mouth. The windows dark eyes staring back at her.

Laura stops, looking inside the doorway and the parlour window, trying to make out any movement. Maybe there are shapes in the parlour. She is unsure.

"What's wrong?" Gareth stopping beside her, looking concerned. "Let's get Sian and go to the gateway and wait for dawn."

"The door is open. I closed it."

Gareth raises his shotgun and leads the way slowly in through the open door into Mortlake. Laura follows him and bolts the door behind them. Darkness and silence inside the house. No movement.

Laura pushes open the door to the parlour. Two figures sit in the chairs around the dining table. Both dressed in white. Ghostly pale in the half light.

Sian rises to her feet. No longer bound. Smiling broadly, giggling happily. Wearing clean white clothes. Laura recognises the clothes she packed to travel here. Sian has been through Laura's bag.

Opposite Sian, Hannah, dressed in her white dress, rises to her feet in greeting. "Laura, we've been waiting for you. We are so glad you're safe. Welcome home."

Sian speaks calmly, all hints of madness gone from her voice. Content. "I'm sorry I misunderstood why you were here. I'm here for you. We're here for you Laura. Stay here with us."

"We need you. You are the future." Hannah steps forward to embrace Laura, who steps backwards defensively.

Gareth steps into the room. "Sian! Let's go!"

Sian answers in Welsh. "Gareth. Leave while you can."

Gareth growls angrily. Knowing this Morwyn with her sister has set her free. Setting Sian loose is making her dangerous again. Making this urgent situation worse. Making his task so much harder. "Come. I'm not leaving without you."

Sian smiles kindly. "I can't leave Gareth... I'm one of the Morwynion now. That is the only thing I've ever wanted. You've seen Cwm Du. The stories are all true. If I leave, I'll die. But it is not too late for you. You haven't drunk the water. Please... go now!!!"

Hannah steps forward between Gareth and Sian, and with one swift movement, Gareth strikes her over the head with the shotgun. He grabs Sian by the hair and drags her towards the parlour door.

Sian screams, trying to fight. She cries out. "Laura, I'm your Morwyn! Help me!!!"

Gareth drags Sian screaming out of the parlour and towards the front door. "You're coming with me!"

Laura follows, unsure whether or not to follow Gareth or remain in the house. Hannah staggers to her feet and puts herself between Gareth and Laura. Gareth pulls back the bolt and opens the door.

Jimmy stands in the doorway. Pale, dead eyed and terrifying.

Laura gasps in shock. "Jimmy??? Where did you go? Are you OK?"

Suddenly a flurry of clicking sounds. Gwyllion emerge behind Jimmy moving forward towards the door, brandishing their slate weapons menacingly.

Laura looks on with terrified and tearful eyes. Jimmy is

gaunt, hurt, obviously sick with sunken dark dead eyes. "Jimmy? What have they done to you???"

Jimmy steps forward. A flash. The sound deafens Laura, taking her breath away. Stopping her thoughts. Her nose and mouth filling with the taste and smell of cordite.

The impact of the gunshot throws Jimmy backwards to the ground and wounds the Gwyllion Warrior closest to him. The Warrior runs away, screaming. Jimmy lies on the ground. Motionless. A pool of blood spreading across this chest. His face pock marked like a teenager. Dead.

Laura looks on in disbelief. She rushes forward to the door. She exchanges looks with Gareth. Shock rising inside her. Her ears ringing after the shotgun blast. The ringing turning into a scream in her head. Then the scream erupts from her soul. "NOOOOOO!!!!"

Laura's scream thumps into the Gwyllion war party knocking them from their feet. They roll with the wave of sound and crawl away trying to escape the power released by Laura's scream. Then silence. Even the Birds of Annwn seem to have quietened overhead. The Gwyllion flee back into the woods now clicking in panic.

The scream is ringing in Gareth's ears. It was deafening. Unnaturally deafening. He shakes his head as he looks at Laura, standing mute, staring at Jimmy's dead body in disbelief. Tears running down her cheeks. Red tears. Tears of blood.

"Jimmy!!!" Laura runs to Jimmy's body. Shaking him. Trying to wake him up. Her bloody tears flowing and dripping on Jimmy's already bloody face.

Gareth steps forward, looking on in shock. This is the second person he has shot. But this one is human. Someone he met only yesterday. He wretches.

Gareth looks at Sian. "Was that the Druidess' scream?"

Sian nods. "The stories are true. I told you Gareth. She

and I belong here now. Please go..."

Hannah steps forward and comforts Laura as she cries over Jimmy's body. Then she looks up. Sensing movement. Getting to her feet, drawing her knife, ready to fight.

Figures emerge from the darkness on the track. Around a dozen of them. Familiar figures she has known all her life.

Idris and his men walk through the gateway to Mortlake. They slow when they see Hannah but stop when they see Laura crouching over Jimmy's body.

Gareth steps forward from the doorway. Training his shotgun on Idris. Aware he only has one shot left. But Idris will not know that. "Let me pass. I have no dispute with you. My sister wants to stay. But I can't stay here... I'm Wyn's son. I'll be your connection to the outside world one day. Let me go."

Hannah turns to Gareth, her hand gently lowering his shotgun. "The Gwyllion caught him. This boy. Laura's friend. And they were using him against her. Just like they used Y Parchedig Huw against Becca. You need to stay with us until dawn. Help us fight the Gwyllion with your gun and ammunition and leave at dawn."

Gareth feels a hand on his wrist. Laura. Face streaked with blood red tears. "Help them. Please." Laura turns away and walks back towards Mortlake.

Idris calls out to her. "Laura. Your place is here. Becca has lost her power as a druidess. You are finding your power. Your scream alone drives the Gwyllion back. Help us."

Laura keeps walking, crying in confusion and grief. Torn. She turns around to speak to Idris but sees Jimmy's body. She runs for the house.

Idris calls out after her. "It's your inheritance Laura!!! It's your duty! Your purpose!!!"

Laura leans on the door and looks at Jimmy through her bloody tears. Sian and Hannah watching her expectantly. At the gateway, Idris and around a dozen villagers who have lived on this borderland for over a century, tasked with keeping it secure so the outside world would be safe. Laura just realising her place in this huge story which unless she intervenes may end tonight. For her there is no life beyond Cwm Du anymore. Jimmy is gone. Her place is here. That is her inheritance. The barman is right. This is her duty.

Laura clears her throat. Raising her voice. "Let's send them back to The Otherworld."

Chapter 30: The Scream of Battle

Becca rises to her feet. She has been sitting on the floor outside the shop for what feels like an eternity. Mary had returned into the shop to prepare Rachel's body, but Becca knows that she was really giving Becca room to gather her thoughts and make a plan for how to deal with this crisis. But Becca hasn't been doing that.

Her mind has been blank. Clouded. Her energy sapped since she screamed. Usually she would recover momentarily, though in all of these years she has only needed to scream once or twice. Keeping order amongst the villagers. Putting down dissent without having to resort to physical violence. A more humane way of governing. Often that was the best way. Now it is not. But she does not know what to do. Idris has taken the men to fight. What if he fails? What if Laura is hurt?

Laura. Why did she let her go? With Wyn's son! One of the few who could understand Cwm Du. But what if he wants an end to it? An end to his family's suffrage to Becca's will.

Becca staggers to her feet like an old woman. Using the wall of the shop to support herself. Mary comes out of the door, wiping blood onto her dress. "Mary. Prepare yourself. We must go into the night. Protect Laura and face the Gwyllion."

Her sense of hearing is returning after that... sound. That noise the young Druidess made outside her cave. Louder than the noise made by the iron stick. Knocking her warriors from their feet and driving them away like cubs from an angry Lack. Atala shakes her head, unable to hear as keenly as before. But thinking. Plotting the next attack.

Her warriors were fleeing, back towards the water and the safety of home. Back to the darkness. Forgetting their promise to take back this world, for the generations who had to live underground, out of light, out of food, out of life. Driven there by Druidesses of generations before memory.

Now those warriors who ran have reached her, standing beside the Knot which they destroyed. The Knot that was to hold them back in The Otherworld. But they shattered it. As they will shatter the young Druidess and the humans who fight with her.

There is darkness now. This place is almost as dark as her world. This place is now like her home. The great light has gone. The light she feared as did they all when they came from the water, and the light they came to love as it showed this world to them with a new sense they did not realise they possessed.

Now the darkness has returned. The humans cannot function in the darkness. Yet here they are coming towards her hordes of warriors, unseeing, unhearing under the creatures moving through the air above her head. The humans do not know they are here. Waiting. Ready to fight. They will know only when they are dead.

Laura walks shoulder to shoulder alongside Idris. Sian and Hannah at her side. Gareth behind her with the ten or so quarrymen. Onwards down the track into the darkness. Even without the thousands of birds now swooping overhead, it is a moonless night. No stars. A heavy leaden night sky. Near darkness. No movement. Any sound drowned out by those damned birds.

They round the curve in the track and Laura can see the gateway. She steps over the dead body on the track. The body which has been there since this morning. That feels like a lifetime ago.

The gateway seems solid. Closed. Laura tries to make out what is there on the track. Then the darkness starts to move. Alive. Alive with Gwyllion Warriors. Scores of them. Lying in wait for her and the others. Unseen.

Laura realises that she is the only one who can see them. Now Hannah sees them. Hannah grips her arm tightly. Laura whispers urgently. "Up ahead. Gwyllion! Dozens of them!"

"Where?" Idris can't see them. Neither can the others it seems.

Laura stops, the others bumping into her as the entire group come to a halt. "In the gateway. The gateway is full of them. Six deep maybe."

Murmurs amongst the quarrymen. Idris whispers in Laura's ear. "Laura. Use your voice. Use your scream. Knock them down so we can kill them."

Laura looks wide eyed. Thinking back to how the Gwyllion ran from her scream before, in the open ground outside Mortlake. Here the sides of the track will funnel the sound. Make it more intense. Focus the sound as water flows down a funnel. And at the end of the funnel are the Gwyllion.

"Ready your weapons. Get down on the ground. Cover your ears." Idris lies down. Everybody follows suit and Laura is left standing alone. She walks forward.

Atala sees the Druidess approaching. Alone. How foolish. Coming to her death. The fight will now be easy. Atala's heart sinks as she sees the Druidess open her mouth.

The scream. Louder than the sound that brought down the Black Wall in times of legend. It knocks Atala back into the warriors behind her. Bodies falling on top of her. Warriors dropping to the ground unable to hear. Clicking wildly to deaf ears. And then the blows begin. The smell of smoking flesh.

Idris and the others smashing their iron hammers and tools onto the helpless Gwyllion. Their bodies burning. Those who can run, escape. But dozens remain, dying under the blows of the quarrymen's iron weapons.

Laura opens her eyes. Alone for a second as her eyes
clear. The blood red tears running from her eyes. An arm
around her. Comforting her. Hugging her now. Sian. She kisses
Laura passionately. "Thank you, my Druidess."

Idris smashes his hammer down on another warrior. Movement
beneath the body. Like a rat under hay. A figure scuttling
away into the darkness. Darting down the track. It must be
heading for the ramp. No. It heads into the woods. So they
will have to clear the woods of these creatures, and if they
won't be driven to the water, kill every last one of them.
"Hurry. They are getting away!!!"

Idris climbs over the dead and burning bodies in the
gateway, and heads on down the track. Others follow.

Moments later, Laura is half carried to the gateway by
Sian and Hannah. Gareth is there waiting. "They've followed
the Gwyllion into the woods. Come on. Hurry!"

A dead body on the ground. Time was when she would be able
to recognise one at a distance, be it friend or foe. But not
immediately this time. Then recognition. Laura's lover. Shot
dead. What happened here? The door to Mortlake is open.
Becca's head reels. Where is Laura?

Becca rushes inside, Mary at her heels. Knowing somehow
that this is the last time she will visit the house which has
been home for at least two lifetimes. Darkness. No sound.
Empty.

Becca goes into the parlour. Looking at the photograph of
her husband. A proud man. A leader of men. Her mother's
leadership was often downplayed and even denied by many of the
villagers of Cwm Du, especially by Huw, so she needed a strong
man in her life.

But he was too headstrong. Going away to war when Arthur
was a babe in arms. What would have happened if that wound he

endured had been fatal? What would have happened if he had
never returned? Would the Black Wall have fallen to the greed
of the company anyway? Or would she and everyone in Cwm Du
have lived short, hard lives in the sight of God?

Becca opens the drawer in her husband's desk. An artefact
that reminded her of him, so she had moved it to the corner of
the room from its place of prominence decades ago. Pushing the
memory into a dark corner. Never able to throw it out.

On top of old quarry letters and documents is her
husband's service revolver. He had taught her how to use it
once, back when there was a threat of a strike at the quarry.
Did he expect her to use it on people she had known all her
life? Would he have used it?

She feels the weight of the gun in her hand. Iron and
steel. Just what she needs to defend herself now that her
powers have gone. The only important thing is to make sure
that Laura is safe, so that she can drive back The Otherworld.

Laura watches the trees go by, trying to gather her
strength. Shattered like the Gwyllion who died in the gateway
behind her. Gareth and Sian carrying her onwards, following
the quarrymen as they move in a line through the woods. Fanned
out as if moving through No Man's Land. Quarry tools rather
than rifles in their hands. Moving swiftly trying to spot
their unseen enemy somewhere out there in the darkness. Laura
is the only one who can see. She closes her eyes.

A minute or two go by. She opens her eyes again. Seeing
into the darkness. Around and beyond the quarrymen who are
before her. She is being carried down what was once a street.
Houses on either side. Green with moss, even in the half
light. Decaying wood on decayed stone. Falling buildings.
Roofless to the sky. Trees growing through them and stretching
up into the night sky towards the birds which are circling
overhead. The sound of the birds drowning out everything else.

So many houses. All long empty. One which has signs of life. Clothing hanging on a branch as if to dry. Someone is still living here? Why would they choose to live here when they could be in the village?

A movement. Or was there?

Laura glances around. More movements behind and inside the derelict houses. And in the trees. She looks the other way. Yes. Movement. Laura gasps. "They are everywhere!"

Up ahead Atala emerges from a building, spear at the ready. Climbing the decayed wall so she towers over the quarrymen below. Clicking quickly as the other Gwyllion Warriors emerge from all around.

Chapter 31: Carving the Knot

Clicking fills the air. The thud of Gwyllion Warriors leaping into battle. The cracks as their slate and stone weapons meet the quarrymen's tools. The iron shattering the slate as it did millennia before.

A stone club hitting home. Knocking a quarryman to the ground. The Gwyllion Warrior smashing the weapon down on the helpless quarryman. Hannah jumping in, knocking the warrior aside. Stabbing at him with her knife. Flesh splitting and burning.

Sian circling Laura with her back towards her. Fending off anyone who would come near her. But they do. Sian ducking and kicking at two warriors who swing at her with clubs. Sian unable to get close enough to them but driving them away. Sian deep in the fight, following them. Leaving Laura alone.

Something tells Laura to turn around. As she turns, a slate spear narrowly misses her. Atala wide eyed, clicking wildly stabs at Laura's belly with her spear. Time after time. Laura dodging. Unarmed. Shattered from her screams. Realising that Atala is stabbing for her unborn child. The creature's features filled with existential hate.

Everything starts to slow down. Laura's primal fear taking over. The spear is thrust again, Laura grabs it, but she is weak. She is dragged back and fore. Atala pushes hard and Laura falls backwards over some fallen rubble. She hits the ground and the spear shatters on the ground beside her.

Atala reaches for another weapon, but there is none. She grabs a rock from the rubble and raises it above her head to hit Laura. Laura closes her eyes. Resigned to her fate. Ready for a blow which will hopefully be mercifully quick.

She is deafened by the sound. Atala's face is smashed by the impact of the bullet from the service revolver. Atala rolls away screaming.

Becca is covered in Atala's black blood. She stands over Laura. Shaking with worry. Laura opens her eyes and Becca smiles. She drops the revolver and reaches out to help Laura to her feet.

Thud! Becca's face changes. Her jaw slackens. Beside her Atala strikes Becca with a rock once again. Becca's body quakes.

Laura tries to scream, but she is hoarse. "Becca!"

Atala locks eyes with Laura. Time standing still. She turns to smash the rock down on Laura but is knocked backwards in a spray of black blood.

Then the sound of the shotgun. Gareth has shot Atala at point blank range. Becca falls forward onto Laura.

Nearby Atala lies on the ground. Dead. The Gwyllion Warriors retreat into the trees. Scattering in all directions.

Only one has not run. Gol stands his ground, swinging his club menacingly. Idris rushes towards him. Gol retreats between some trees. Idris follows him, stopping short as Gol swings his club. The club slams into a tree and is stuck. Idris steps in swiftly and smashes Gol's head with his hammer. Gol drops to his knees. Idris smashes his hammer down on Gol's head once more. A spray of black blood and smoke as Gol's body falls to the ground.

Laura sees the Gwyllion's eyes shining in the darkness. Sees them grouping between herself and the way they came into the abandoned village. "They're over there!" She points and the quarrymen turn and advance on the creatures in the dark woods.

Then the eyes are gone. The Gwyllion are running. The snap of branches in the woods as they rush away. The quarrymen pursue them into the darkness.

Laura feels Becca moving beside her. Hannah, Mary and Sian join Becca and Laura who lie on the ground, side by side.

Becca is looking up at the birds flying overhead. She

turns her eyes to Laura. "This is the borderland, Laura. This is your home."

Laura nods, looking deep into Becca's eyes. "I know. But what do I do?"

Becca shakily removes the slate amulet from around her neck and pushes it into Laura's hand. "Take this. You'll know what to do. It's in your blood. You need to be strong. Darker things may come."

Laura glances away, unable to hold Becca's desperate stare. She sees the body of Atala nearby. What darker things could come? Is The Otherworld coming into our world not the worst thing that could happen? She swallows hard, turning her gaze back to Becca who is bleeding profusely. Black blood. Just like the Gwyllion blood on the ground nearby. Laura nods. "I will be strong. So will my child. Don't worry."

Becca smiles through her bloody tears. "That water in the lake isn't deep enough to hold back The Otherworld. You've seen that. You need to take my place. This will be your life's work. Do you understand me?"

Laura nods. "Yes."

Becca smiles as she cries. "Good. Welcome home Laura." She looks at Hannah, Mary and Sian. "All three of you. Protect her. Help her."

Hannah joins Idris in the trees. He is looking down at Gol's body at his feet. Hannah crouches and using her knife cuts at Gol's throat. Idris looks on, blank. Back in battle where he hoped he'd never be again. He turns away, unable to watch. Sian is standing feet away, watching intently. She walks away across the darkness of the abandoned village.

Sian crouches near Laura and Becca and decapitates Atala. Laura looks on aghast, while Becca nods. "Well done my daughter."

Sian holds up Atala's head and screams. Hannah appears out of the darkness carrying Gol's head. Idris comes out of the darkness behind Hannah. "Come. Let's drive them back to The Otherworld!"

Sian, Hannah and Idris follow the remaining quarrymen through the woods back towards the flooded quarry. Movement in the woods ahead of them. Gwyllion seeing them in the darkness. Seeing their leaders' heads held high by the two women, and the quarrymen following behind. The Gwyllion run.

Out of the trees, across the track and down the ramp towards the black water under the black sky. They rush into the water, wading out until their heads disappear under the black surface of the lake. Only to reappear again further out from shore. Along with dozens more. Scores of Gwyllion waiting offshore in the rising light. The first light in the sky beyond the massive slate stacks at the eastern edge of the quarry. The light rising slowly over the mountains beyond.

Gareth helps Laura carry Becca through the woods. Mary walks beside them, watchful, checking constantly for any Gwyllion remaining in the woods. Moving through the trees. Onwards until they reach the slate track.

Gareth looks up at the brightening sky. Ahead of him his sister's white clothes are now covered in black blood, some of it from the severed head she is holding aloft. Beyond her the last of the Gwyllion are on the shore of the black lake below, retreating into the water. Their grey bodies silhouettes in the rising light.

Gareth passes Becca to Mary and walks to his sister. "Sian. I have to go. Come with me. Dad misses you."

Sian turns, smiling warmly. "Go Gareth. I'll see Dad again at the gateway. I'll see you at the gateway for the rest of your life. This is not goodbye." Sian kisses Gareth on the cheek.

Gareth looks to Becca and Laura. "I wish you luck. Keep the borderland safe. I'll be outside with anything you need.

Goodbye." Gareth is gone in the gloom.

Laura watches him disappear into the gloaming, empty shotgun in hand. She turns her gaze to Becca, sinking fast in her arms.

"Take me to the shore." Becca nods towards the ramp. Laura and Mary carry her down the ramp. Sian and Hannah lead the way holding up the severed heads whilst Idris and the quarrymen form a guard around them.

The sky is brightening above the black water, but the water does not reflect the light. Out a hundred feet from shore the heads of a horde of Gwyllion Warriors can be seen watching the shore. Watching as our world becomes closed to them once more.

Gareth runs along the slate track. The pre-dawn light allowing him to see ahead of him. The birds still swarming overhead screaming out drowning out the noise of his feet smacking on the slate track,

He rounds the bend and sees the gateway up ahead. Beyond it open mountain. He arrives at the gate, breathless. He checks all around to make sure he has not been followed by any of those creatures from Hell. But he is alone.

He turns around to see his quad bike a few yards away outside the gateway. He glances backwards to see the sun just appearing over the mountain of slate waste beyond Cwm Du.

He runs, his feet no longer on the slate track, but on the old stone surface overgrown at the crossroads to nowhere he discovered his father used to visit every morning. But right now, he is alone. With his quad.

He climbs on the vehicle and turns the ignition key. The engine roars into life. Gareth looks up at the open mountain ahead of him. Nothing but open land beyond the crossroads. Cwm Du has gone.

The birds circle screaming overhead. The water of the black lake laps on the shore.

The amulet cuts into the slate. Marking it. One continuous line. Folding back on itself digging deeper into the soft rock's surface.

Laura is carefully carving curves into the slate guided by Idris and watched by Becca. Her hands bleed as she works. Behind them stand Hannah, Mary, Sian, the surviving quarrymen and the remnants of the Villagers. All watching Laura work and watching the black heads on the surface of the black water in the rising light.

Laura puts the final touch in place. The Knot is complete, filling with Laura's blood. Becca smiles at Laura and her eyes close.

"Is the Knot correct?" Laura looks to Becca for approval, but she does not reply.

She exchanges looks with Idris whose eyes are full of tears. "She has left us, Laura."

Laura looks out across the lake, seeing the heads of the Gwyllion warriors still visible. Creatures once of this world, driven away millennia ago by her mothers. Too much time, too much blood, too much hatred has flowed for there ever to be peace. These creatures and the pestilence they carry would overrun the world should they be given an opportunity. And the person to stop that opportunity is her. For the rest of her life. Maybe for many times her expected lifetime. Just like her great great grandmother who lies beside her.

Laura's eyes fill with tears. Clear tears for a great grandmother she never thought to meet. Tears for Jimmy and a life she has now left behind. She looks around her at her new neighbours. Her new tribe.

The loss hits her. The loss of family, love, and way of life. She is on the borderland. This thin place. Her role to hold back the Otherworld.

She picks up the piece of slate on which she has carved the same knot that is now around her neck. Becca's Knot. Before her, Myfanwy's Knot. And before that...

She can feel the emotion rising inside her. As if coming up through her feet out of the ground. The power from within the land burning through her, rising through her core, burning in her mind, forward into her eyes which fill with bloody tears.

Laura screams! The powerful scream travels out filling the quarry. The shockwave skimming along the surface of the black water, creating a wave. It hits the Gwyllion smashing them, pushing them downwards into the black quarry water. Gone from sight.

Above the birds are thrown from the sky falling to the water below. They are sucked beneath the surface and are gone. Back to Annwn. Back to The Otherworld.

Silence across the water. Silence across what was once the quarry. Silence as the gateway to The Otherworld is shut once more. Laura places the Knot at the edge of the black water.

THE END.